Praise for *Four Seasons*

"I've been privy to all of Chris Widener's work, and this, by far, is his most impactful book. It is filled with invaluable insights and lessons on living a life of purpose told in the most compelling way. You truly will not be able to put this down! Priceless!"

—**Greg Provenzano**,
President and Co-Founder, CAN Inc.

"Chris Widener has written a beautiful and meaningful novel dealing with the most important question: How do you find meaning in life, especially if you only have one year to live? *Four Seasons* is a powerful story that will make you look at your life in a brand-new way and bring meaning to your story."

—**Jeffrey J. Fox**,
Author of Several International Bestsellers,
Including *How to Become a Rainmaker*

"Chris is an insightful and powerful author whose books inspire and instill in us a desire to be the best version of ourselves. *Four Seasons* is another compelling read that will elicit all ranges of emotions as you walk in the footsteps of a man facing his own mortality [who eventually comes to the] realization that he has been given a gift to repair, enhance and cultivate relationships with those who mean the most to him. This story is a poignant reminder of what is most important in life and how the greatest legacy we can leave is our faith and love."

—**Jennie Norris**,
ASPM, BTS, ISC, SRS, STRS, SSS, LHS, CDE, SMS,
Chairwoman of International Association
of Home Staging Professionals

T0043628

"Want to finally learn the answer to the age-old question of what is more important, time or money? Start here!"

—Patrick Snow,
International Bestselling Author of *Creating Your Own Destiny*

"*Four Seasons* is one of those books that will alter the significance of your life!"

—Ryan Chamberlin,
Author, Speaker, and CEO of the True Patriot Network

"Chris Widener has transformed his own life and career beyond the biggest dreams of most people. He has truly had a positive impact on the world, and it continues to expand. This story is told in a way that will cause you to reflect on your deepest values and life goals. It will also touch your heart."

—Jim Cathcart,
Mentor, Speaker, and Author

"There's a saying that 'time heals.' But time also reveals. I've had the pleasure of not only being mentored by Chris Widener but considering him a dear friend. Chris walks his talk. He is leaving a living legacy and impacting generations. Learning to discover what you would give your life for helps you know what you give your time to, and for that, *Four Seasons* is priority straightening wisdom."

—Donna Johnson,
Sr. Entrepreneur and Author of *My Mentor Walks on Water*

"We tend to live life like we're immortal, even though that fantasy doesn't make any sense. In Chris Widener's new book, he takes us on a vicarious journey with a highly successful has-it-all character who has to face mortality sooner than expected. And in doing so, we are compelled to look deeper at our own relationships, values, and priorities and reconsider how we want to live. What more would you want a book to do?"

—Brian Walter,
CSP, CPAE, President of Extreme Meetings Inc.

"Very little is guaranteed in life, but we know *Four Seasons* are. How we work through them, grow through them, learn from them, and still find joy in the midst of it all is pertinent to our happiness. I know I want to be a shining light for my loved ones, and this book will help us all to do just that."

—Cyndi Walter,
Owner of Cynergy, Inc.

"We all face changes. We all face challenges. And, one day, we will all face our final *Four Seasons*. The wisdom, insight, and heart of Chris Widener's powerful book will help every reader navigate those times with greater peace and hope. Bless you, Chris!"

—Robert Hotchkin,
Minister, Author, and Speaker

"I can't wait for the world to read Chris's new book *Four Seasons*. So many focus their time on this earth making a living and never get around to making the life God designed for us. One year… four seasons to do just that. What will you do?"

—Curt Beavers,
Entrepreneur

"*Four Seasons* mirrors the reality of each person's life. Whether lived only for success in this world's economy OR for the beauty of living a life of God's best blessing: the rich life of family, friendship, and influence that lingers into lasting life legacies. May we so live!"

—Naomi Rhode,
Professional Speaker, CoFounder of Smart Practice

Four
Seasons

One Family's Transformation
Through Tragedy and Triumph

Chris Widener

MADE FOR
SUCCESS

Made for Success Publishing
P.O. Box 1775 Issaquah, WA 98027
www.MadeForSuccessPublishing.com

Distributed by Made for Success Publishing

First Printing

Library of Congress Cataloging-in-Publication data

Widener, Chris
    FOUR SEASONS: One Family's Transformation Through
    Tragedy and Triumph

        p. cm.

LCCN: 2021943355
ISBN: 978-1-64146-658-5 (*Paperback)*
ISBN: 978-1-64146-659-2 (*eBook*)
ISBN: 978-1-64146-660-8 (*Audiobook*)

Printed in the United States of America

For further information contact Made for Success Publishing
+1-425-526-6480 or email service@madeforsuccess.net

CONTENTS

PREFACE

ALL AROUND THE world today, someone's precious child will die. Some of those people will be 10 years old; others will be 90. In any case, the person who dies is special to someone. Such is the story of this drama that we call life. There is the inexpressible joy of living, and there is the inescapable inevitability of death. Each and every one of us will travel this wearisome course. All of us will watch as our friends and family pass from this life to the next. We must remember that each and every one is important, no matter what our state is in this world. Every person is valuable to those in our families and, above all, to God.

Four Seasons is the story of a man and his family confronted with unavoidable tragedy and their journey through this year of their life. The story shows the commonness of the lives we all live. From the poorest of the poor in third-world countries, to the wealth of an East Coast publisher's Northern New Jersey estate, the people of this world encounter the grandest of joys through the celebrations that mark the passing of special events of life, as well as the withering sorrows of the painful paths we are all called to travel at different intervals of time.

This story pursues the joys of a family's good times, set against the background of the ultimate finality of death, the four seasons of every life that come and go: Life and Death, Joy and Sorrow.

While *Four Seasons* is a story set amidst power, wealth, prestige, and privilege, it is still the story of Everyman. Every person, every family experiences the four seasons of life. Great wealth and fame are not shields from the sorrows of life nor guarantors of joy. Indeed, every human being, at one time or another, experiences the same: the ebb and flow of both positive and negative experiences and circumstances.

The four seasons of life are guaranteed. They will come eventually to everyone. This is the story of how the four seasons came to one family and how they lived through them with courage, strength, emotion, and purpose.

SPRING

March 10, 3 p.m.

A S JONATHAN BLAKE turned off Roxiticus Road and into his drive, he pushed the console button that would open his gate, and the massive, wrought-iron gates began to open. While waiting, his gloved hand on the stick shift, his eye caught the marker on the brick post. It read "Three Lakes." When the gate had opened far enough, Jonathan eased his black luxury car through and continued up to the house. Jonathan had always cherished Three Lakes, but this afternoon, he loved it more than ever. Moving slowly up the mile-long driveway, he surveyed the land on which he had lived for most of his life. The massive, glorious trees that guarded the front entrance created a secluded tunnel leading to the first of the three lakes sitting just off to the right, a quarter-mile up the driveway. Lush, rolling terrain that occupied most of the rest of the 157 acres that made up the estate welcomed him warmly this afternoon.

The drive from Manhattan had taken him roughly an hour and 15 minutes. Having until two years ago been the owner of some 50 city and county newspapers up and down the East Coast, Jonathan had driven in and out of Manhattan thousands of times during his lifetime. This trip was different, though. There was so much to think about today, so much weighing on his mind. Monumental events loomed on the horizon—events that would affect Jonathan and his family profoundly and change their lives forever. Normally, the drive from the city to Three Lakes was a calm and soothing one, changing slowly along the way from the sterile, high-rise atmosphere of the fastest-paced city in the United States to the natural, colorful scenery of the area surrounding Far Hills, New Jersey, deep in horse country. The drive usually drew Jonathan through an inner change, taking him from the overworked executive to the relaxed husband and father, ready to spend time with his family. Not so this day. The mind-numbing thoughts racing to and fro had made this drive seem nonexistent. By the time he approached Three Lakes, he was dull from the desperate mental exertion. He negotiated the drive on autopilot.

Nearing the house, Jonathan reached to touch another button, and the second stall of the five-car garage opened, making way for him to park. He slowed down and eased the car into its resting place. Turning off the engine and climbing out of the car, he pressed the opener again and closed the garage door behind him. The first stall, closest to the door to the mudroom, was reserved for his wife Gloria's car, but seeing that it was gone, he knew that the house was his, at least for a time.

He rarely felt this way, but today he was glad Gloria was gone. He needed some more time to himself before revealing the tragic news.

The house on Three Lakes was enormous. At 23,000 square feet, the English Tudor-style home built by Jonathan's father on the rolling landscape outside of Far Hills was the quintessential Northern New Jersey estate. It had five bedrooms in the family quarters, a two-bedroom guest wing above the garages, and a formal dining room that seated thirty-two when the large cherry table was extended. The huge kitchen was where wonderful family memories began, where feasts were prepared for the hungry family to enjoy. In addition, there were formal and informal living rooms, a den, a recreation room complete with a billiards table built in 1865, and two offices, one for Jonathan and one for Gloria. The two rooms that set Three Lakes apart from the other large homes in the area were the library and the ballroom. It was Jonathan's mother, Charlotte, who, indulging a lifelong love affair with books, made sure that her husband, Edgar, included a library when he built the home. It was 2 stories high, with bookshelves all the way around its 1,800 square feet, holding 20,000 volumes. All of the great books of history were there, and Jonathan, also a book lover and avid reader, had spent hundreds of hours in the library reading them. The room was decorated exquisitely with overstuffed leather couches, recliners, and study tables in the corners, complete with a banker's lamp on each. Providing access to the volumes on high shelves above your head was a two-story, rolling oak ladder that moved around the perimeter of the room.

The second special room was the 4,000-square-foot ballroom. Throughout their years together, Edgar and Charlotte had hosted many a party there and always engaged the most popular bands and ensembles to entertain their friends, relatives, and business acquaintances. A large chandelier hung like a sparkling beach umbrella in the center of the room, while off to the side were sitting areas around the wooden dance floor where tired dancers could talk, enjoy good food, and drink their wine or champagne. A huge fireplace dominated the outer wall, and in the winter months, guests looked forward to the warmth of a crackling fire. Large, two-story windows around the room gave way to broad, sweeping views of the gazebo, the front gate below, and the largest of the three lakes. The room was, quite simply, breathtaking.

Edgar and Charlotte Blake had built the home as a place in which to raise their two children, Betsy and Jonathan, away from the hustle and bustle of the city. It was their permanent family retreat. When Jonathan was 20, his older sister died in a freak drowning accident. Edgar and Charlotte then lived alone after Jonathan left for college, their solitude punctuated with frequent visits home from Jonathan and later, Jonathan and Gloria.

When Edgar died at the age of 64, he left the house to his wife, Charlotte Wilson Blake. She died four years later, and the house in which Jonathan had grown up became his. Jonathan, Gloria, and their four children had lived there ever since.

After entering the house through the mudroom, Jonathan moved quickly through the kitchen, stopping only briefly at the preparation island in the middle of the room to see what had come in the mail that was laid out there. He quickly perused the stack and came to the conclusion that there was nothing important, at least not compared to what else had been occupying his mind since this afternoon. He left the kitchen cutting through the formal living room, down the hall, through the main foyer, and into his haven, his office.

Jonathan always felt safe and at home in the office that had originally been his father's. Scores of books were nestled in the bookshelves, surrounded by dark, rich, mahogany woodwork and leather furniture. He settled into his favorite chair next to the glass cabinet that held his favorite hunting rifles and shotguns, slipped his tired feet out of his shoes, and raised his legs to rest on the ottoman. Reaching over to the table next to him, he opened a small humidor and took out an Opus X cigar, one of the small pleasures of his life. Jonathan never smoked more than one per week when he was working, as he didn't want them to become commonplace but to remain a special privilege he allowed himself as a reward for making it through another hard week at the office. Since retiring, though, sometimes he would allow himself an additional cigar during the week. After cutting the tip off, he took the lighter from the table and lit the cigar. Jonathan savored the rich aroma of the cigar. He loved the smell and had since he was a little boy when Edgar would relax with an occasional cigar.

There he was, home by himself and left to his own thoughts. The quiet of the house was deafening as he sat motionless, his head resting against the back of his chair. He stared out the window toward the backyard, where he could see the gazebo and the fields beyond. He looked longingly over his land and dreamed of what the future might have held.

"How will I tell them?" he wondered. "When will I tell them? What will they think? What will they do? How can I let them down like this?" As a cloud of cigar smoke curled into the air, his eyes turned toward what the Blake family affectionately called "The Wall." The walls of the office were covered with artwork, plaques, and diplomas, but "The Wall" was reserved for the special photos that, taken together, told the story of his life. Jonathan put his cigar down in the ashtray and walked deliberately to the wall to gain a closer look. There stood Jonathan Blake. He was a tall, good-looking man. At 6-foot-1 and 175 pounds, he was still in good shape, though in these later years in life, he had lost a little weight as some of his muscle mass had disappeared. In his younger years, he had weighed close to 190, a picture of good health. Now, his hair was dark, with just a touch of gray, the symbolic mist of wisdom framing his temples. His eyes were steel blue. All in all, he had leading-man good looks.

Set among the pictures were his 12 favorites. He buried both hands deep in his pockets and, moving from left to right along "The Wall," he considered each picture and the time of life it represented. There was the picture of Jonathan and Betsy, aged 10 and 12, along with their parents, out in the back of the house next to the original gazebo, still full of vim and vigor, ready for life. He remembered the day well. It was warm and sunny, and he was a typical boy. His mother and father had asked him repeatedly to settle down and leave his sister alone so that they could get on with the picture taking. It was an amateur family portrait, but it captured this family, and that was what was significant. It showed them on the land that they loved, together for a moment in time. Jonathan thought of what a beautiful woman Betsy would have been had she lived. She had a broad, white smile that was infectious. Jonathan wished that his family could still be together. Now, as the other three were gone, this was an important picture, an important memory, for Jonathan.

It was a connection to his past, his original family, his blood. His eyes turned to the picture of him and Edgar fishing in Pennsylvania. Charlotte had captured this on film when Jonathan was 14 on one of the family's vacations. Edgar loved to fish and hunt, a passion that he eagerly and successfully instilled in his only son. In this photograph, Jonathan, not Edgar, was reeling in the big one, something that didn't happen very often. Jonathan's boyish grin was the center of the picture, his father's smile of pride in his only son a close second. Jonathan looked just like Edgar, simply younger.

Just below that was a picture of Jonathan's lacrosse team at the Delbarton Catholic Boys High School outside of Morristown. The Blakes were Presbyterian, but Jonathan, and then Jonathan's two boys, Michael and Thomas, all attended Delbarton because it provided the finest education money could buy in that area of New Jersey. Thomas, the youngest of Jonathan and Gloria's four children, would graduate that spring from Delbarton and then go on to Princeton University, another family tradition.

Delbarton had taught Jonathan to love a classical education and given him an outlet for his love of the written word. It also taught him to place God in the center of his life and to remember that he had a responsibility to his Maker and his fellow man. Delbarton was also where Jonathan pursued his passion for sports. He always played team sports, and he was elected the captain of the lacrosse team in both his junior and senior years. Many of his fellow students came from wealthy families, so it was always a source of inner satisfaction for Jonathan, knowing that it was his leadership abilities and athletic skill, not his father's money, that got him voted captain by his teammates. His senior year, the lacrosse team went to the state finals but lost, despite Jonathan's valiant effort of three goals.

The team picture brought that game to mind, and Jonathan studied each member of the team. He saw young men about to graduate from high school, go on to college, and then into the real world. He had kept up with most of his teammates and knew at least where most of them were and where their lives were taking them. As with all senior classes, some went on to do great things, others to more mundane and ordinary lives. Some, like Jonathan, attained great fame and wealth. Others lived simply, content with an average existence.

Jonathan thought about each of these teammates, so childlike then, so energetic, so full of dreams. Life had taken them in many directions. He wondered how many of them were truly happy now as they neared the twilight of their lives. He wondered how much longer they would live and what legacy they would leave for others. He wondered if any were truly making a difference in the lives of those around them or if they were just waiting life out, distracted by a plethora of activities.

In the middle of "The Wall" was a large picture of Jonathan and his precious mate, Gloria. He was a sophomore at Princeton, she a freshman at Drew University in Madison, about an hour away. Gloria had come to know Jonathan through her brother Martin, a classmate of Jonathan's who now lived in Germany and taught at a university there. The picture was taken in front of one of the restaurants on Palmer Square. Jonathan noticed how young they looked. Their faces were so... taut. *Age takes its toll on your skin first,* he thought. There they were. Gloria was beautiful. Not striking, but naturally good-looking. Her light-brown hair caught the sunlight just so in the picture. At the time of the picture, they had been dating only two months, but they were in love and about to realize they would spend the rest of their lives together. He reminisced about Gloria. She was a spunky but brilliant young woman from South Jersey. Jonathan was bright, to be sure, but his family's network of relationships definitely played a part in helping the Princeton admission process go smoothly. After college, Gloria taught school until Jennifer was born four years into her teaching career. How he respected and adored Gloria. He still caught himself looking lovingly at her across the room when she was not aware of him. Occasionally, she would catch him looking, and he would just smile a smile of love and appreciation.

Beside the picture of Gloria and Jonathan was a picture taken at a restaurant in Paris while on their 10th-anniversary trip. Jonathan had been to Europe many times before, but Gloria had only dreamed about it. Jonathan arranged to surprise her with this trip. It was the only time they went to France, and it was memorable for the setting as well as the occasion. Around that photo were four others, each one with Jonathan and one of the four children. There was Jonathan and Jennifer, the oldest of the Blake children, eating cotton candy at the zoo when she was 9. She was a small version of her current self with her brown hair, blue eyes, and a wide smile. How he loved Jennifer. He remembered when she was born, how he had cradled her in his arms so tenderly that first time. He had gazed into her eyes, amazed at the gift of life that God had bestowed upon him. How would he care for her? How would he be able to provide all that another human being, his child, needed? He had felt deeply the awesome privilege and responsibility of another life under his care.

Jennifer had grown up to be a strong woman, a lawyer. She was beautiful, proud, and self-confident. Yet Jonathan knew that her life was not perfect. Jennifer and her husband Scott, who was also a lawyer, were obviously not happily married. This caused Jonathan and Gloria much pain; they had many discussions on how they might possibly be helped. Jonathan pondered what might happen to them in the future. He didn't know. And now, more than ever, he felt completely unable to provide any help. He wanted to do something, anything, to steer them in the right direction. He made a mental note to work on that soon.

There was also a picture of Jonathan with Michael, his second child, wrestling on the living room floor, both of their faces beaded with sweat and looking directly into the camera as if they had stopped and posed. How does a father describe his love for his first son? Jonathan breathed deeply, letting the air out in a heavy sigh. Jonathan had dreamed of a life of partnership with Michael, and his son had not disappointed him. Michael had also graduated from Princeton and was becoming a young man who would, in a few years, be ready to partner with his father in life and work. Jonathan had for years vividly pictured in his mind late nights plotting the next adventure with Michael, alternating between bestowing fatherly wisdom and eagerly embracing the vigor of a young man pursuing a higher goal. Michael was now married to Patty, a charming young woman whom Jonathan and Gloria considered the greatest find Michael could have made. Grandchildren would come from these two first, he figured. The thought of grandchildren was important to Jonathan—even more so now.

A picture of Samantha, Jonathan and Gloria's third child, and her dad dressed exquisitely for a high school, father-daughter dinner was next to the picture of Michael and Jonathan. Jonathan wore a dark-blue, double-breasted suit. He had looked dapper, he thought. Samantha wore a dark-blue dress to match. Samantha. Now she was a pleasant enigma to Jonathan. She was the tenderest of the Blake children. A typical middle child, she was quiet and deferred to the strength of the older children and the attention shown to her younger brother. She usually played the role of the quiet helper in the Blake family. Jonathan admired Samantha for her calm spirit. He appreciated her servant's heart immensely. He thought the world of her. The problem was simply that he didn't know her very well. Yes, this picture placed him at a certain time and date in her life, but the reality was that if any of the Blake children had been lost in the shuffle of Jonathan's busy life, it was Samantha. Jonathan hadn't spent much time getting to know her while she was growing up, and now he regretted that. Soon she would be marrying William Moore, a young Presbyterian minister, and begin to develop her own life and family. He had thought ever since the engagement that the chances of delving into his daughter's heart and life were growing increasingly slim. He had often pondered recently how he might find time to make a place for himself in Samantha's life. This, too, he would make a priority now.

A picture of the youngest, Thomas, about age 14 and looking a lot like Jonathan did in the picture with Edgar, and Jonathan holding a shotgun in one hand and a duck in the other, completed the collection of pictures of Jonathan and his children. Thomas had brought a sense of completeness to Jonathan. He had always wanted four children. His slightly morbid reason being that he wanted to make sure he had more than two children in case anything happened to one of them. While Michael had been groomed to be a businessman, Thomas had been groomed to take up Jonathan's leisurely pursuits such as hunting and fishing. He was smart and did well in school, but his passion was in sport. Michael could obviously handle a rod and reel or a shotgun, given the scores of trips he had taken with his father to pursue fish, elk, and deer, but Thomas was a young master in Jonathan's eyes.

Yes, Jonathan pondered, each of the children had their strengths and weaknesses, as do all people, but all in all, they were good kids, leading good lives. Jonathan was very proud of them all and loved them as only a father could. Finishing off "The Wall" were pictures of the family on the beach in Florida, a picture of the combined staffs of Jonathan's newspapers taken at one of their annual Christmas parties, and, next to the picture of Gloria and Jonathan, was a family portrait. Here was the Jonathan Blake family, attired in suits and dresses, standing on the newly renovated gazebo in the backyard. It was a beautiful summer day, and there was a lot to be happy about. The family was all together, they had attained wealth and status that only a few ever achieve, and above all, they were healthy.

All of the pictures on Jonathan's wall boldly declared one thing: family man. Jonathan Blake had remained married and faithful to his one true love for his whole life, had succeeded in business beyond anyone's expectations, including his own, provided jobs for literally hundreds of people, and had raised four fine, upstanding, God-fearing children who would most likely repeat the pattern in their own lives. His life appeared to be a success.

As he stood there staring at the family portrait, thinking more of the trouble he was now facing and the dread with which he faced it, knowing the impact it would have on his family, he heard the mudroom door swing open and then close again. Gloria was home. Jonathan's heart began to race. He stood there, hands still deep in his pockets. He didn't move. He didn't need to. Gloria would surely look for him in his office first. She would be there soon enough, asking questions Jonathan didn't want to answer. He didn't want to have to do what he would be required to do in the next few minutes. In fact, he loathed the pain he was about to cause his love.

"Jon?" Gloria called toward his office.

"God, why do I have to go through this?" Jonathan asked, looking heavenward momentarily.

Gloria came through the door and into the office. "I figured you would be in here. What did he say?"

Jonathan was again staring at the pictures. As he turned slowly to face his bride, his demeanor told Gloria that she was not about to hear good news. Her face showed panic. "What did he say, Jon?" she repeated, this time more frantically, her voice rising sharply.

"It's not good at all, Gloria. It is cancer." Trying to remain calm, he took a deep breath and blew it out. "And it has spread throughout my body."

Gloria began to cry. "What does that mean?" she sobbed.

"It means that they think I have six months to a year to live, and there is nothing they can do about it. They did say that they could perform some treatments but that none of them would do anything except waste our time and money, and in fact, would probably make me feel even sicker than I would feel without the treatment."

"There has to be something," Gloria retorted brusquely. "We can't just say, 'Well, that's it. I guess we call it a life.' There has to be a second opinion, some sort of experimental medicine, something. Jonathan, what are we going to do?" Jonathan had asked all of these questions of their family physician and the oncologist who had performed the tests. All of the results pointed to impending death.

Jonathan stood silent and then said, "Honey, I went through all of those options with the doctors. It is quite clear from all of the tests that there really is nothing they can do. They suggested that I just accept it and make the most of the rest of my time here."

They both stood speechless. There was nothing left to say. The judgment had been pronounced, and, unfortunately for the Blake family, it was final. After a few seconds, they moved toward each other, Gloria beginning to cry harder, Jonathan took her into his arms, feeling half sorry for her and the kids, half sorry for himself. They were quiet, standing there in each other's arms. Jonathan held Gloria tightly, rubbing his right hand up and down on her back, trying somehow to calm and comfort her. He thought of the many years that he and Gloria had already enjoyed together. Now all the future years they had planned on were being stripped away in what was supposed to be the prime of their lives. He moved his hand up to the back of Gloria's head and ran his fingers through her hair. He loved the silky feeling of Gloria's hair. He nudged his nose into her neck and took in a deep breath. Gloria wore the best perfume, always the faint smell of a florist's shop. He held her in his arms for some time. Finally, pulling away, Jonathan suggested they sit down. He wanted to share some of his thoughts.

When they were seated, he began. "Gloria, I know it will be hard to keep this inside, but please don't tell anyone, not even the kids. I want to pick the right time and the right place to tell them myself. I'm thinking that I would like to wait until after Samantha's wedding. That way we'll be able to enjoy our anniversary, Tom's graduation, and the wedding. I wouldn't want to put a cloud over any of those. I want them to be wonderful memories. We will tell the kids in time, and they will surely be distraught, so if we hold off telling them, at least we will be able to enjoy the good times that we have coming to us." Gloria didn't respond. "Okay?" he asked, prodding.

She was quiet, her face now buried in her hands. This was not at all the outcome that she had imagined. Jonathan had not been entirely healthy since early last winter, and their doctor had decided to run some tests, suspecting that something could be seriously wrong. Gloria had assumed, though, as many loved ones do, that they would go through the testing process and come out the other side with simply a bad scare. She assumed that ultimately everything would be all right, that perhaps Jonathan would have to go on some sort of long-term medication, but never did she entertain the thought that he might have a terminal disease. "Is that all right, Gloria?" Jonathan asked again, breaking into her thoughts.

She looked up slowly, breaking her stare at the floor. "Yes, I guess that's okay." She tossed her hair away from her face and turned to look out the window. She nervously held one hand in the other, wringing it. "Listen," she said. "I really need some time to think this all through. I never thought..." She paused. She really didn't know what to say. She was shocked and completely unprepared to deal with this, let alone carry on a conversation about it. "Do you mind if I go upstairs, and we can talk more over dinner?" she asked. Gloria was the type who needed time to think things—even small things—over. She would frequently retreat when faced with decisions, not to run but to prepare and consider all the options. This approach had served her well in the past, but now it was not as if anything could really be done.

"Yes. How about we go out for dinner? We can go up to Chester," Jonathan suggested.

"Oh, I don't know if I..."

Jonathan cut in. "Come on, Gloria, it will be a date." He got a smirk on his face. "I'll treat." Here was Jonathan, the strong one, trying to keep Gloria from breaking under the crushing weight of the news. The irony hit him. He was the one dying, but Gloria was the one hurting. He was pretending it wasn't so bad to help her not hurt while he was dying. It's a funny way humans postpone feeling the emotions that they are supposed to feel when things like this happen. "We'll be sad tomorrow." He continued, "It's Friday. Tom is gone for the weekend, and we have nothing to do. Tonight, let's enjoy each other. I'm still healthy enough for a trip to Chester."

"I suppose," Gloria relented, "What time shall we leave, 6 o'clock?"

"Fine. Take a nap or just relax. I need some time to myself to think about things, too. We'll go at 5." With that, Gloria shuffled out of the room, entirely disconsolate.

As she left, Jonathan called after her. "Gloria, be strong." She would be, eventually. Jonathan watched the door for a moment, then turned back to his chair. His cigar had burned down and fallen into the ashtray. As he sat down, he picked up and puffed what was left of the cigar. Eerily, words he had memorized some 37 years ago for a speech in a classical literature class at Princeton came into his mind. They were from John Bunyan's *The Pilgrim's Progress*.

> My sword I give to him that shall succeed me in my pilgrimage, and my courage and skill to him that can get it. My marks and scars I carry with me, to be witness for me, that I have fought his battles who now will be my rewarder. When the day that he must go whence was come, many accompanied him to the riverside, into which as he went he said: 'Death, where is thy sting?' And as he went down deeper, he said: 'Grave, where is thy victory?' So he passed over and all the trumpets sounded for him on the other side.

At the time he had committed these words to memory, he didn't know why he had picked them, other than that they intrigued him. Today, a lifetime later, perhaps he knew why they had.

Jonathan Blake had lived a privileged life until now. Born to wealthy parents, he attended the finest schools, experiencing the best prep school and an Ivy League education, and enjoyed a head start in the business world. At age 36, he inherited his mother and father's estate—well over $100 million and one of the finest homes in the Northeast. As a publisher armed with a huge treasure chest, he forged ahead and bought out the newspaper he worked for. For the next 19 years, he leveraged the buying power of his businesses and went on a buying binge, purchasing every paper he could, eventually owning more papers than anyone in the Eastern United States. At the age of 55, Jonathan decided to end his publishing career. He sold out to a large, international conglomerate for almost $2 billion cash. The last two years had been spent enjoying his family and helping others. He had lived it all and had done so in a noble fashion. Now, he was face to face with his own mortality, and he wanted to die the way he had lived.

One more year to live, he thought as he snuffed out what remained of his cigar. He considered how he might live it. He pondered how he might make the most of this year for his family. He thought about how he would settle his affairs. Jonathan knew that most people don't have the advantage of knowing that they will die soon. Many perish quickly, leaving much undone to be strung together by loved ones left behind. Friends and relatives are left to wonder about the life they have lost. He would be different, he decided. He had the chance to do what so many others didn't. It was a bittersweet pill. A long, drawn-out agony and physical pain were the price to pay for the opportunity to take his time on the path to the grave. It was a price he was willing to pay—as if he had the choice. He would have the luxury, if one could call it that, of creating memories, of tying up loose ends, of telling people the words he had always thought yet never spoken. Words of thanks, of praise and encouragement, words of challenge and advice. He would be able to steer his children in the direction that he wanted them to go for the remainder of their lives. He had the chance to make sure that Gloria and the kids knew clearly how much he loved them. He had one other opportunity.

"A year to say goodbye," he said softly to himself.

Gloria decided as she walked up the grand, broad stairs to the master bedroom that she would draw herself a bath and soak while she contemplated what Jonathan had just told her. Moving sluggishly down the hall and through the bedroom, she went directly to her opulent bathroom and started the bath water running. She added some bubble bath. Back in the bedroom, she undressed without thinking, dropping her clothes one article at a time in a messy heap, her subconscious taking over as she became almost completely numb. She finally sat down, naked, on the side of the bed, staring endlessly out the window. There were no thoughts in her mind, just a blank, bland, dead feeling that overwhelmed her emotions. The seconds passed into minutes as her gaze remained riveted on the window. The bath continued to fill.

The phone rang, startling her with its shrill chirp. At first, she wasn't going to answer it but then decided it might be Thomas calling one last time before he went to Vermont for the weekend with a friend and his parents. Gloria picked up the phone just as Jonathan began talking on the other end with a friend about some sort of business investment they were involved in. She listened for just a moment.

How can he think about that kind of thing right now? she thought as she hung up the phone quietly. *I can barely think. I feel like I'm living a nightmare.* Jonathan had always been able to separate his emotions from the reality of what was happening around him. Gloria had both admired and despised that trait in him. At times, it had been a source of strength for her and the kids; at others, it provoked frustration. It had always baffled her.

Gloria became aware of the tub running and snapped to attention. She got up off of the bed and walked quickly into the bathroom. Carefully, she stepped into the tub, a little over half-full. Slowly, she lowered herself into the steaming hot water, hoping to unwind, yet knowing it wouldn't happen. Soon she was thinking. *Life isn't supposed to turn out this way. Jonathan and I were supposed to live longer than this.* Her thoughts turned to Edgar and Charlotte. Edgar died at an early age, too. She remembered the night vividly, the events burned forever into her memory. She and Jonathan were at home with Jennifer and Michael when, at about 8:45, the phone rang. It was Charlotte calling to tell them that Edgar had just been killed in an automobile accident. They all rushed to the hospital and then drove with Charlotte back to Three Lakes. There they sat, not saying much of anything, drinking coffee into the middle of the night. The young children slept upstairs, unaware that Grandpa was gone forever. One day Edgar was there; the next day, he wasn't. There wasn't even a chance to say goodbye. At least Jonathan would have that.

Charlotte had always been such a strong person, admired by those who knew her as a woman of inner fortitude, but after Edgar passed on, she became almost timid, as though there just wasn't anything left to live for. She died four years later, probably quite literally heartbroken, of a heart attack. Those four years passed so quickly, like months. There seemed to be very little joy left in the family gatherings and outings; Edgar was missing, and he just wasn't supposed to be, at least not according to anyone who loved him.

Now it was Jonathan and Gloria's turn. Every generation gets its turn at this thing called death. "But I don't want my turn, not now," she said quietly, whimpering, her face beginning to curl up. "I don't want my turn now. Please, God, don't let Jon die. Please don't let him die. Please don't let him die." She repeatedly whispered that futile phrase before drifting into silence, staring at the tiles at the head of the tub.

Gloria soaked for more than an hour, occasionally adding more hot water into the bath to replace that which had gone down the overflow, thinking all the while about Jonathan, about what she would do when he was gone, and especially how the kids would take the news. The kids would not handle this well at all, she was sure. They all practically worshipped their father. He had always been so good to them. Gloria decided that she would help Jonathan plan the right time and setting to tell them. Then she would make sure she spent time with each of them, helping them sort through it all.

She wondered how long he would actually live. Sure, he was given six months to a year, but what did that mean? He could take a turn for the worse and go in three months. She wondered if Jonathan would actually see Thomas graduate or Samantha and William get married. Her heart began to race with panic. There was no guarantee that Jonathan would even last a year. That was it. Jonathan was going to die. Not wanting to think about it, she tried to relax again.

"Pull yourself together, Gloria," she finally said out loud to herself. "This is what life has given you; you will just have to deal with it." With that thought, she got out of the tub, reaching to flip the water release latch as she rose. She grabbed a fluffy, white towel and dried herself off, then threw the towel into the hamper and turned to go into the bedroom to get dressed for dinner. She had made her decision. She would do her best to help Jonathan live this last year the way he wanted to. That decision would prove easier made than lived. As the coming months played out, she would often have a hard time admitting that all of this was a reality.

Dinner at the Publick House had been very good as usual. The quaint little restaurant and hotel on Route 24 in the middle of Chester had been a favorite of theirs over the years. It was decent food, reasonably priced, close, and they liked the decor. They had discussed how and when to tell the children about the cancer. They had decided on a family dinner sometime after Samantha and William's wedding in July. Gloria had again asked, twice actually, whether anything could be done to battle the disease. Both times Jonathan had answered that the doctors all said there was nothing to be done except to administer pain relievers as the disease progressed. It wasn't as though Jonathan had given up and chosen to die. It was just that he had just always been very pragmatic, and he assumed that the doctors knew what they were doing. Dr. Kidman had been their family doctor for many years, and his and the other doctors' decisions could be trusted. Why fight the inevitable?

It was late now—10 o'clock. Jonathan and Gloria were in their bedroom. Actually, Jonathan was in bed already, and Gloria was in her bathroom brushing her teeth. "How are the preparations for the wedding coming?" Jonathan said loudly to Gloria.

He heard what he deciphered to be "Wait 'til I'm done brushing my teeth," so he began to read an article in the magazine that was on his nightstand.

A few moments later, Gloria came into the bedroom, switched on the lamp on her nightstand, and crawled into bed. "Now, what did you say?" she asked.

"How are the wedding preparations coming?" he asked, setting the magazine down again.

"Oh, they're fine. I talked to the florist again today and the caterer. It's coming together, knock on wood. Samantha is so excited."

"Yes, I know she is. I talked to her yesterday," Jonathan said. "She's the second-to-the-last one. Thomas will get married soon enough, and we'll be officially done." The thought hit Jonathan that Gloria would have to do the "finishing" by herself, as he wouldn't be around. The thought shocked him. Gloria, sadly enough, realized the same thing nearly at the same time. They both were quiet, not knowing what the other was thinking.

"I wonder what our kids will be like in 20 years, what their lives will be about, what their kids will be like?" Jonathan asked.

Gloria looked at the ceiling. "I don't know," she said. Her earlier resolve to deal with this head-on quickly dissolved under the weight of the terrifying reality that Jonathan would be gone soon.

It became obvious that they had both had enough deep and emotional thought for the evening. They were simply too tired and emotionally drained to have any more. Jonathan rolled over and took Gloria into his arms.

"How could I be such a lucky guy to get such a beautiful woman like you?" he asked.

Gloria laughed. "I wouldn't count me as such a catch. You're the prize in this family." They both smiled. They kissed. Jonathan said, "Good night."

"Good night Jonathan."

"I love you."

"I love you too."

The lights went out, and in a few minutes, the most difficult day in their lives up until now was over for Jonathan and Gloria Blake.

March 21

JONATHAN HAD DECIDED the day he found out that he was going to die that one thing he would surely do before his time here ended would be to get to know Samantha better. He also knew that he would have to do so sooner rather than later, to get the process moving along before her wedding. After the wedding, he knew, Samantha would be too busy getting used to married life to spend much time with her father, and rightly so. He knew it would be hard enough before the wedding, what with all of the busyness of the preparations, let alone afterward. The idea of pursuing a relationship with Samantha scared Jonathan quite a bit. He didn't have any idea how to go about it or really what he hoped to accomplish, for that matter. He realized, though, that he wanted, even needed, to make the effort. He secretly hoped it wouldn't prove to be too daunting of a task.

This day he had arranged for Gloria to go out with a couple of her girlfriends for dinner, hoping to be able to take Samantha out to eat, just the two of them. Thomas was always home late on Tuesdays because of club meetings at Delbarton, so Jonathan didn't worry about him being alone.

About 5:30, Samantha came in through the mudroom and into the kitchen. Jonathan was seated at the kitchen table reading the evening paper, a cup of coffee next to him.

"Hi, Dad," she said, dropping a couple of bags into a chair next to Jonathan.

"Hi there. How was the day?"

"Oh, pretty good, I guess. There have been better. There have been worse. Nothing exciting. Where's Mom?"

Samantha was just doing what she had been trained to do: Talk briefly to Dad, then move on to deeper things with Mom. He was to blame, he knew. Not that anything was ever really wrong between them, just shallow. Gloria had always paid so much attention to Samantha, whereas Jonathan had always been rather indifferent, so it was natural for Samantha to be drawn to her mother. This is exactly why Jonathan knew tonight was the first step in the right direction in changing that, if even for the short time that remained for him.

He wanted her to always remember after he was gone that he had recognized his mistakes and had made the effort to restore their relationship. "She went out with a couple of friends for dinner."

"Oh." Samantha paused. "Well, I'll just grab some soup or something then. Do you want me to make you some, too?"

"I have a better idea," Jonathan replied, pushing the newspaper away and slapping both palms lightly to the tabletop. "How about if your dear old dad takes his lovely third child out on a date?"

"Me?" Samantha asked, pointing to herself.

"You are my third child, aren't you?"

"Just you and me?"

"Yes!" Jonathan was grinning in disbelief by now. "It won't be that bad. I promise not to slobber when I eat. I won't ruin your reputation."

Samantha giggled. "Oh no, Dad. I don't mean it that way. I just... I just don't know that we've ever gone out, just the two of us. I mean, other than a special occasion or two."

"Well, it's never too late to change a bad habit, is it?"

"Yes, I guess so. Okay," Samantha agreed. "When do you want to go?"

"Whenever you're ready."

"Well, great. Just let me go upstairs and put some stuff away, and I'll be back down."

"Sounds like a deal," Jonathan replied. "I'll pull the car around front."

"Okay, I'll only be five minutes." Samantha gathered up the bags she had put down and went upstairs. Less than 10 minutes later, Jonathan and Samantha passed through the gates of Three Lakes on their way to dinner. The trip to Morristown seemed to go quickly. Jonathan knew he could get mileage out of a discussion of wedding plans. The talk was predictable: flowers, pictures, people, and food. When they reached Morristown, Jonathan maneuvered the car to the north side of the Green and parked in a lot. He and Gloria had a favorite little Italian restaurant right across from Headquarters Plaza that they snuck off to about once a month. Jonathan thought Samantha liked Italian and that she might enjoy it, too.

"Have you ever been here?" Jonathan asked as they entered.

"No, I haven't. I've seen it a lot, though. I guess when my friends and I want Italian, we usually go for pizza instead. It sure smells good, though." Samantha was simply excited about being with Jonathan and his seeming newfound interest in her, though she, like Jonathan, found it a touch uncomfortable at times.

"This happens to be one of your mother's and my favorites."

"Yeah, I've heard her talk about it. I'm excited to try it."

Jonathan and Samantha waited a few minutes in the small front waiting area before being seated. Garlic aroma filled the entire place. After looking intently through the menu, the waitress arrived to take their orders. They each decided on a Caesar salad. Samantha also ordered spaghetti, Jonathan ravioli. As they sat eating, their window allowing them the view of the street beyond, Jonathan began his job of getting to know Samantha better. He tried poking and prodding around different topics that he thought might be of interest to her but never really got anywhere. The fact was, he was wholly at a loss as to how to connect with Samantha, the conversation again and again falling flat and meandering into painful silence.

Finally, over dessert, he asked a question that started to break the ice. "This may seem like an odd question, but what do you really like about life?" he queried.

Samantha looked up from her dessert. Actually, she did find it an odd question. She looked at her dad for a moment. Jonathan looked down at his plate.

"Well," she finally began, "I guess I like people the most."

"What do you mean? I mean, what about people?" Jonathan fidgeted. This wasn't easy for him.

"I like the differences in people. The variety. Every person I meet provides me with a new experience. Some are so easy to get along with, you know, like your best friends. They are just easy to spend time with, no work at all, and such a pleasure. Other people are an effort, not in a bad way, just that it takes work to get inside, to know them, to understand them. Everybody has this intricate inner person that is shaped and molded by their past and by their personality." She drifted off for a moment. "I don't know; it's just fascinating to me to live life with so many different kinds of people. I guess I just like variety, and people provide that for me. Sometimes it is bothersome, but most of the time it is enjoyable."

"It sounds like you and William will be in the right profession then, won't you?"

"Well, the truth be known, I never imagined myself to be a minister's wife growing up, that's for sure. I do think I'll be good at it, though."

"I think you will be great at it," Jonathan said.

They each ate for a couple of minutes before Samantha spoke up. "Dad, can I ask you an odd question?"

"Sure. Anything."

"Do you like William?"

"Of course, Samantha. Have I given you reason to believe otherwise? If I have, I'm sorry."

"No, no, not at all. It's just that you never really know for sure what other people think unless you ask them point-blank. Too many people just keep their true feelings to themselves. So, I know you like him, but maybe 'What do you think of him?' is a better question."

"I think William is a terrific young man. Your mom and I like his family. He seems like a very intelligent young man, responsible. Yes, we like him very much. And he seems to fit into the family well."

"What about the fact that he's a minister?"

Jonathan paused to think. "I must admit that I never figured anyone in our family would marry into the clergy, but I have no problems with it. In fact, you know how much Reverend Wilton has meant to our family. I only hope that you and William will be able to mean so much to other families. It's a big job being a minister. I know I could never have done it."

"What do you mean that you couldn't have done it?"

"Oh, I guess I like being in control too much. I'm very cut and dried, so to speak. I don't know if I would have the compassion or tolerance for all of the ups and downs of life that a minister is involved in as he works with people. I like being able to go home and be off duty for the evening. It's not like that for a minister, you know."

"Yes, I know. So, what do you like about life, Dad?" Samantha asked, turning the tables on her dad.

"Hey, I'm supposed to ask the deep questions." He kept eating.

"I'm serious, Dad, what is it you like?"

"Here's one for you," Jonathan said, turning the question right back at Samantha, "What do you think I like about life?" he asked.

"That's easy," Samantha responded instantly.

"Oh, I'm that much of an open book, am I? No hesitation at all?"

"Well, I didn't say that, but actions do speak volumes."

"Okay, so what is important to me?" Jonathan was now intrigued by Samantha's assurance in what he liked about life.

"Money, for one."

Jonathan pondered that one before responding. It seemed like a bold thing to say, considering what he thought it meant. "How so?"

"I don't mean you love money in a bad way or anything. It's just that it sure must be a priority in your life. Grandpa left you a lot of money, more than you ever needed anyway, right?"

"Some would say that." Jonathan squirmed in his chair. He hardly felt like he wanted to be interrogated by his own daughter.

"It just seems that you worked awfully hard to make so much more. And maybe some other things fell through the cracks."

Jonathan suspected this would come, and he was now dreading it. "Without trying to sound defensive, I didn't work to make more money. I worked because it is right to work hard. Working hard, being in the right place at the right time, a little luck, all of that together is what made me more money. I also enjoyed my work. I provided hundreds of jobs for families that depended on our business." They both now recognized this was uncomfortable. He got back to the topic at hand. "What fell through the cracks? You mentioned things falling through the cracks."

"To be honest, I feel like I fell through the cracks." Samantha's eyes were filling with tears. She had finished her dessert, and the waitress cleared her plate away.

"Darling," Jonathan said, ignoring the server and reaching out to touch her hand. "I know. I know that I have made mistakes with you. That's actually why we're here tonight. I wanted to spend some time with you, to get to know you better." Samantha touched her napkin to her eyes and dried them. Jonathan continued. "I always just felt like you and I were so different; we didn't seem to have much in common."

"I know," Samantha said.

"You know what?"

"Well, with Michael, you always had business, Thomas was hunting and fishing, and Jennifer is just so much like you, business-oriented. You always talked about law with her. With me, there never seemed to be any common interests." She stopped to let it sink in. "It's nothing to feel bad about. It's just the way it is."

"Well, I do feel bad about it, Samantha, and I want to change it. In fact, I'll do whatever it takes to get to know you better. I want you to know that I have always respected you and admired and appreciated you, but I've realized this was lacking because we didn't know each other very well. I want to change that now, okay?"

"Okay," she accepted.

"Samantha, I know that I have hurt you for many years. Will you forgive me?"

Samantha looked at her father. "Yes, Dad, I forgive you."

Jonathan finished his dessert, paid the bill, and soon he and Samantha were driving the short way home again. Before going upstairs, Samantha went into Jonathan's office where he had gone to work. "Dad?" she said, peeking in.

"Yes, honey?" said Jonathan, turning in his chair.

"Thanks."

Jonathan rose and approached Samantha to give her a hug. "You are very welcome. If anything, I owe you a thanks for being so patient with me."

"Aww, it's nothing, Dad. You're great." Samantha now wore a beaming, brilliant smile on her face as she once more left Jonathan to himself.

The road to a closer relationship with Samantha had begun. It was difficult for both of them, but they had been able to bring to the surface some of the feelings they had held so deeply for years. Gloria finally arrived home about quarter after 10. Jonathan had already put on his pajamas and was reclining in bed reading a new biography of Thomas Jefferson, a favorite historical figure of his, when Gloria came in.

"Hi, honey," he said. "Did you have a good time?"

"We sure did. We decided to go into Hoboken and then take the train into New York. We ate in Chinatown and then caught a cab to Fifth Avenue for some shopping. But I want you to know that I restrained myself and bought absolutely nothing. I only window shopped."

"You are a pillar of self-control in your old age, Gloria."

"I know, aren't I great?"

"You sure are."

"So, tell me, how did your dinner go with Samantha?" Gloria asked.

"It went well, albeit a little uncomfortable at times."

"Oh? How so?"

"Well, Samantha brought up that she thought I put money and work before her. I already knew that I had neglected that relationship some, but she connected it to loving work too much. That's just not the case, though."

"But it is her perception, and for her, that's reality, which affects the way she relates to you."

"Well, I do have time to change that, don't I?"

"Yes, and Samantha's easy. She'll appreciate anything you do to get to know her better." By this time, Gloria had gotten her pajamas on as well and was climbing into bed.

"I think you are doing the right thing with her," she said as she snuggled up to Jonathan.

"Thanks. I'm trying." With that, he kissed Gloria, turned off his light, and rolled over to go to sleep.

April 16

EASTER WAS A joyous occasion in the Blake home as it is for millions of homes across America. The flowers were starting to bloom in the gardens at Three Lakes and the surrounding countryside of Far Hills, the weather was turning warmer with each day, and Jonathan always appreciated the message of hope that the Easter Sunday sermon focused on. Deep down, Jonathan was an optimist, always trying to find the good in people and circumstances, and Easter seemed to bring it out in him even more so. As usual, the Blake clan dressed up in their Sunday finest for the trip to New Vernon Presbyterian church. After arriving in separate cars, the whole family congregated just to the left of the steps leading into the small white church. There they enjoyed the fresh spring air and talking about the events of the past week. As other gathering parishioners arrived, the Blakes greeted them cheerfully.

Finally, the church bells began to ring, and it was time to enter and find themselves seats. The service was wonderful, as it always was, with the choir singing "Christ the Lord is Risen Today" so beautifully, but the sermon is what struck Jonathan this morning. Turning to 1 Corinthians 15, the minister made a statement that struck a chord deep within him. "And if Christ has not been raised, your faith is futile; you are still in your sins. Then those also who have fallen asleep in Christ are lost. If only for this life we have hope in Christ, we are to be pitied more than all men. But Christ has indeed been raised from the dead, the firstfruits of those who have fallen asleep." The minister placed the Bible back on the pulpit and began to expound on the passage.

"This passage shows us one crystal-clear truth about eternity. While most men live their lives here on earth totally consumed with the temporal nature of this earth and its ways, there is waiting for them another life, and it is eternal in nature. This life is given to us through Christ. The truth is that we do not have hope simply for this life! Yes, God walks with us, yes, even carries us through the peaks of the highest mountains and the lows of the lowest valleys, strengthening us, encouraging us, and empowering us through our lives. But the greatest hope for humanity is that Christ has enabled us to live not only for these 70-some years that He grants us here on this earth but also to live with Him for all eternity. If our hope is only for a better life here, then indeed, we are to be pitied. Our hope is for eternity."

Jonathan didn't hear much after that. He was thinking now about his own life. He had never really thought about dying much. He had never had to, personally. Yes, he was grieved through the deaths of his family, but he never got to the point where he actually realized that he himself would someday perish. He began this morning to think about eternity, about what heaven would be like, about whether or not there were really streets of gold and mansions to live in or if those were merely figurative analogies used to demonstrate the bliss one lives in eternally. He knew that he would soon find out for sure.

The thought of heaven intrigued Jonathan. He certainly had lived on his own slice of what many would call heaven on earth. Now, soon, Jonathan would make that far-away journey. He didn't want to go. Not now. There was too much to look forward to. His thoughts drifted about for the rest of the service. Even the final song he sang mouthing the words but thinking of impending death.

He snapped back to attention when the service was over, and someone was tugging at his arm. It was Ethel Wilson, the perpetual church lady if ever there was one. Ethel was always at the church and gave every ounce of her energy to make it a family place. She was the definitive grandmother of the flock, you would say.

"That was a wonderful service, wasn't it, Jonathan?" Ethel asked, more stating the fact than asking the question." Her face was beaming, connected to a slanted head, looking up at the tall Jonathan from her position a mere five feet from the floor. Her dress was new, floral. She had probably made it herself.

"It was, indeed, Mrs. Wilson," Jonathan replied. He had liked her ever since he was a young boy. Back then, it seemed as though she always had a plate full of chocolate chip cookies extended for little boys and girls to sample from. She also had such a simple faith and was so adept at bringing the joyful aspect of that faith into others' lives. Jonathan remembered that because she had been his fifth-grade Sunday School teacher, and it was one of the better years he spent there, if he remembered correctly.

"Now, Jonathan, I told you when you graduated from Harvard that you weren't to call me Mrs. Wilson. You should call me Ethel. When you become an adult, you call me by my first name."

"Princeton," Jonathan said.

"What?"

"Princeton. I went to Princeton University."

"Oh yes, Princeton. Princeton, Harvard, Yale, they're all the same thing."

Michael was standing next to his father and rolled his eyes. "Still, you call me Ethel, okay?"

"All right, it's a deal, Ethel," he said, finally relenting.

"You know," Ethel continued, "when you get to my age, looking death in the face, you take a sermon like that a little more seriously than a person does at your young age. I'm going to be a bit quicker to Gloryland than you will, so I've got to think of these things."

"Well, I'm trying to learn to take all of the sermons I hear seriously nowadays. They all seem to hit home in my life."

"You don't worry, though. You have plenty of years left in this ole' world." She paused and started to turn away, off to the next person who could lend an ear, then turned back to add an afterthought. "And if you don't, the good Lord will meet you on the other side anyway. You just have to trust Him. Trust Him here and trust Him there; that's what I say. You have a good Easter with your family, now."

Ethel Wilson was gone as quickly as she had come. Her words were more prophetic than she could have ever imagined. Jonathan looked to the ceiling briefly. Jonathan finally turned to find that his whole family was just exiting the building. All of them, including Michael now, were caught up in conversation with others. Jonathan pushed past a few families to catch up to Gloria. Once out in the parking lot, they all said goodbye and agreed on a time for dinner back at Three Lakes.

Jonathan and Gloria walked across the parking lot, stopping every so often to chat. Finally, they climbed into their car.

"That was a beautiful service," Gloria announced.

"That it was, dear."

"And I thought the sermon was presented well, didn't you?" she asked.

Jonathan didn't immediately respond. He was thinking about the sermon.

"Honey, didn't you think the sermon was good?"

"Oh, yes, dear. I'm sorry I didn't answer you. I was just thinking about a couple of his points."

"Which points?"

"Well, the part about having hope only for this life, and if you do, then you are to be pitied." Jonathan gripped the steering wheel tighter.

Gloria had done her best not to think much about Jonathan's illness. It was impossible, of course, but she just didn't want to think about it. Besides, Jonathan was still in relatively good health and didn't have outward signs that would remind her that he was dying. Not yet anyway. There was the occasional pain, but Dr. Kidman had prescribed Jonathan some pain relievers, and he took them whenever he began to ache. This kept others from seeing the deterioration right away. She knew where Jonathan was going with this, and she wasn't sure she wanted to talk about it on a day like Easter that was supposed to be a joyous occasion. She needed to respond, though. She looked casually out the window.

"What about that made you think something in particular?" she asked.

"As he mentioned, sometimes we become so temporally minded that we forget that most of a person's existence is the other side of death, not in this world. It struck a chord with me."

"Do you feel like you haven't been aware enough of the future?" She couldn't even get herself to say the word "death."

"Yes, that's right. I feel like I have been pretty focused here. For years, I've been absorbed in business and the many tasks and relationships that brings. In a way, it's imperative that one keep their eye on the ball, so to speak, but I'm not so sure that I have thought much about death and what comes after this life." Gloria bit her bottom lip when she heard the word "death."

"Well, let's not think about that today, shall we?" This is Easter, and it's supposed to be a day of celebration and joy."

"I think that's the point I'm trying to get at, Gloria. This is a day of celebration and joy because it gives hope to people like me, dying people." Gloria still looked out the window. "Gloria, we have to face this, not ignore it, and what he said today made sense in that it reminds me that I don't just have this life. Sure, I may not know for sure what will come afterward, but because of Easter, I can have some measure of joy, of hope."

Gloria turned and looked at Jonathan. He briefly looked at her but turned back to the road ahead. Gloria began to cry softly. "Jonathan, I'm just so scared. I don't want to be without you.

I don't know what I'll do without you." Jonathan squeezed her hand. He knew that Gloria was having a tremendously difficult time accepting the truth of the situation. He felt like they needed to deal with it openly, but he also didn't want to put a damper on their Easter. He decided not to carry it any further today. They rode the rest of the way home in silence.

Once the family had all gotten back to Three Lakes, Gloria told them that dinner would be in about an hour. Michael and Patty stole away for a quick nap. Jennifer and Samantha helped Gloria in the kitchen, and William read the Sunday paper in the living room. Thomas and Jonathan played pool while Scott watched on.

Thomas slowly drew his cue stick back and then slammed it forward to break. He sank the four-ball. "Looks like you're solids," Jonathan said.

"Yes, sir. And I left myself set up to run the table on you, so you can have a seat."

"Always the dreamer, you are," Scott chimed in. Jonathan laughed.

"What do you know about the hunting in Montana, Dad?" Thomas asked as he moved around the table for an easy shot at the two-ball.

"Oh, enough. What do you want to know about it?"

"Well, I saw an article talking about the fishing and elk hunting out there and just thought it might be fun to go out there sometime. We always tend to stay around here or go up into Canada." Thomas sank the two-ball and moved to the opposite corner for a hard bank shot at the seven.

"I went out there with some friends about 10 years ago. It was pretty good fishing," Jonathan replied. "When were you thinking of going?"

"Actually," Thomas said, again drawing his pool cue methodically back. "I thought maybe we could rent a ranch out there sometime, maybe next year after I get going at Princeton, and take the whole family. What do you think? I could get some information on it."

Jonathan initially started to get excited. He loved family vacations, and the Blakes had had some wonderful ones in the past. Suddenly, the thought struck him that he most certainly wouldn't be here long enough to carry a trip to Montana out. He was sure that his face had turned ashen, and his heart began to race out of control. This was one of the first times of many that Jonathan would come to the stark realization that, for him, life would soon be over. Very few opportunities were left for him to enjoy his family. Plans for future vacations and celebrations would only prove futile. There were those they already had planned, but for them, he merely hoped to live through and enjoy as much as he could.

"Well, we'll just have to see how it works out," Jonathan forced the words out.

"Maybe I can check into it." He hoped that Thomas and Scott didn't notice his panic.

"You have to reserve those ranches early," Thomas said as the seven-ball barely dropped into the pocket.

"We'll see," Jonathan said. Changing the topic, Jonathan turned to Scott.

"How's work going, Scott?"

"Oh, pretty well, I guess. I'm in the middle of a pharmaceutical acquisition right now. I can't really say what it is, but it's one of the big boys taking out a little guy who happened to stumble upon a pretty effective pain reliever. It should make them a tidy little sum in the next 10 years."

"Hmmm. Sounds interesting. It sounds like you're glad to have switched your focus."

"This is a little more my style. Dividing up the estates of divorcing 50-year-olds was not very challenging, not to mention that the bickering gets to you after a while. So, yes, I'm enjoying it."

Thomas continued to clear the table and sink the eight-ball, all without letting Jonathan have even one chance. "I taught you everything I know about pool," Jonathan said to Thomas when he won.

"Ha! You'll do anything to take credit. Even when you lose."

"That's what dads are for, my son," Jonathan said as he handed his cue to Scott. "Here you go. I'm going to go to my office for a few minutes before dinner. Hopefully, you can take a little wind out of my baby boy's sails. We wouldn't want him to become arrogant."

"I think I'm up for the challenge," Scott replied. "All those late nights I should have been studying in law school made me a better pool player, if you know what I mean." Thomas was already collecting the balls to then rack for the next game.

Jonathan turned and walked out of the room. "Practice up, and I'll give you a rematch," Thomas called to his father.

"Keep talking, and I'll sell the table," Jonathan retorted without looking back as he turned down the hall to his office. Scott smiled at his father-in-law's humor before beating Thomas in two of their three games.

Finally, it was time for dinner. The Blake family gathered together and sat around the table. Jonathan gave thanks for the meal. "God, thank You for this day to enjoy with my family. Thank You for this meal and Your provision of it. We especially thank You for the knowledge that this day gives us hope beyond ourselves, hope for something more. Bless this food to our bodies. Amen."

"Amen," came the chorus from around the table, which was decorated beautifully with an assortment of fresh-cut flowers from Gloria's gardens.

"The flowers look beautiful," Samantha said.

"Thank you," replied Gloria as she stood passing dishes around the table.

"So, what did you think of the sermon?" William asked to no one in particular. Gloria glanced at Jonathan.

It was Michael who spoke first. "I thought it was well done. I just have a hard time thinking about eternity and death and such. It just seems so far out there, like it will never happen to you, always someone else, someone older."

"I thought the same thing," Jennifer said. "I mean, you know that you are going to die someday, but you just don't think about it much. There is too much life to live right now."

"What about the part about hope?" William asked another question.

"The older you get," Gloria started to reply. "The more you realize that death is a part of life." She paused and got teary. She couldn't believe that she had entered the conversation. The children all noticed her tears and wondered what was going on. "I loathe that, you know. But like the minister said, there is hope. It is something we take by faith…"

Jonathan finished the sentence for Gloria. "And that is why this is such a special day. We remember that faith isn't a historical event and that it isn't misplaced. There is hope, and this is a day to be joyful about. So let's quit talking about death and start talking about all that we have to live for."

"That sounds good," Samantha said, still wondering what her mother's tears were all about. "Let's change the subject."

It isn't that anybody had any idea of what was going on or that they couldn't handle the topic. No, Gloria's sudden change in demeanor stunned everyone. Most of them figured she was just getting older and was probably asking questions that most people their age simply haven't reason to ask yet.

The Blakes spent the remainder of their Easter dinner together eating, discussing the upcoming week and all of the other things that families discuss. After dinner, they all found things to do around the estate, and eventually, those who lived elsewhere drifted home. Another Easter. It would be Jonathan's last. Next Easter, he would be elsewhere. He remembered that there was hope while at the same time beginning to see that there really was an end coming. His contemplation tossed back and forth between the positive and the negative emotions he alternately experienced. Hope and despair, faith and futility, side by side, roaming Jonathan's heart.

April 27

"HELLO," JENNIFER ANSWERED the phone in her study at home.

"Hi there, Jennifer." She instantly recognized her father's voice.

"Oh, hi, Dad. What's up?" Jennifer sat in her chair and thumbed through file folders, looking for one she needed.

"Well, I called to see if you want to go to lunch tomorrow."

"I think so. I'll have to check my calendar at work, but I think I'm free. I usually don't schedule much on Fridays so I can get my work done for the weekend. Eleven-thirty will probably work."

"Okay. So when will you let me know for sure?"

"How about we just plan on it. I'll call you by 9 if I have something, but I don't think I do. Where do you want to meet?"

"I'll come to your office, and we can decide on where to go, then walk there."

"Sure, that sounds fine. What's the special occasion anyway?"

"I just want to see how you're doing, catch up, that's all." He wanted to get off the subject for tonight, so he asked about Scott. "How's Scott doing?"

"He's gone for two days in Pittsburgh on business, so I'm holding down the fort. He'll be back Saturday morning. It's nice in a way because I can get a lot of work done around the house and still sneak in some time with the books I've been trying to make it through."

"You enjoy your time then, and I'll see you at 11:30 unless I hear from you." They both said goodbye and hung up. Gloria walked into the office just as Jonathan was putting the phone back on the desk.

"Who were you talking to?" she asked.

"Jennifer. I'm taking her to lunch tomorrow."

"That will be fun. What are you going to talk about?"

"You know, I'm starting to get a little paranoid. Every time I want to spend some time with a child of mine, everybody thinks it's a national event."

Gloria laughed. "Well, sir, it's just that you aren't in the habit of just calling up, spur of the moment, and going out with the kids. So what do you want to talk to her about?"

"Oh, you know me too well, Gloria. I want to see how she and Scott are doing. I'm still a little concerned. It won't be anything heavy. I just want to find out how they are doing and encourage her a little."

"I'm sure she will appreciate it. She respects you so very much, you know."

"I hope so. Prodding into people's lives isn't always appreciated or welcomed with open arms."

Jonathan arrived at Jennifer's law office at 11:25 the next day. As he walked through the massive glass doors, the receptionist greeted him by name. It surprised him a little, but most people in the area knew who he was. "Hello, Mr. Blake," she said.

"Good day, how are you?"

"I'm fine. Here to see your daughter, are you?"

"I sure am. Is she in?"

"She is. I'll ring her." The receptionist pressed a few buttons and spoke into her headset. "Jennifer, your father is here to see you." She paused. "I'll tell him." She then turned to Jonathan, who had by this time found a seat and was reading the latest issue of *Forbes FYI*. "Jennifer says she'll be out in a few minutes."

"That's fine," Jonathan responded.

Just a few minutes later, Jennifer emerged from the hallway leading to the back offices. "Ready to go," she declared.

Jonathan jumped to his feet, laying the magazine back down on the table. "Hey, you look sharp today," Jonathan said, noticing the bright red dress Jennifer was wearing.

She flipped her hair to the side as she walked past her father. "I always look sharp, Dad," she said only half-jokingly, opening the door.

Jonathan looked at the receptionist again, who was smiling now. "I've created a monster," he said.

"Come on, or I'll have to charge you by the hour," Jennifer called, reminding Jonathan that she was ever the lawyer.

Jonathan and Jennifer walked the three blocks to a small deli just south of the Green in Morristown. After ordering two sandwiches, two soups, and two sodas, then picking them up at the end of the counter, they sat in a booth looking out over Route 24, which winded through Morristown, out through Mendham, Chester, and Long Valley and continued west over Schooley's Mountain.

"So, how's the day going?" Jonathan asked.

"Pretty well, actually. Standard stuff, but I'm having a good day. How about you?"

"I must say that retirement is pretty good to your mother and me. We slept in; I got to read the paper and drink some hot coffee, checked into what was happening in the markets, then had breakfast with your mom. What a morning! It sure beats the pressure of meeting the daily deadline."

"You don't miss the papers at all?"

"Not one iota."

"Come on."

"No, really. Your mom and I are loving the relaxation and freedom retirement provides. I worked too hard for too many years. The newspaper business is a deadline a day, and that grinds on you."

"I guess. At least I have weeks and months to prepare for my work." Jennifer changed the subject. "So, what's the topic of conversation today?" she asked, just before biting into her tuna salad sandwich. She knew she shouldn't have tuna when she had to go back to work because of what it did to her breath, but it was her favorite, so she gave in.

"I wanted to catch up with you, but I also wanted to find out how you and Scott are doing." Jennifer rolled her eyes and swallowed while setting her sandwich down. Of all of the marriages in the Blake family, Scott and Jennifer's was the one that gave people the most to worry about. Scott and Jennifer met at Wilson, Banks, and Smith, the law firm where Scott was an attorney. Jennifer worked for another law firm, Thompson, Carr, Dunn, and Hart, that did occasional work with Wilson, Banks, and Smith, and she met him one day while delivering some legal briefs to his office. He engaged her in conversation and found a reason to get her phone number. Shortly after that, they went on their first date.

They had a stormy but torrid romance and were married not too long after meeting each other. Both Jennifer and Scott were terrific people, but there was definitely something missing in their relationship. They had tried quite hard at times to make the relationship work, but with the busy schedules they both carried, there had been precious little time in which to commit to what would make the relationship right. They had also tried off and on to have children with no success—which was probably for the better, considering the state of their marriage. Deep down, they both truly loved one another, but their work, their lack of time, and a slight selfish streak in both kept them from the kind of fulfilling marriage that could be theirs. Divorce wasn't an option for either of them, mainly because of commitments they both made to each other, which were strengthened by the resolve they developed after seeing the many divorces that go through their law offices.

Scott and Jennifer lived in Mendham, about 15 minutes north of Far Hills. They purchased a house there on Mountainside Road three years ago. It was a standard colonial, the first home they owned. The past three years had been spent decorating the different rooms, and of course, fixing the problems that the last owners conveniently forgot to tell them existed. It was a good house, one large enough to raise the family they would eventually have in comfort. Right now, though, they needed most to work on their own love.

"Scott is Scott," Jennifer replied. "He is simply self-absorbed, and it drives me nuts at best, makes me furious at worst. But I love him." She added the last as an afterthought.

"That's it? That's how you sum up your entire relationship? That doesn't sound too healthy to me." Jonathan grimaced in disbelief at what he was hearing.

"Dad, of course, it's not the whole thing." Jonathan relaxed some. "The downfall for us is that we are both so busy we are able to ignore the problem and keep our minds centered on other things. I know in the long run that we are going to have to deal with it head-on. Especially before we have kids."

Jonathan smiled. "Are you pregnant?" he asked, hoping.

"Ha. No, but you'll be the first to know, I promise. No, we have absolutely no plans on that front yet."

"Oh. Well, your mother and I are concerned, Jennifer. We've noticed that you two aren't exactly the lovebirds you once were."

"I know. I wonder if anyone stays that way, though. I would like to do something about it, but he is just so obstinate."

"Jennifer, if I may be so bold, which I may, being your father, as it has been put before, 'It takes two to tango.'"

"Dad, I try really hard..."

"But you are partly to blame, aren't you?" he asked, cutting in on Jennifer's sentence.

She stopped talking. Lifting a spoonful of soup to her mouth, she paused in thought. "I am partly to blame," she finally conceded. Jennifer looked out the window. The noon-hour traffic was hustling by. Busy people on their way to their busy destinations.

"What are you going to do about it?" he asked. "You can't simply disregard the problems. I've learned with your mother and I that when something comes up, you have to deal with it sooner rather than later, or it festers and becomes a bigger problem. Or problems. If you want my opinion, and I can only speak to you at this point, though I may try to spend some time with Scott soon as well, I think you need to learn the fine art of forgiveness."

"What do you mean by that?" Jennifer asked, somewhat indignant.

"Here. I have failed your mother constantly for years—in many different ways. The one thing I could count on, though, was that when I did, she forgave me rather than hold it against me. It is entirely freeing, Jennifer. Then I didn't want to fail her. I wanted to honor her forgiveness. What would happen if the next time Scott really blows it, you forgive him rather than beat him up with it?"

"You're kidding, right?"

"No, Jennifer, I'm not. Listen, you can be the tough lawyer at work, upholding the law and all there, but at home, the best thing you could do would be to dedicate yourself to being the second part of a two-way relationship where the people involved are working together and willing to forgive one another for the sake of the relationship."

"What about all the times he does me wrong? Frankly, it's tiring, Dad."

"What are your options, Jennifer? You could get vindictive and pay him back tit for tat, causing yourself to be in a war that would most likely end in a divorce. That's one. You could ignore him, allowing your relationship to continue the way it is, but that will only cause more severe problems down the road. That's two. Or three, you could commit to working everything out, discussing it like adults, and forgiving each other when you fail. I mean, face it. Scott is going to fail you. That is a given. And, I might add, I know as a fact of life that you fail him regularly as well. It's part of being human. So your choices are to forgive him when he fails or don't forgive him when he fails. Take your pick. One leads one way, to pain and bitterness, and the other leads to peace and a life of fulfillment." Jonathan could tell that she was beginning to get the idea. He could almost see her brain working to grasp the logic of forgiveness.

"Well, you should have been a preacher, Dad." Jonathan should have smiled but didn't. He cared too deeply to laugh at the moment. Instead, he waited for Jennifer. After a few moments, Jennifer finally cracked a bit. "I'll take it under consideration, Counselor," she said, implying in a lawyerly way that she got the point and would make the adjustments. Jennifer did want her relationship with Scott to work. She had seen so much of a caring side to him when they were dating, but like many couples, they began to drift into the patterns of life that prove to be the undoing of the countless masses that give up rather than commit to the more difficult task of loving and forgiving.

"I'm glad that you will. And I'm sure you will both be the better for it. Say, let's change the topic. I've said my piece, so you can think about it."

Jennifer took her father up on the idea of changing the topic. She had heard him loud and clear, and, though she hated to admit it, he was right. The way she usually handled Scott's mistakes tended to be a bit severe, especially for one who wanted the relationship to get better. They spent the next 15 minutes eating and talking, then Jonathan walked his beloved oldest child back to her office.

At the entrance to the building, Jonathan stopped and held the door open. "I'll let you go up by yourself. Thanks for lending me your ear."

"No problem, Dad. Thanks for the lunch. And thanks for the advice. I know that I needed it, as hard as it is to hear."

"That's my job—to keep my kids going in the right direction. I know it's tough, but you'll make it if you do what is right."

"Thanks, Dad. I love you." Jennifer reached up and gave Jonathan a peck on the cheek.

"I love you, too. We'll talk later."

Jonathan was happy now. Driving home to Three Lakes, he hummed to the music of Tchaikovsky playing loudly on the stereo.

Sticking his nose into others' business wasn't something Jonathan relished, but this was his daughter after all. And his time to make a lasting impression, one that would benefit her for the rest of her life, was drawing to a close with each passing day. He felt good about how his meeting with Jennifer went. He had wondered beforehand whether she would become defensive or not. She hadn't, and that was good.

As the gates opened to Three Lakes, Jonathan tapped his fingers to the music on the steering wheel. "Another day, another child pointed in the right direction." He gunned the engine and took off up the driveway.

May 13

I T WAS 5 O'CLOCK, and Michael Blake was standing near the window of the bedroom that he had grown up in. He was 29 now and had been out of the home for 11 years. Still, when he and his wife Patty spent the night back at Three Lakes, this was their room. Gloria had taken down all of the sports posters that had once covered the walls, but there were still remnants of a teenage boy. There was a bin with five baseball bats in it, a Nerf hoop still on the closet door, and a sign on the desk that read "Michael's Room."

Michael gazed out the window, looking toward the front gate and the few cars driving up the driveway and parking in the small, freshly mowed field just north of the house. Michael was a good-looking young man. He had similar features as his father, but his younger brother Thomas was the one who looked the most like Jonathan. Michael actually looked most like Gloria's father. Michael had graduated from Princeton and gone straight into business at a local consulting firm. It was small but prestigious. He was an astute businessman for his age, which was due, in large part, to growing up being mentored by his father; but it was true that the partners there figured the Blake name would also carry with it a large Rolodex of connections. It certainly wouldn't hurt to have someone working for them, they figured, who could call his father any time he was in a dilemma and instantly get the number of virtually anyone on the

East Coast with any power to solve the problem. Michael worked hard, made good money, and brought in his share of business to the firm, in fact, rarely relying on his family connections.

This Saturday night would be spent honoring two great people and one great accomplishment. Tonight was Jonathan and Gloria's 35th wedding anniversary, and Michael and his older sister Jennifer had received Jonathan's permission to organize a grand party to honor them. Jonathan had granted Michael a stipend to pull the whole thing off, and he tried to keep Gloria out of the loop as much as possible. Eventually, about two weeks before the party, she found out about it, but not how big it would actually be.

"The people are starting to arrive, huh?" Patty Blake asked as she came out of the bathroom, her head tilted to one side, trying to put the back on her earring.

"Yeah, this is going to be a great night," Michael responded. He was so proud of his parents, and he adored his dad especially. Michael had never been a problem growing up. There had never been any rebellion of any kind: no drugs, no smoking or drinking, no trouble with the law, not even a speeding ticket—at least none that Jonathan knew about. Now, standing in his bedroom with his black tuxedo on and his bowtie hanging untied around his neck, he contemplated again in his mind what it was going to take to pull tonight off in the manner he wanted to. There was the short cocktail reception, the eight-course dinner under the tent they had erected in the back, the music, the speeches, and the dancing, probably until midnight or later, that would take place in the ballroom. He had carefully organized the evening but still worried a bit that the affair wouldn't come off as planned. Above all, his desire was to have his parents enjoy themselves and know that people loved them.

"How many people do you think will come?" Patty asked, now on the floor looking in the carpet for the back of her earring she dropped.

"Well, we had 125 RSVPs, so probably that many, give or take a few."

Patty found her earring back and finally got it together. She moved up behind Michael and put her arms around his waist. "You're a great son. You've done a great job organizing. Don't worry about tonight. It is going to go just fine. Besides, the rest of us kids are pulling up some of the slack."

Patty had read Michael's mind, as was usual. Since they met at Princeton nine years ago, she always had the knack to know what Michael was thinking. When his thinking was wrong, she also had the ability to help him change it without making him defensive. She was a perfect match for Michael, and so Michael had made her his wife four years ago.

Cars were still coming in, but as the time approached 5:15, Michael knew it was time to get going and start mingling with people as they arrived. He quickly tied his bowtie, kissed Patty on the cheek, and moved to leave.

"See you downstairs," he said as he turned and walked down the hall. Patty forgave him for leaving without her, even though she was ready to go downstairs herself. She knew he was a little flighty when he was nervous. "See you downstairs," she laughed to nobody in particular as she started out the door behind him.

When Michael arrived downstairs, his sister Jennifer was already out in front of the home greeting people and directing them around the corner of the house to the white, 80-foot-by-80-foot tent that had been erected the day before. Michael went out and stood next to Jennifer to help greet the guests as they arrived.

"Mr. and Mrs. Adcox. How are you tonight?" Michael asked.

"We're doing fine, Michael." They extended hands to greet one another. "This is a wonderful idea that you and Jennifer had. We are so glad to be a part of it," Reginald Adcox responded. Mr. Adcox is a private banker in Manhattan, and he and his wife had been friends of Jonathan and Gloria for many years. The two couples had even taken a cruise together through the Caribbean in 1987. Adcox and his band of bankers and venture capitalists had provided much of the financing needed to purchase the newspapers that Jonathan owned. They had been rewarded well by investing in Jonathan's Midas touch.

Michael pointed the way for the Adcoxes, and he and Jennifer continued to welcome people as they arrived. After welcoming a few more of the guests and pointing them in the right direction as well, Michael noticed Albert Manning walking up behind some others, so he turned to Jennifer and asked her to continue without him because he would like to talk to Albert alone.

"Uncle Al, hi."

"Hello, Michael. Were you worried that I would forget my best friend's anniversary party?" Albert asked as he came close to Michael.

"No, I knew that you would be here. I just want to talk a bit before we start and let you know what the schedule is."

Albert Manning had been Jonathan's dearest friend ever since their days at Delbarton together. After Delbarton, they attended Princeton and were roommates for all four years. Both Jonathan and Albert majored in literature. Jonathan, of course, after inheriting his parents' wealth, went into publishing, while Albert became a writer. As the years progressed, he had become one of the most famous political satirists in the country, with his column being one of the most highly syndicated columns in America. Many a politician had melted under Albert's scathing wit and satirical scrutiny. In addition to his writing, he had done television and speaking and was a frequent guest on the Sunday morning news shows. Albert is also single, having never found anyone to marry. He liked to say that he was married to his work. In a way, Albert Manning was Michael's stand-in uncle. Many a Thanksgiving day was spent with Albert joining the Blake family to watch football and enjoy a scrumptious meal.

"So, are you ready?" Michael inquired, already knowing the answer. One doesn't get to Albert Manning's status by ever being unprepared.

"I am, indeed. Would you like to hear it?"

"No, but I do want to let you know that you will be the second speaker right after dessert is served. Reverend Wilton will go first, then you, then my brothers and sisters all want to say something, then the Blake kids will dazzle everybody with a song, and I'll conclude with a few words. After all that excitement, we'll all go into the ballroom to dance the night away."

Albert was impressed. "That sounds terrific. Your mother and father will remember this for the rest of their lives. The only regret I have in not getting married is that I never had children like you. But at least the way it has been, I was able to enjoy you for a time, and your parents had the hard jobs like bailing you out of jail." They both chuckled. Albert slapped Michael on the shoulder and said, "Excuse me now, I'm going to see if any of your mother's single friends have arrived." As quickly as he had come, Albert had gone to the back of the estate.

What a piece of work, Michael thought to himself as he smiled. Walking back over to Jennifer, he informed her that he was going to go to the back of the house. Soon after Michael left, Scott came from inside the house and joined her out front.

"So, you're the official greeter, are you?" Scott asked as he approached Jennifer.

"Yes," Jennifer said without turning, "Michael was here for a bit, but he went to the back of the house to make sure everything is running smoothly there."

"It looks like it's going to be a full house tonight," Scott said as more cars made their way up the drive, just trying to make small talk.

"I'm so glad that so many of Mom and Dad's friends are going to be here. It will mean a lot to them."

After a moment, Scott asked, "I wonder what our 35th wedding anniversary will be like?"

"I sometimes wonder if our 35th wedding anniversary will actually happen." Jennifer let the words out harshly, realizing the instant that she did that she was moving into territory she didn't want to venture into, especially tonight. Not on this special night. She should have waited to restart their previous argument some other time, sometime later. She didn't mean the words, but the resentment she felt toward Scott had just reached a boiling point.

Scott realized he was about to enter into an argument that they would both regret later, so he tried to shrug it off. "Sure it will, if I have any say about it. I'm going to go see if Michael needs any help. I'll see you later." With that, he turned and disappeared behind the house.

Jennifer bit her lip. She knew she had made a mistake, and she appreciated that Scott had sense enough to ignore her and not exacerbate the problem. She thought about the words Jonathan had spoken to her a few weeks back. Forgiveness. She pondered the word as she watched the guests arriving. She would talk to Scott later and apologize, she decided. Right now, she had to devote her full attention to making this night a success for her parents.

"Hello, Mr. and Mrs. Allen," she said to the next couple approaching the house. "Please, go around back. There are a number of folks already there." And so it went for the next 15 minutes until the final guests had arrived. When they did, Jennifer joined the rest of the family and guests.

Michael went to the podium promptly at 6 o'clock and began to speak as the crowd milled around eating appetizers, greeting one another, reuniting with old friends, and meeting new ones. The party was already starting out to be a joyous one. "Ladies and Gentlemen, if I might have your attention, please. We would like to get started, so if you would be so kind as to find your seats, we would be grateful."

After a few minutes, the guests had all found their respective seats and waited for further instruction, still all of them involved in their conversations.

Michael continued as those gathered quieted. "I am Michael Blake, and I would like to warmly welcome you on behalf of my brother and sisters and myself, as well as our guests of honor tonight, my mother and father, Jonathan and Gloria Blake. We are truly privileged to have you here with us to celebrate 35 years of marriage. The next four or five hours should prove to be a marvelous and memorable time.

"For your information, the night will progress as follows. In a few moments, we will be treated to a superb dinner, followed by a few special people who have some kind words and reflections for Mom and Dad, and then we will close the evening with dancing in the ballroom, where we are excited to have the Morris County Strings playing some of our favorite music." Jonathan and Gloria's many friends nodded their approval.

"Again, I want to thank you for being here for this special occasion. Enjoy your meal and the company you share it with."

As Michael left the podium, the waitstaff began to bring the meals to the tables, and the night was officially underway. Jonathan and Gloria sat at the head table, along with Michael and Patty, the Reverend Wilton, Albert Manning, and Gloria's sister, Margaret, and her husband Bob, who had flown in from their home in Charlottesville, Virginia, to celebrate with the Blakes. Gloria's brother Martin and his wife were unable to attend because of commitments in Germany, but they did send a beautiful floral arrangement which was on display in the foyer of the entrance to the house. Gloria beamed most of the night, enjoying the food, the guests, and Jonathan. Oh, how she loved her dear Jonathan. Every 10 minutes or so, she would reach under the table and squeeze his knee and twinkle her eyes at him as he looked at her.

"So, Jonathan, do you still love my sister as much as you did when you first got married?" Margaret asked.

"Margaret, I love her infinitely more than I did when I first married her."

"I remember that wedding day. I was so excited that my sister was getting married. You were my hero, Jonathan, what with me being just a teenager and all. You were so handsome in your black tuxedo. I couldn't believe that Gloria was getting such a fine catch."

"Oh, you stop it, Margaret," Gloria said, mocking jealousy, her hand on her sister's shoulder.

"Besides," said Margaret's husband Bob, "You were the one who ended up with the real catch."

"I couldn't agree with Bob more," Jonathan added.

"Spoken like the humble man that you are," Margaret said, looking back over her shoulder toward Bob. She turned back to Jonathan and Gloria. "Seriously though, you two, we are so happy for you. You two are the greatest."

Reverend Wilton looked at Michael. "You must be very proud of your mom and dad."

"In this day and age, you really realize what a treasure they are."

"And it looks like you two are doing well?" he added, looking briefly toward Patty.

Michael smiled at Patty and reached out to take her hand in his. "Yes, we are. She is the joy of my life. Just a few short years but getting better with every day."

"Well, you follow in the footsteps of your parents, and someday you two will celebrate your 35th wedding anniversary too, I'm sure," Reverend Wilton pronounced. Just then the conversation stopped momentarily as the waitstaff served the table.

Thomas was sitting with a group of his parents' friends, and he was the youngest at the table by a good 40 years. He felt remotely comfortable, though. Of all the Blake children, he was the one with a shy streak, and this made it hard at times around new people, especially older ones. For his parents, though, he would make the most of it, answering all of the questions of his inquisitive tablemates.

"So I suppose it's off to Old Nassau for you next year, yes, Thomas?" It was Jim Blair, a friend of Jonathan's from the Wall Street Journal. Blair had also been a year ahead of Jonathan at Princeton. They met sitting next to each other in a history class and had been friends ever since. Most everyone knew that the Blake family all made their way to Princeton. Thomas decided to have some fun with Blair.

"Old Nassau, Sir?" he feigned misunderstanding.

"Yes, Princeton. You haven't heard your father call it 'Old Nassau'?"

"Oh, yes. Well, actually, I am leaning heavily toward Duke. I've always wanted to go to the South, and I think that it is in the same class as Princeton academically," Thomas said, stuffing a forkful of food into his mouth, nonchalantly and avoiding eye contact. You could see the pained, disappointed look on Jim Blair's face, while all the while, he was trying to cover it with a smile.

Before he could say anything, though, Thomas relieved him by pronouncing, "I'm just kidding, Mr. Blair. I am going to Princeton. I've already been accepted, and I'm just waiting to hear about my room assignment." The table roared with laughter, knowing that Jim had been taken.

"Well," Blair said, slapping Thomas on the arm, "you had me scared for a minute there. So, what are you thinking about studying?"

"I don't know yet. I have a few things I'm interested in, but I'll have to see when I get there. I have a while before I have to decide."

"Are you thinking about something that will lead you into journalism?" Blair asked.

"No, one big shot journalist in the family is enough," Thomas retorted, again to a table of laughter.

"Well, you'll find the right pursuits, I'm sure," replied Mrs. Blair. "Besides, you have two wonderful parents to help guide you and help you along. You will do just fine."

The table began to drift into old Princeton stories after that as a couple of other gentlemen at the table had also attended there. Thomas quickly became bored, feeling like he was at a class reunion. He wondered to himself if he would ever voluntarily utter the words "Old Nassau."

Jennifer and Scott sat at their table of eight, carrying on superficial conversation with the other guests, all the while thinking of their earlier spat. All throughout dinner, they each wondered how the night would progress and whether or not it would end on a positive or negative note.

As soon as the main course was through, Jennifer had decided to resolve the problem so she leaned over and whispered to Scott. "In a few minutes, I'm going to excuse myself. Would you wait a few minutes and then excuse yourself and meet me in the library?"

Scott nodded. He wanted to put this issue to rest, too, as well as a few other issues that had been bothering him and causing dissension in his and Jennifer's marriage for some time.

As she had indicated, Jennifer waited a few minutes then excused herself. "I'll be back in a few moments. Is there anything I can get for anybody while I'm up?" The others at the table declined her offer, and so Jennifer began weaving her way through the other tables and disappeared into the house. Scott excused himself soon thereafter.

Scott entered the library and quietly shut the massive oak doors. Jennifer sat without a word on one of the couches in the far corner. Scott walked over and sat down in a chair to her right, still remaining silent himself. They each eyed the other. Finally, after a few moments of quiet, Scott asked the obvious. "So, you're pretty angry with me still?"

Jennifer, who had remained calm on the outside, was obviously angry inside, as the coming barrage would show. "Scott, I'm furious. I am so sick and tired of you breaking your promises to me. You told me that you would stay home with me this morning and help me with some things around the house. And then, we were going to drive down here together. You are so thoughtless!" She was almost screaming by the end.

Scott started to respond. "Look, Jennifer, I..."

"You what? You broke your promise again," she interrupted. "And frankly, I'm not going to take it anymore." Excitedly, Jennifer was standing now. She hovered over Scott, who was sitting deep in his seat, filled with shock at his young wife's rage and beginning to genuinely feel sorry that he had caused it.

Jennifer continued, "You knew last night that you were going to go in to work this morning, yet you didn't even have the courtesy or the courage to tell me. You let me believe until this morning that you would help me. You should have told me. No, I take that back. You should have not gone. When is it going to end, Scott? When will you simply do what you say? When will I come first in your life? I know that you are busy. We're both busy. I keep you first in my life, though, and that's the difference between us. I put you first, and you only get around to me. I'm so tired of it."

Jennifer, with this, began to cry. She turned away and moved back to the couch where she flopped down again. She put her head in her hands. Scott knew that he had an apology to make, and that he had better make it sooner rather than later, so he got up to move over to the couch. As he did, Jennifer tried to recompose herself, dabbing at her eyes with a tissue, so as not to smear her makeup. Scott sat down next to her.

"Honey, look, I really had to go in today. There was some work Wilson wanted done, and—"

Jennifer interrupted again, her eyes wide with anger. "And you should have told him you would do it tomorrow afternoon or that you would have done it Monday morning. Period."

Scott looked to the ceiling while he thought for a moment. He was so very tired of all the bickering and arguing. He knew that he and Jennifer would have to do something soon to turn their relationship around. Not that it was ready for divorce, but he knew that they were developing severely unhealthy patterns of communication that would certainly come back to haunt them if left alone. He also knew they would each have to give a little. He decided to be first. "You're right, Jennifer. I should have. I just want to do well there, you know. I just want the partners to think I'm willing to do the job." He faded out and turned his head to look out the window.

Jennifer was still extremely angry but knew that they had to get back out to the party, and it was some consolation that Scott was at least showing some remorse for his actions, so she touched his hand. "Scott, you do a great job there, and everybody knows it. One morning would not have made a difference."

"I know," Scott replied. He turned and looked at Jennifer. "Will you forgive me?" he asked.

She thought for a few moments, her father's words again ringing in her ears. As much as it wasn't in her nature, she found herself saying, "Yes, I will." She was cooling down a bit now. She squeezed his hand. "I still want to talk some more about this, though. We can do it later. Right now, we need to get back out to the party. Promise we can talk about this later this week?"

"Yeah, we can," Scott said.

They were smiling now, slightly forced as it was. They held each other's hands for a few brief moments, then got up to go. Before they started to leave, Scott pulled Jennifer close to him. "I love you very much, you know." He said, looking deep into her eyes.

"I love you too," she said.

"I would never, never, do anything to purposely hurt you, either."

"I know," she said.

Scott motioned with his head to indicate, "Come on," and they walked back out to the party hand in hand.

As everyone was beginning their dessert, Michael came once more to the microphone. "I hope that your dinner was as delectable as mine was." Heads nodded throughout the tent. "While you are enjoying your dessert, I would like to introduce a few people who have some words for us tonight. The first person is a man who has known my folks for many years. In fact, he performed their wedding ceremony. Charles Wilton has been a pastor to Mom and Dad, but he has been far more than that. He has been their close friend, advisor, and mentor. We asked him if he would share a few thoughts with us tonight. Reverend Wilton?" The guests clapped.

The Reverend Charles Wilton rose and strode to the podium. Reverend Wilton was getting on in years. He was tremendously respected in the region. He not only was the most respected elder statesman in the Protestant church in the area, but he also had the ear of some of New Jersey's most prominent families. He knew how to take something seemingly abstract like faith and make it understandable to the businessmen he had worked with so passionately over the years. Though he was officially retired, he now led a weekly study on Friday mornings that hundreds of men came out for. For a few years, he had even written a column for a few of Jonathan's newspapers. He was indeed a highly regarded man, and the people gathered this evening looked forward to his words.

Grasping both hands to the lectern, he began: "1 Corinthians 13:4-8 says 'Love is patient, love is kind. It does not envy, it does not boast, it is not proud. It is not rude, it is not self-seeking, it is not easily angered, it keeps no record of wrongs. Love does not delight in evil but rejoices with the truth. It always protects, always trusts, always hopes, always perseveres. Love never fails.' And 1 Corinthians 13:13 reads, 'And now these three remain: faith, hope and love. But the greatest of these is love.'

"Thirty-five years ago, I read these words at the wedding of Jonathan and Gloria Blake, just as I read them at most every wedding I am involved in or officiate. Over the years, I have performed literally hundreds of weddings at the many churches I have pastored. I have been involved in countless thousands of lives and marriages. Yet very few marriage relationships do I come to a great admiration and respect for. Those that gain my esteem do so by living out continuously, over the period of many years, those characteristics of love found in 1 Corinthians 13. Patience, kindness, humility, self-sacrifice, trust, hope, and perseverance are the marks of a truly great relationship. As I have known Jonathan and Gloria these many years, I have seen these qualities in their lives, both public and private, and in their marriage relationship. It is because of their undying love and commitment to one another, no matter what trials should come to them, that allow us to be here today, celebrating their lives and their love."

Turning to look at Jonathan and Gloria, he concluded, "Jonathan. Gloria. Thank you for the shining example you have set for your friends and family. Thank you for being a bright light in a society of throw-away relationships. May God give you many more years together, and may He continue to bless you richly."

With that, Reverend Wilton went and sat down, and the people gathered together applauded their appreciation for his words. Michael Blake came to the microphone to introduce Albert Manning.

"Thank you, Reverend Wilton. Now I would like to introduce you to one of our family's closest friends. He and my father went to Delbarton together, and both Mom and Dad attended college with him as well. I could go into who he is and what he does, but the reality is that if you don't know him, you live on a deserted island anyway. Ladies and gentlemen, Albert Manning."

Albert Manning strode confidently to take his place addressing the crowd. He was collected and at ease there. "To use your words, Michael, the reality is that after having to listen to me speak, many here today may wish they lived on a deserted island." The crowd chuckled.

Albert Manning got his initial fame and fortune through his writing, but he was also an accomplished speaker who could captivate an audience for any given period of time, all without ever using a note. His sharp and brilliant mind allowed him to memorize what seemed like volumes of information and then recall it at any given time. This evening, he was in fine form.

"Henry van Dyke wrote a charming little poem entitled *A Wayfaring Song*. It says so much about what I want to mention this evening." Looking out to the crowd, he began the poem he had memorized.

O who will walk a mile with me
Along life's merry way?

A comrade blithe and full of glee,
Who dares to laugh out loud and free
And let his frolic fancy play,
Like a happy child, through the flowers gay
That fill the field and fringe the way
Where he walks a mile with me.
And who will walk a mile with me
Along life's weary way?
A friend whose heart has eyes to see
The stars shine out o'er the darkening lea,
And the quiet rest at the end o' the day -
A friend who knows, and dares to say,
The brave, sweet words that cheer the way
Where he walks a mile with me.
With such a comrade, such a friend,
I fain would walk till journey's end,
Through summer sunshine, winter rain,
And then? Farewell, we shall meet again!

When Albert had finished the poem, he paused for dramatic effect, then began with his own thoughts. "I have had a best friend for many years. It has been a tremendous honor to know him. We have walked many countless miles together, both literally through the woods while hunting and across the schoolyards of Delbarton School and Princeton University. We have walked many miles figuratively as well as we both have lived this enigma we call life. We have relished just about all of life's pleasures and sorrows together, having gone through most of life's stages at each other's side. Every human being has an innate need to have that person whom they call their best friend. He was that for me. And my best friend has fulfilled all of the obligations a best friend can have in the life of the other.

"There has only been one letdown in that relationship, though, something that I have thought about for many a year. It is the fact that while I have considered this man my best friend, I knew that I was forever relegated to being second in his book. This maddening effect was increased by the knowledge that I had indeed actually held the number one position for the first six or seven years of our friendship. Then, to my amazement, out of nowhere, this beautiful, fantastic really, little waif came into my best friend's life. She was everything I wasn't: First, she was humble." The crowd laughed enthusiastically. "Jonathan actually had the opportunity to speak when she was near, which was quite the opposite of when I was around.

"Secondly, she was pleasing to look at with her God-given beauty. Now, understand, while I may never grace the cover of *Gentlemen's Quarterly*, I am no dreadful beast either. Nevertheless, she was slowly and methodically wooing my best friend away. She was naturally brilliant while I had to work so awfully hard at it. She so easily made friends with everyone, making them feel as though they were the center of her universe, all the while, for some reason, everybody seemed to think that I thought I was the center of my universe. Above all else, suddenly I realized that my best friend was falling for all of this! Imagine my fury! My indignation!" Jonathan and Gloria were laughing hysterically now.

"My best friend began to spend a considerable amount of time with this woman, almost every weekend to be exact, but since he had much too much integrity to just sacrifice poor old me because he had met someone of the female gender, he let me spend much of my time with the two of them. Lo and behold, even I started to like this woman! She had cast this mysterious spell on me, of all people.

"Well," he said, waving his hand in the air. "To make a long story short, I was no longer Jonathan's best friend. I had been surpassed by dear miss Gloria. To this day, I know that Jonathan is my best friend, but Jonathan's best friend is and always will be Gloria Blake. And this is, much to my chagrin, rightly so. I only take refuge in that, if I had to lose out to somebody, I'm glad it was someone of her stature.

"After all of these years, looking back on the delightful way Gloria has treated me and the hospitality that she has shown me, not to mention the many ways she has challenged me to grow through the manner in which she conducts her life, I have come to another conclusion, and that is that Gloria Blake is my number-two best friend. I even suppose if she could shoot a shotgun or cast a line, or if she would break down and enjoy a good cigar once in a while, she could probably give Jonathan a run for number one because, frankly, she always smells so much better than him!

"Anyway, before I babble on anymore as I have the propensity to do, let me just say that you two Blakes are the finest friends any person could ever have, and I am so very privileged to have you in my life. May God grant His manifold blessings on you and the rest of your lives. You are wonderful people!" With that, the crowd applauded, and Albert Manning returned to his seat.

Michael again approached the microphone. "You know, most people would think of Jonathan and Gloria Blake as a high-society, distinguished couple, and that they are. However, they both have a touch of—what does my younger brother Thomas call it—*goofball* in them. There was one Blake ritual that I am sure no one outside of our immediate family knows about that took place weekly. Growing up, we kids at first laughed about it, and then, to be completely candid, we were embarrassed by their actions. We certainly thought that they could have behaved a little more dignified."

The crowd sensed something funny coming and began to smile. Jonathan and Gloria, smiles also on their faces, puzzled as to what it might be that Michael was leading up to. Jonathan did have a funny side to him, exclusively reserved for his family and, on occasion, Albert Manning, but only when they were alone.

Michael continued. "It was a ritual that, as we look back on it, we realize that it was the play of two people completely in love. While it was done in jest, it was at the same time serious. You see, every week our whole family sat down and watched a television show together. At a certain point in the show there would come a song."

Jonathan and Gloria suddenly got it. "Oh no!" Jonathan said with mock horror. "Michael, don't." Gloria giggled like the young girl she once was.

"Every time that song came on, Dad would grab Mom, and they would stand and sing together with the two people on TV to an audience of four. If my brother and sisters would join me now, we would like to sing that song for you." Thomas, Samantha, and Jennifer all came to the front and joined Michael. Samantha had a bag with the costumes. Two big, bushy mustaches for Michael and Thomas, long brown wigs for Samantha and Jennifer. Scott went to the back to cue the tape they had prepared.

"Now, the two who used to sing this song have since gone their separate ways, which means that this song no longer applies to them. But it does apply to Jonathan and Gloria Blake, who sang that song week in and week out, and continued to sing that song even after the show was canceled. I'm sure if we could bug the house, we would still hear Mom and Dad sing this song to each other from time to time."

The tape began, and the four Blake children brought down the house with their rendition of Sonny and Cher's "I Got You Babe."

The gathering was still laughing, some of the women in tears of jocularity, as Jonathan came to the microphone, shaking his head in disbelief at what had just happened and laughing aloud. "I wish it weren't true," Jonathan said to those gathered, "but it is." All laughed again. "Just call us Sonny and Cher! Seriously, friends, we are so pleased that you all have taken the time to be here to share this very special evening with us. These past 35 years have been truly wonderful and extremely fulfilling. We as a family have experienced the best that this life can offer. And I have been blessed with the most wonderful wife on the earth. I hope that you all have just half the happiness that we do. If so, your life and marriage will be fantastic.

"I don't want to speak too long here, so thank you to the kids for organizing the party. It took a lot of preparation. Thanks to all of you who have graced us throughout the years with your friendship and tonight with your presence, and above all, thank you to the stunningly beautiful and charming wife of my youth—Gloria."

Jonathan and Gloria's friends gave them a standing ovation. When they were done clapping, Michael came and gave instructions for the rest of the evening. "At this time, you are free to venture into the ballroom. In about 15 minutes, we will have dancing for the rest of the night. And, of course, there will be champagne and food later as well. This will be the last I will address you tonight, so I would like to say thank you for coming and making this a most memorable night for Mom and Dad. Have a great night."

The guests arose and slowly moved into the house and, eventually, found their way to the ballroom. Some of the women gathered together in the living room to discuss their dresses, the dinner, the decorations, and such matters. Some of the men retired to the recreation room for billiards. All were passing the time, waiting the few minutes it would take for the musicians to move to the ballroom. Many talked about the obvious love that Jonathan and Gloria had for one another. The children, too, were the topic of discussion. So many thought that they had turned out so bright and charming. Not all children represented by their parents that night had turned out so well. Certainly, few whole families did.

The Blakes were admired by many people. There were the obvious admirers, those who saw Jonathan and Gloria's pictures in society magazines and such. They merely admired them for their money and possessions, though. This was thin admiration, to say the least. The admiration that counted the most to the Blakes was from those who were their peers, those who knew what kind of people they were. There are many people who have vast wealth, though not many with the kind of money Jonathan Blake has. Rare is the family with riches who has a true treasure, the treasure of a complete and happy family. Many of the men wondered how Jonathan did it, managing a huge business, shaping the society around him, and keeping a contented wife and children. This is the most difficult of balances.

The women were admirers as well, though at times, more often than not, it took on the air of innocent envy. Jonathan was a man who had vast wealth, but it surely did not have him. His family garnered that honor. To his very core, his family had Jonathan Blake. Many women could only dream of a husband who placed the family as his first priority. Even the greatest wealth couldn't cover the pain of having your husband love the mistress of business.

"The music is about to begin," Gloria said over and over again, moving through the house, encouraging everyone to join them in the ballroom. "Come and dance."

The rest of the evening was filled with dancing to the finest music. Almost all of the guests stayed until the end. Food, friends, and the joy of life. It brought out the best in everyone.

As the guests danced, Michael stood on the side, next to the fireplace, watching. Patty was out helping for a few minutes in the kitchen. They had already danced a few times before she was called out. Thomas, who had excused himself from the evening after dinner, came downstairs into the ballroom and stood next to Michael.

"They call this music?" Thomas quipped.

"They sure do," Michael responded. "You'll like it too when you get a little refinement in you."

"But of course, Charles," Thomas said in his best impression of a British butler. "But of course."

Thomas turned to go back to his room. As he was leaving, he walked past his mother and father, who were dancing and enjoying themselves. "Boogie down, Dad," Thomas said as he walked by. "Don't pull a muscle, though."

"Isn't it past your bedtime?" Jonathan asked to his youngest son's back as he moved to the door.

The night was continuing to turn around for Scott and Jennifer. The celebration of marriage and the slight reconciliation they had in the house earlier had given them both a touch of hope. They decided to enjoy it to the fullest. In the middle of the ballroom floor, Scott had taken Jennifer for a dance. They moved about the floor to the music. They both danced well. Jennifer had taken dance lessons while growing up, as had all of the Blake children, and they had taken lessons together before their wedding so that Scott could be nimble on his feet at their reception. He had learned quite fast, and now they loved to put their skills to action. They whirled about, and the argument of earlier in the evening seemed to slip away into the distance. They gazed at one another longingly and lovingly.

Scott looked deep into Jennifer's eyes. He pulled her tighter in his arms, now around her waist. "You know, you are the most beautiful woman on the face of the earth," he said.

The compliment washed over Jennifer like water over the dry, parched ground. She smiled. Who said flattery wasn't welcome? She thought that perhaps she should return the compliment, but two-fold. "And you are the most handsome and brilliant man that has ever lived," she said, hoping the patronization wouldn't damper the effect.

"Ha! Now that is the most egregious form of exaggeration there ever has been," Scott said, pausing before announcing, "But I'll take it." They both laughed.

"I really do want to work on our relationship," Scott said, turning serious. "I'll do whatever you want me to, to make things better." Jennifer just listened as they continued to dance. "You know," Scott continued, "You make me so happy, even when we aren't getting along. You make me feel so complete, so fulfilled. I don't know how I could live without you. And yet, I know that I often don't show that to you. I want to, though."

"We'll get it right soon enough," Jennifer said. "The most important thing is that we both commit ourselves to fixing the problem."

"Jennifer, I told you when I married you that I would love and cherish you for better or for worse, and I will. I mean, I do."

"I know you do. And I do, too." They just looked at each other for a few moments then she continued. "We can talk about this later. I like to dance and enjoy myself, and so do you, so let's say you squeeze me a little tighter, kiss me every once in a while, and we'll cut a rug for this old crowd."

"Sounds like a great idea to me."

As the night progressed, Jennifer and Scott's problems seemed to continue to fade away. They hadn't, of course, but for the moment, they were headed in the right direction. They lost themselves in the emotion of the night and once again allowed themselves to feel for the other, rather than clinging to the selfish defense and justification of their own positions and rights. They were once more acting like human beings in love rather than lawyers. Finally, Scott decided the time was right to whisk Jennifer out of the party and home to a romantic conclusion to the night. They slipped out to the driveway and climbed into their Audi sedan.

"I hope nobody minds that we didn't say goodbye," Scott said as they drove down the driveway.

"Oh, nobody will even notice," Jennifer said. They both reached out their hands simultaneously to take hold of the other's. It was a perfectly beautiful night, not a cloud in the sky, and the stars shone so brightly. Scott let go of Jennifer's hand just long enough to open the sunroof. The rest of the trip home was filled with the warmth of the late spring night and of two people falling back into love.

As they pulled into their driveway, Jennifer reached up and pushed the garage door opener for Scott. As Jennifer got out of the car, Scott met her, and they embraced. They kissed passionately. Slowly, they moved their way into the house. Scott began to sing a song that they had been dancing to earlier. They danced to the foot of the stairs where Scott picked Jennifer up in his arms and carried her to the bedroom door. There he put her back down, and again, they kissed. Scott opened the door, and they moved into their bedroom. In but a few weeks, they would find out just how much this rendezvous would change the rest of their lives.

May 31

THE LARGE MAHOGANY door swung shut, and Ted Sampson invited Jonathan to sit down. "So, time to revise the will, Jonathan?" he asked. Ted had been recommended as a top estate-planning attorney to Jonathan a few years ago. They had begun the process then, but Jonathan, out of a lack of time to do the necessary paperwork, stopped short of completing what really needed to be done to protect Jonathan's vast wealth from the ravages of the federal estate tax. He had been meaning to get back into Ted's office but had been remiss in doing so. Now he had to take care of his final affairs, whether he liked it or not.

"Actually, Ted, we are going to have to do a lot more work than we've done up to now. I have cancer."

"Oh, my. Jonathan, I'm so sorry to hear that. I'm sorry, too, about the flippant comment about the will. I mean... I mean, sure, we'll do whatever it takes to set everything straight." He paused while Jonathan simply listened. "When did you find out? Is it, is it fatal?" Ted hated to ask the question, but he wanted to find out whether or not Jonathan had a fighting chance.

"I found out in March. Yes, it's fatal. It is growing through organs where they just wouldn't be able to get it all. They said that I had about a year at the most."

Ted grimaced. He had had a few people that had come into his office facing death's certainty before. He hated being involved in those circumstances. It reminded him of his own mortality. The others, those who were just making preparations but who were still in good health, never bothered him as it seemed like it was just a game where no one really died. But when people came in with just months to live, this bothered him. One because of the human factor—he couldn't imagine what their life must be like having to plan to die. But two, being a pragmatist, he simply wasn't able to do the kind of work he would like to do for them in regard to protecting their estate. Ted knew that the best thing for large estates like Jonathan's was a single payment, last to die, life insurance policy for the estimated amount of taxes due at the time of death. Nobody would give Jonathan a life insurance policy now.

"Well, let's start by moving over to the table." He pointed to a conference table over on the side of the office as he arose and moved across the room. Jonathan smiled and thought to himself as he followed Ted that the estate business must be good, considering the size of Ted's office.

"Would you like something to drink? Coffee? Tea? Soda?" Ted asked.

"No, thanks, I'm fine."

They each sat down at the table, one on either side. "Let's start with the obvious—life insurance. Obviously, you won't be able to get any now, but how much do you already have?" Ted asked.

"I knew you would ask that, so I checked. It's bad news, I think. It's about three million. Not much now, I guess, but before I sold the papers, it seemed like enough." Ted grimaced as Jonathan continued. "I just never thought about it much. I've never had any personal debt, and taxes, well, I didn't think much about those. At least not in regard to my estate."

"Hmmm. We'll have to work at this, but we'll be all right. We'll just do what we can."

Over the next two hours, they talked about Jonathan's family, his values, and the things he would like to accomplish with his wealth after he passed on. They had to take into consideration the children's ages, as Jonathan didn't want any of the kids to come into too much money before they were 30 or 35. He also wanted them to take possession of their money part by part. The best way to do all that Jonathan wanted was to place the money into a number of trusts. This would allow most of it to pass through without giving significant amounts to the government, although the IRS could look at the timing of the trusts, within three years of death, and still go after the estate aggressively. This way would allow Gloria and the kids the opportunity to receive income from them and would eventually, at a time predetermined by Jonathan, turn over entirely to each of the kids.

After they had hammered out all of the basics of the plan, the question came down to who would control the trusts. Ted began his suggestions. "Now, as for who will control all of this. You can go one of two routes, as I see it. You can have a family friend, per-haps a business partner or someone else you trust, or you can hire a lawyer to be the trustee. I would suggest the latter as I've seen a few unfortunate cases where the family didn't like the way the money was handled, and they turned on the old family friend. It is not a pretty situation. If you do decide to go with a lawyer, I can give you a few names of some who do quite a bit of this."

"Well, Ted, I've been thinking about this, and I don't think either of those options will work."

"Oh," Ted was a little surprised. "What idea do you have?"

"I'd like my oldest son to manage it."

"Ah." He was going to do his best to put this tactfully without sounding accusatory. "You can do whatever you like, but I certainly wouldn't recommend that situation. As I see it, there is just too much that can go wrong. Arguments of money, mismanagement, you name it. This really has the potential to destroy a family."

"I expect you to say that, and I appreciate it. I think you are probably right on about 99 percent of the families, but Michael will do all right. Gloria's okay with this." Jonathan left it at that. He had already made up his mind, and Ted got the message clearly.

"Okay, Jonathan. You made it; you can do what you want with it. I'll start working on the papers tomorrow. My secretary will work with you to get all of the information that we'll need. I think that's about it."

"Good." Jonathan stood up, and Ted followed suit. "When do you think we'll be able to start putting it into place?" he asked.

"Oh, a month. Maybe a little shorter than that. We'll have to get a detailed list of pretty much everything you own. I'll have a few people get a hold of you next week."

"Okay. Let me know what I need to do."

"Sure, Jonathan. There will be plenty to do. I'll keep in touch regularly."

"Fine. Thanks, Ted." Jonathan shook Ted's hand and turned to walk to the door.

"Jonathan?"

"Yes?" he said turning back.

"I am sorry. I'll do my best work for you."

"I know that, Ted. Thanks again."

The financial work had begun.

June 2, 4 p.m.

DELBARTON SCHOOL IS a prestigious, all-boys junior and senior high school set in the rolling hills of Northern New Jersey, about three miles west of Morristown. To the discriminating parent, Delbarton, along with only a few other schools in New Jersey, offers their children the opportunity to combine an excellent classical education with strong religious instruction. For some 500 boys, Delbarton is the first step on the way to a distinguished university and then into the business world.

Delbarton is a serene, heavily wooded campus of some 400 acres adjacent to Jockey Hollow National Park that was purchased by the Order of Saint Benedict in 1926. Originally, the campus was a house of theological studies, and the current school was founded in 1939. As you drive up the driveway, you notice the beautifully kept and landscaped grounds, the ball fields for various sporting events, and, set right in the middle, Old Main, a field-stone mansion originally built by Luther Kountze, a wealthy New York financier, to be used as his vacation estate. Slightly to the west is the Abbey Church.

Graduation day is quite an event at Delbarton, and Thomas Blake would be the third Blake to graduate from Delbarton. His father and brother had both preceded him. The Abbey church was full this afternoon. It was filled not only with people but also with dreams and expectations, primarily of these young men's future plans and aspirations, but also with those who reflected on their own past and their thought of brighter tomorrows. The church today was brimming with hope.

Everyone is happy on graduation day, albeit perhaps hectically happy. The rush of everything going on can set a frantic pace for most anyone, but the overall tone is one of excitement and joy.

At 1:55, the whole Blake family, minus Thomas, sat in the pew, waiting expectantly for the graduation service to begin. Jonathan leaned over to Gloria and whispered in her ear. "It seems like just yesterday I was here going through this same ritual." Gloria looked at Jonathan and nodded affirmatively before Jonathan turned and looked forward again. He was just stating a fact, not looking for a conversation.

Next down the pew, Jennifer and Scott sat holding hands, Scott gently caressing Jennifer's hand. Their relationship had taken a step in the right direction since Jonathan and Gloria's anniversary. They had been spending much more time together and had been treating each other with a lot more tolerance and understanding.

Patty and Michael were next, sitting quietly, Michael himself reflecting on his years at Delbarton. It was only 11 years ago that he sat up front here in this room, listening to speakers and waiting impatiently for his well-deserved diploma. Thomas had then just been a 6-year-old, squirming in his seat, waiting for the service to end. "Twenty-nine," Michael thought to himself, "I shouldn't feel old. I'm not old."

"Sooner than we know it, it will be our kid's graduation we're at," Michael said softly to Patty.

"Oh brother, we don't even have any children, Michael," she said back, a smile coming over her face.

"I know, but, well, you know…" He stopped talking and looked to the ceiling, still in deep thought. Patty chuckled quietly.

Samantha and William sat next to Michael and Patty, cuddled together just as you would expect from a couple that was only a month away from their wedding day. Every once in a while, William would tip his head over and whisper something in Samantha's ear, and she would giggle and slap him playfully on the leg.

Promptly at 2 o'clock, the service began with giant organ music. The graduation ceremony itself was like most graduation ceremonies, music, speeches, awards, diplomas... The weather was typical June weather, and the room was unmercifully hot and muggy. All over the chapel, people used their bulletins as fans to bring some sense of cooling to themselves. This busy flutter continued throughout the service.

The main speaker today was Blaine O'Reilly, a 1970 Delbarton graduate who went on to Columbia and Harvard and had been the New York City NBC affiliate news anchor for the last seven years. His topic for the graduates was "Making a Difference in Society."

"In conclusion, may I leave you with one final quote and one final thought as you exit these safe doors of the Delbarton School. The great Catholic writer G.K. Chesterton once said, 'It is not so much that Christianity has been tried and found wanting, as much as Christianity has been found difficult and left untried.' May I say that you have all received a fine education here. In fact, in my opinion, the best high school education money can buy. This education will serve you well, and most of you will further enhance your academic skills at a university. I have no doubts that you will be prepared academically as you enter the workplace. My challenge to you is to be prepared spiritually as you enter the workplace.

"The world we live in today can be a frightening place. I report every evening on the evils of a society and a world run amok. There is a world of people out there waiting for someone, some group, to lead the way back to a sane society, to bring hope and relief to those who are stricken with real grief. I believe that you young men here today, if you are willing to put your Christianity into practice, as difficult as that may be in a world given to secularism, can make a difference in this world. You can make this world a better place.

"Now you have come to the end of your time here, and you've memorized the answers for your religion classes, but will you practice those answers? Benjamin Franklin said that well done is better than well said. May the Delbarton School graduating class of 1995 be doers rather than talkers. Gentlemen—to your future! May God grant you peace, happiness, and success."

After Blaine O'Reilly had taken his seat, the diplomas were handed out in the usual fashion. Thomas Blake came near the beginning, receiving his diploma as well as recognition as a Garden State Scholar. All in all, the service lasted an hour and a half, and while everyone enjoyed the service, they were more than delighted to get out and catch the slight breeze that blew through the hills that day.

The Chancellor's reception for the graduates and their families was held in the gardens off the west side of Old Main. Cheeses, fruits, and crackers were the fare. Caterers busily moved about, replacing empty platters and punch bowls. The Blakes had congregated near the middle of the gardens, each with a cup of punch in hand. The men were in suits and ties, the woman in an array of radiant dresses. Thomas, of course, was decked in a black gown.

Patty teased Thomas. "You look nice in a black dress, Thomas." The family laughed, but Thomas decided the comment wasn't worth a reply.

Just then, Mark Jacobs, another Delbarton graduating senior, came up to the group. "Hello, Mr. and Mrs. Blake, everybody," he said as he nodded to each of the others.

Jonathan spoke to Mark. "Are you coming to the party tonight?" he asked.

"I wouldn't miss it," Mark replied.

As part of Thomas's graduation present, Jonathan decided to throw a dance and pizza party in the ballroom at Three Lakes for Thomas and his classmates and their dates. All told, they were expecting just over 100 guests. Jonathan figured that it would be a way to honor Thomas but also to give the young men and their dates a place to go and a special way to spend one last time together.

For the next hour, the Blakes ate and drank and spoke to the other graduates and their parents. The sun was shining, the company was good, and Thomas was now a graduate. All in all, it was a great day.

There was one dark spot, though. Jonathan was beginning to feel his sickness. He had dropped a few pounds, he ached a little, and a cough had begun to haunt him quite a bit. No one else besides him and Gloria noticed, though. The others were too involved in celebrating the moment, as well they should.

As the caravan of cars arrived back at Three Lakes from the graduation, Jonathan parked out in front of the front door of the house. No one thought it odd that he parked outside instead of in his garage, as they merely figured that he was planning on going somewhere else this afternoon. This was good because it played well into his plan.

As they got out of the car, Jonathan asked Thomas to fix the garage door. "Say, Thomas, would you do me a favor before you come in? I was trying to take a can of paint out through the last garage door the other day, and I couldn't get it to open. Would you go around and see if you can get the security code to open it from the outside? If it does, you can come in through the mudroom. If not, I'll have to get someone to look at it this week."

"Can I do it a little later, Dad?" Thomas asked. "I'm a little tired."

"Oh, it won't take you too long. Why don't you just get it over with?"

"All right."

Thomas relented and disappeared around the other side of the house as the rest of his family went in the front door and into the kitchen to wait for him to come in through the mudroom. Thomas lifted up the cover of the security pad and punched in the code, 4-5-1, which is the temperature at which paper ignites. The family thought it was rather odd, but that's the number they had used since the security system was installed. No one in the family would admit to being the one to come up with the code—most normal families use a birthdate or some such thing—but they kept it, nonetheless.

After punching in the code, the door immediately began to open. Thomas thought to himself about how his dad had to get up to speed with technology. "He can't even get the garage door security system to work."

As the door arose, it revealed tires behind it.

"That's weird," he thought. "Whose car is this?"

As the door got past the halfway mark, the meaning of the car became clear. Sitting in the last stall, one that is usually empty except for occasional boxes used for packing odds and ends, was a brand-new black Jeep. Wrapped completely around it was a red ribbon and bow. On the front windshield that faced him was a hand-made sign made from poster board that read: "Happy Graduation, Son! We are very proud of you! Mom and Dad."

Thomas stood for a moment, hands to his side, wide-eyed and mouth agape in shock. Suddenly, he ran to the window and quickly looked in. There it all was. This one was fully loaded. Up until now, Thomas had driven an old Jeep that his dad had originally driven, but now he had his own.

Thomas ran through the garage, in through the mudroom, and threw open the door to the kitchen. There stood the entire family to greet him. "Surprise!" they all yelled in unison.

Thomas stopped dead in his tracks. "Mom. Dad. Thanks. It's awesome!" Jonathan and Gloria beamed as broadly as Jonathan.

After some hugs, Jonathan and the kids went back out into the garage to look at the new Jeep. Jonathan handed Thomas the keys, and he pulled it out into the driveway so everyone could see it. After about 10 minutes of admiration, Jonathan suggested that they all go in. "Hey, we can look at this later. We need to get some naps in before dinner. Then we still have a big night tonight. Everybody will start getting here around 8. That's just a few hours." Most of the siblings agreed and dissipated into the house. Thomas jumped in the Jeep and headed out for a drive.

By 9 o'clock that evening, the party was in full swing. Forty-seven young men and their dates arrived for a night of dancing, food, and farewells. The energy was ubiquitous. These were young men who were celebrating. They were celebrating youth, achievement, and the next mountain they would surely conquer. They were stunningly handsome, and their dates, beautiful. Radiant young men and women, together for one last time.

Jonathan, Gloria, Michael, and Patty were the chaperones. Jonathan and Gloria attended to the foyer and library, with an occasional stop in the kitchen to oversee the pizza distribution. Michael and Patty stayed in the ballroom, watching the dancing and talking to the new graduates. This certainly wasn't a rough crowd. They were a well-behaved group, if ever there was one. This wouldn't be a night of trouble but a night of memories.

Patty was by the windows overlooking the back grounds, discussing dresses with some of the girls whose dates had gone for something to drink. It was just about dusk, and the last bit of sun coming through the windows, combined with the radiance from the chandeliers, brought the room to life. Patty herself had gone out and purchased a semi-formal dress just for this night. Michael stationed himself by the huge double door entryway. From time to time, he spoke to some of the kids he knew through Thomas, but mainly he stood alone.

The DJ pounded out contemporary music at quite a high level, and the kids enjoyed every minute of it. Every so often, he would play a slower song, and the boys would eagerly take their dates in their arms for the chance to slow dance. They would hold them tight, laughing the way young people do, nervously, when they're infatuated with another. Slowly, they would dance, looking into each other's eyes, enjoying one another. Before they knew it, though, they were back to the fast-paced dancing of modern pop music.

During one particularly "contemporary" song, Jonathan came into the ballroom to see how the dance was progressing. He came and leaned against the wall near the entryway, next to Michael.

"They call this music?" Jonathan asked Michael.

Michael laughed, remembering Thomas's reflections on the music at Jonathan and Gloria's anniversary. "Yes, Dad, they do."

"Hmmm." That was all Jonathan could muster as he listened.

June 3

THE SUMMER HAD definitely arrived. The weather was warm most every day now. The trees were full of leaves, and the flowers decorated the countryside and the gardens of the homes of Far Hills. Jonathan was on the couch in the living room, resting. He had been reading, but his lunch was settling in now, and the sun was shining in, beaming on him and pushing him into a lethargic slumber. He was just about asleep when Gloria came in with a glass of iced tea. "Here you go, my love, a little iced tea to enjoy while you read your book." As she came around the end of the couch, she realized that Jonathan had been trying to sleep. He shook his head a bit, waking himself again, and processed what Gloria had said.

He reached out his hand. "Well, thank you."

"Oh, I'm sorry. I didn't know you were sleeping. Do you want me to leave you alone?"

Jonathan began to sit up. "That's all right. I would rather spend some time with my gorgeous bride anyway." He took a long sip of tea. "Ahh, that, Darlin', is very good tea." Gloria grew her own mint in their garden, and she usually added some to the tea, just enough to give a hint of flavor.

Gloria sat down across from Jonathan and put her stocking feet on the wooden coffee table. "Well, you did it."

"I did, did I?" Jonathan asked.

"Yes, you did."

"Okay, I'll bite. I did what?"

"You got all of your children through high school without any major problems or mishaps."

"Oh. Don't you mean *we* did it?"

"Hmm. Yes, you're right. We did it." She raised her tea toward Jonathan.

"Another chapter is done," he said, raising his glass toward Gloria.

They each drank and relaxed in the quiet living room. Gloria looked down at her fingernails. It was time to paint them again. She had intended to before Thomas's graduation but didn't get to it. Jonathan looked out the windows at the trees slowly swaying in the light breeze of summer.

"Gloria?"

"Yes?"

"I've been thinking, and I have a decision to make. Do you think I should be cremated or buried?"

"Oh, Jonathan, let's not talk about that."

Jonathan became irritated. He was frustrated that Gloria seemed to want to pretend that he wasn't really dying. "Gloria, when will we talk about this? We have to at some point. Are we going to talk about it when I'm a week away from dying? Or maybe after I actually die? We need to talk about this, so why not now?"

Gloria was quiet. She obviously didn't want to have this conversation. She certainly wouldn't be the one to lead the way in it.

"Gloria? Do you have any preference? I do."

After a few moments, Gloria finally gave her opinion. "I've always assumed that we would be buried, I guess. I thought that you and I could have our headstones next to each other like most couples do."

"Yes, it does seem to me like we should be buried. I feel a little uncomfortable with the idea of cremation. Not that I think it's immoral or anything. I just... I don't know. I'll have to call the funeral home soon to take care of all of this." Gloria just looked into her glass of tea. "Will you come with me and help me make the decisions?" he asked.

"Yes, of course. Would you like me to call and set it up?"

"No, I can do it." Again, quiet. "Enough of that. I've been making the arrangements for the family trip in December."

"Oh, good." Gloria perked right up, happy that Jonathan wanted to talk about something else. She loved taking family vacations, and this was going to be another great one, while most certainly the last.

"Yes, I've got the house all lined up. And it sounds like the kids are working out getting the time off. I hope that they can all make it. It sounds right now like they will all be able to. It should be fun."

The phone rang, and Gloria picked up the line on the end table. "Hello? Oh, hi, Margaret."

Jonathan stood up. He knew that Gloria would now be on the phone for a while. "I'm going up to take a nap," he whispered as he pointed upstairs. Gloria nodded and dove into conversation with her sister.

SUMMER

June 4, 1:30 p.m.

MICHAEL WAS OVER at Three Lakes for lunch and to spend some time with his parents this afternoon because Patty was home visiting her parents for the weekend. William and Samantha were with some friends, and Scott and Jennifer were in the Poconos for a weekend away, the rehabilitation of their marriage getting stronger with each passing day. Thomas was at a Yankees game in the city.

That left Jonathan, Gloria, and Michael. They sat together in the kitchen nook, eating ham and cheese sandwiches, chips, and sliced vegetables. When she was done, Gloria excused herself to go outside and work on some gardening. It was probably too hot for Gloria to be working outside, but with church that morning, this was the only time she had to do so. Most of the grounds at Three Lakes were kept by a professional landscaping crew, but Gloria had always kept one patch of about 20 feet by 20 feet, just off of the kitchen area, to herself. She loved to spend hours primping and preening her plants. It had been a few weeks since she had given them the care she liked to give them, so she had been planning for a few days to get a couple of hours in this afternoon. Besides, she knew that Jonathan wanted to tell Michael about the cancer and that they would need some time together alone.

"I'm going outside to love on my garden a little. It's been so long since they've seen me, I should probably wear a nametag so they'll know who I am."

"Have fun, Darling," Jonathan said.

"Tell the lilies 'hi' for me," Michael called after his mother as she put on her wide-brimmed hat and walked out the back door.

"She sure loves that garden," Jonathan said to Michael.

"Yeah, always has. At least as long as I can remember."

They kept eating, stopping only for the occasional sip of iced tea. "I wonder if there's a baseball game on television?" Michael asked.

"I don't know, but I was thinking we could take a walk. Maybe we could go down to the gate and back."

"Sure, that sounds good. It will work off the lunch."

After finishing his lunch, Jonathan went upstairs to his bedroom to change out of his church clothes and into a jogging suit. Michael set his plate and glass on the counter and then went out to his car to grab some old Levi's and a polo shirt he had brought to change into and went upstairs to his old bedroom to change as well. They met back down in the television room where Michael was trying to find a baseball game.

"Ready to go?" Jonathan asked.

They began the walk down to the gate. The smell in the air was the delightful aroma of summer. The trees and flowers smelled so good in the warmth of the summer air. They talked a little about the upcoming wedding, but mostly they talked about the stock market. About two-thirds of the way down the driveway, right next to one of the lakes, Gloria had created a sitting area by the lake so they could stop and watch the ducks that frequently gathered there. Jonathan suggested they stop and watch the four that were there now.

Jonathan and Michael took a seat on each end of a bench. Jonathan looked closer at a wildflower he had picked up before sitting down. Then he glanced at Michael out of the corner of his eye. Michael looked a little like Jonathan at that age, but he had the exact same heart as Jonathan. And now, Jonathan knew that he had to break that heart. "Michael, there is something we need to talk about, but we have to keep it confidential at this point, all right?"

"Sure, Dad, what is it?" Michael was still looking slightly away from Jonathan, watching a duck swimming across the pond.

"Well, you know that a few months ago, I was getting sick frequently. I went to Dr. Kidman, and he was more than a little concerned with some of the signs that he saw, so he had me go to a specialist in Manhattan. It was there that they found what the problem was. I have cancer, Michael."

Michael didn't immediately respond. Instead, he turned his head away even more, assuming the next part that was still to come. He stared into the lake. "And," Jonathan continued, Michael already feeling what was coming, "it is fatal. They give me about another nine months to live, on the outside, but it could be sooner than that."

Michael still could not look at his father. Multitudinous thoughts flew through his mind, none of which were comforting. What were you supposed to feel when your beloved father, your best friend in the world, tells you he is dying?

Michael began to cry. It was slow at first, a whimpering, really. His eyes filled quickly, and the tears began to stream down his cheeks. He bent over at the waist and buried his head in his hands. His stomach knotted inside. He began to cry heavier, the sobs coming more rapidly. His body began to convulse as it alternately heaved loud, moanful cries and breathed to restore itself.

Jonathan was a little surprised. He expected Michael to be upset, perhaps to even cry a little, but he was certainly unprepared for such an emotional outburst. The Blake family would never have been described as emotional but rather steady, reserved. Today would be different. There was no one here to impress with a cool and collected reaction. Michael could be himself and react naturally to the news. Jonathan placed his hand calmly on his oldest son's back.

A few minutes passed, and Jonathan finally spoke again. "Son, I know it is very hard." He paused as Michael began to control himself a little. "This is what we call life. It was inevitable that it would happen someday." Jonathan was making excuses now. They were excuses he didn't need to make, but those that he thought might help Michael understand and cope. They didn't.

"How can you say that?" Michael asked as he finally snapped his head toward his father. "How can you just write your life off in just one sentence? 'It's life; it's inevitable.' That is just not true." Michael waited for his dad to reply, but Jonathan remained quiet. Michael had other questions. "So, when do you start treatment?"

"There is no treatment, Michael," Jonathan said quietly.

"There is no treatment? What about chemotherapy? What about radiation?"

Michael didn't know what he was talking about. He was merely throwing out words that he knew were associated with cancer. Michael had never actually known anyone with cancer, but, like most everyone who has read even a little, he knew that when you got cancer, you underwent radiation or chemotherapy.

"There is no treatment, Michael," Jonathan reiterated. "By the time I started feeling the pain and then got around to going to the doctor, the cancer had spread too far. It is spreading quite rapidly, actually. There is just nothing I can do."

Michael was not in the mood to tolerate the fatalistic attitude his father was showing. "That isn't true," Michael said. He stood up now and backed away from his Dad. He turned and, half yelling, said, "That isn't true. There has to be something. You can't just give up, Dad." Michael was exasperated now. He turned toward the house. "Are you just going to roll over and die and leave Mom to live in this gargantuan house all by herself? She can't do that!" Michael could hardly control himself as he began to rage with anger. No one was going to tell him that his dad was going to die.

He turned and began to run toward the house, leaving Jonathan sitting in stunned silence, looking not at Michael running away but at the serene lake in front of him, where the ducks had come up onto the grass in front of them. There was nothing Jonathan could do. He wouldn't be able to console Michael now. Later he would be able to talk to him but not now. Now, Michael must be allowed to fully experience the pain of knowing his father would be gone in less than nine months. Jonathan knew that that would be a terrifying feeling for anyone. Jonathan remained sitting by the lake, trying to think if there was another way he could have told Michael. He realized that there wasn't, really.

By that time, Michael had reached the top of the hill where the house sat. He jumped into his red Miata and turned the key. He didn't want to be at Three Lakes anymore. He needed to drive and think. Michael would often drive when he was upset. Sometimes when he and Patty fought, Michael would drive west on Route 24 through Long Valley and over Schooley's Mountain. He sped down the driveway toward the entrance.

Jonathan had heard the engine start and looked toward the driveway. He stood up and now saw Michael speeding toward him on the drive. He thought that Michael was going much too fast to time himself going through the gate. There was a pad built into the drive that triggered the gate, but a person driving could only be going 15 miles an hour or slower; otherwise, they would reach the gate before it opened fully. Michael went by Jonathan at about 40 miles an hour, disappearing into the tunnel of oak trees lining the front portion of the driveway. As soon as he hit the pad, Michael realized that he would have to brake rather quickly. He did, and he came close to slamming into the edge of the gate as he passed but slid right through and came to a slight stop at the edge of Roxiticus Road.

He turned north toward Mendham and began to speed up. All along the long, winding road Michael was driving much too fast. About three miles before Mendham, the road turned fast to the right, then down a steep hill, then back again to the left. Michael was driving dangerously, even for a small car with good maneuverability.

Just at the bottom of the hill, his tires broke free from the pavement, and he began to spin out of control. Fortunately, there was nothing to careen into that would kill him. There was only an open field with some sheep wandering through. There was, however, a 4-foot-high wooden fence between him and the pasture. The small car tore through the fence and threw the wood like kindling in all directions. When the car hit the slippery grass, it sped up again and slid another 100 feet, turning all the way before coming to a rest. Michael sat in the car, dazed. He didn't think the car had flipped, and it hadn't. There was obviously much damage to the car, but that was not what angered him. He pounded his fist three times on the steering wheel.

"No!" he screamed at the top of his lungs before resting his head on the steering wheel and beginning again to weep. "No," he said again, quieter.

From up on a bluff across the road, the owner of the house and of the field that Michael's car was now sitting in had been in his front yard and had heard the tires squealing and had seen the wreck and was now making his way down the hill and across the street. He heard Michael scream to himself. He walked briskly right through the gap where he used to have a fence and across the field.

Bill Tappen was his name. He was about 5-foot-10, slight of build, a head of gray hair. He walked up to the car. Michael didn't even know that he was there, so he just watched Michael cry for a few minutes. Tappen was in his mid-50s and could tell that Michael was still in his late 20s or early 30s. He wondered what could make this young man so upset. He couldn't imagine that it was just the car.

"Are you all right, Son?" Bill finally asked Michael. The question surprised Michael, and he snapped his head to the left to see who was talking to him. As he turned, he revealed a small cut above his right eye that was bleeding, not dangerously, but enough. A slight trickle of red ran into the corner of his eye.

Michael wiped his eyes. "Uh, yes, I am, though I don't think my car is." Both of the men laughed nervously.

"Well, let's get you out of the car and have my wife look at your eye. Then you can call someone to make arrangements for your car."

Michael pushed open the crumpled car door and got out. Together they walked across the field and toward the main house. Bill tried to make small talk. "Going a little fast around that corner, huh? That can be a tough one the first time you travel it."

"Well, I've traveled it a lot, actually. And as fast as I was going, it's tough even if you've driven it a hundred times."

"You're from around here then?"

"Yes. Far Hills."

"Well, I'm Bill Tappen." He extended his right, somewhat dirty hand to Michael.

"I'm Michael Blake," Michael said, reciprocating the gesture.

Bill Tappen recognized the Blake name. "Related to Jonathan Blake, the newspaper man?"

"Yes. Former newspaper man, though. He's my father."

Bill thought he could lighten the mood a little now. He put his arm on Michael's shoulder. "Well, I guess you won't have a problem paying for my fence then, will you?"

Michael smiled just a crack. "No, I'll manage." The smile then faded. Reality set back in, and he grimaced. A frown took over where the smile left off. That drop of blood now ran down his cheek, mixed with a tear.

"Something wrong?" Bill asked.

Michael thought for a fleeting moment of baring his soul and telling this stranger, this new acquaintance, just why he was speeding so fast through this dangerous valley. He knew that he couldn't, though, as much as he wanted to talk to somebody. "No, nothing really," he answered.

When they reached the house, Mrs. Tappen put a bandage on Michael's eye and wiped his face. Michael used the phone, an old rotary dial, and called a tow truck and a cab. Bill thought it odd that the young man hadn't called his family, but he wasn't one to pry much by asking too many questions. Before he left, Michael gave

Tappen his name, phone number, and insurance information. He thanked the man for coming to help him and being understanding enough. Bill Tappen was a gracious man and assured Michael that it was no problem.

The cab eventually came and took Michael home. He spent the rest of the day in his house alternately crying and yelling, the latter which was quite out of the ordinary for him. Patty wasn't due home until Monday night, so Michael called into his office and took a personal day on Monday. He spent the day alone, thinking.

Gloria had called on Sunday night to find out how he was doing, and Michael assured her that he was just fine, though he didn't tell her about the car wreck. Gloria and Jonathan figured that, given a little time, Michael would come to grips with Jonathan's sickness.

June 6

AFTER DECIDING NOT to talk to Patty, as per his father's wishes, Michael knew that he needed to talk again to Jonathan. He needed to apologize for his outburst on Sunday afternoon. Early Tuesday morning, Michael called Jonathan at home and asked if they could get together for lunch. Jonathan's day was free, so they met at noon at a deli in Bernardsville.

They both arrived within minutes of each other and greeted one another before walking together into the store. They sat themselves in a booth before realizing that they had to order first and then take their sandwiches to their seats.

Neither of them had been to the deli before. It had only been open about three months, and many people thought their food was outstanding, especially the potato salad, which was gaining a local reputation. They each ordered a half sandwich, some chips, the potato salad, and a drink. They waited a few minutes, Michael leafing through the sports page until their food was ready. They then went back to their booth.

Michael started the conversation. "Dad, I'm really sorry about Sunday. I acted foolishly."

Jonathan finished sipping his iced tea and put the glass down. "Son, I must admit that I was a little surprised, but then I thought about it, and there really isn't any right reaction. You reacted the way you reacted. It obviously hurt. It's okay."

"Well, it gets worse. I was so angry that I was driving too fast, and I wrecked my car."

Jonathan was good at hiding his shock. "Where did you wreck?" he asked calmly.

"Oh, you know that curve down through that valley a couple of miles before Mendham?"

"Yes..."

"Right there. I spun out, went through the fence, and ended up in the pasture."

"Well, I'm glad that you weren't hurt. Maybe you need to think about the way you reacted after all."

"I know."

"Listen, Son. I'm sorry about this. There is just nothing that I can do. You know that if there was, I would. Hey, I feel worse about this than you do, believe me. We have some time left, I'm sure, so we will have plenty of opportunity to grow together and say our goodbyes. I plan on making this last year the best ever. We still have the wedding in a few weeks, Thanksgiving, our family vacation, Christmas..." His voice trailed off because he knew from the prognosis that he couldn't promise much after Christmas.

"Is there anything that you want me to do, Dad?"

"For right now, just keep it quiet. Only you and your mother know, except for the doctors. I am going to tell the rest of the kids after the wedding. I don't want to put a damper on William and Samantha's special day. I'll tell Reverend Wilton and Albert sometime soon as well. It will be after the kids, most likely. Other than that, just help me make this year a good one. You are going to be the man of the family after I am gone, so maybe you can start taking some leadership in the coming months. I'll help you. And if you ever want or need to talk, please, Son, let's talk."

"Thanks, Dad."

They spent the rest of their lunch talking, reminiscing about old times. The lunch was short, though, as Michael had to get back to work. He had accomplished his task of apologizing, which is what he had set out to do, and he started the process of saying goodbye to his father.

June 9

JONATHAN ARRIVED HOME about 3:30 from a doctor's appointment. Dr. Kidman wanted to continue checking up on him, to keep an eye on the progression of the cancer, particularly to help Jonathan through what would surely be a definite increase in the pain he would be suffering. The appointment went quickly.

Jonathan's cancer wasn't increasing rapidly, at least not as the doctors feared it might. There was a little more pain than at the last appointment, so Dr. Kidman prescribed some more pain medication. He said that it would probably cause nausea.

Jonathan came into the kitchen from the garage and started flipping through the large stack of mail. Jonathan was always amazed at how many catalogs Gloria received. As he was about halfway through it, Gloria came in.

"You're home," she said. "I didn't hear the garage close. How was the appointment?" She hugged him.

"Fine. He told me that it was slow going, a slight increase in the pain, so he prescribed some medication for me. He expects at some point it will accelerate, though he doesn't know when it could be. For now, it's a waiting game."

"I still can't believe that they can't do anything."

"It's just spread into places they can't do anything about. They could go in and cut some out, but they would never get it all."

Gloria changed the subject. "Oh, I almost forgot, you got a card in the mail today. The return address is ours, so it must be from Samantha. It looks like her handwriting." Just then, Jonathan came across it and eagerly opened it. It was, indeed, written on Samantha's stationery and written in her handwriting. Jonathan began to read.

Dear Dad,

I've been meaning to write this since our lunch together, but I am just now getting to it. First, I wanted to say thanks so much for taking the time for me. As I've thought about what we talked about and the things you said that you have come to see in regard to your relationship with me, I realize how difficult it must have been for you to take the step that you did. I want you to know how much I appreciate you doing that and how much you mean to me. I look up to you so much and have for the longest time admired you far more than you will ever know.

So often growing up, I would lie in bed at night, crying, wondering when my dad would notice me, when he would take the time to care about me, about what I thought, about what I cared about—about who I am. I know that we have never had any bad things happen between us, but you and I both know there wasn't the depth that there needed to be. Then, you took the time.

I feel like now we can finally talk, like we can finally connect. I'm so glad, too, that it happened before William and I get married, as I know that then so much of my attention will be in that direction.

I am glad, though, that we have so much time left, rather than if this had happened 20 years from now.

I guess this is all I wanted to say, so I'll close.

Dad, I love you very much. Thanks for taking the first step.

Samantha.

Jonathan had tears in his eyes by the time he was finished reading. They were tears of joy from knowing that he had opened up a relationship with his daughter. They were tears of pain in knowing that he would never be able to fulfill what Samantha now was hoping for.

"What did it say?" Gloria asked, noticing that Jonathan's eyes had welled up.

Jonathan handed the note to Gloria, and she read it. When she was done, she set the card down on the counter and embraced Jonathan. "It seems like she is very happy that you took her out and talked with her."

"Yes, but the pain I've caused her. All she wanted was her dad's love, affection, and attention. Gloria, how could I have missed that?"

"I don't know, Jonathan."

"I mean, I have always tried so hard. I've always thought so much of Samantha. I never intended to hurt her in any way."

"I think that she knows that. She's just glad that you finally realized it. And I'm sure that she forgives you."

"And now there is so little time left for me to do anything about it."

"But at least you have the opportunity, short as it may be. Don't be discouraged by that note. That was a positive note. She's reaching out to you." Gloria squeezed tighter. "Come on, see it for what it is and make the most of it."

"You're right, Gloria. I will."

June 17

THIS SATURDAY WAS a typical Blake family day. As the two older kids had gotten married and Samantha had fallen in love with William, and as young Thomas had grown into a popular young man with a driver's license, the weekends together had become fewer, but this weekend would be as they all had been when they happened. The whole family was gathered there for the weekend. During the summers, Saturdays would see the kids playing all sorts of games, such as touch football, tennis, and badminton. They would all spend some time around the pool. Jonathan and Michael would barbecue a wonderful dinner, usually elk meat from one of Jonathan's previous hunts. They would perhaps watch a movie at night while eating popcorn. Some of the family would stay up and play cards until late at night. The others would go to bed early to be ready for church the next day. William would leave about 10 o'clock in order to be ready for his responsibilities at church the next morning.

On Sunday, the rest of the family would meet William at New Vernon Presbyterian, where he was the associate minister. After church, they would all go out for lunch, then back to Three Lakes for an afternoon of rest and relaxation. Sunday night, they would eat dinner together and discuss the coming week. They were together, a family, and, quite frankly, content with themselves. There wasn't a great need for outside entertainment or stimulation. This family simply enjoyed each other. That in and of itself sets the Blake family apart from so many others. Even the children enjoyed the fellowship of their parents and didn't seem anxious to get away.

Sunday night, Patty and Michael would go back to their home in Chester, Jennifer and Scott to theirs in Mendham. Samantha was still living at home until after the wedding, so she and Thomas would be with Jonathan and Gloria at night.

The weekends were always eventful and drew the family close together again, even as the kids grew older and moved out onto their own, developing their own lives and families. The weekends, whether in winter or summer, would always revolve around being with one another, taking time out for God on Sunday, and reconnecting while rejuvenating themselves for their hectic schedules the following week. There would, of course, be the occasional spat, but the Blakes simply are not the temperamental types, given to fighting. You could say that it just wasn't in their genes.

This weekend was like most. They did the things they expected to do. No one knew about Jonathan, and no one suspected that anything whatsoever was wrong. The weekend went perfectly, and that is exactly how Jonathan wanted it to go.

July 1

B Y NOW, JONATHAN was beginning to find it a bit harder to get out of bed in the mornings. The cancer was spreading more and more and was starting to take away some of his mobility. This lack of mobility was particularly pronounced in the mornings before he worked the pain out. Gloria knew how hard it was becoming for Jonathan, so she decided to get up early and make him breakfast in bed so that in his first moments awake this morning, he would be able to relax and enjoy.

At 7:15, she came into the bedroom and opened the shades. Sunlight poured in and beamed on the foot of the bed and brightened the whole room. Jonathan had already begun to wake up, and the sunshine completed the task.

"Good morning, my love," Gloria commented as she saw Jonathan's eyes open and look her direction. "I have here for you an incredibly scrumptious breakfast for you to start your day off." Gloria set the tray across Jonathan's lap. Two eggs, over medium, four strips of bacon, hash-browned potatoes, and sourdough toast.

"This smells fabulous!" Jonathan was wide awake now.

"And that's not all." She reached down and picked up his coffee cup, then turned and went over to the table where she had set the pot of fresh coffee. Pouring the coffee, she asked back to Jonathan, "Would you like a little cream or sugar, Sir?"

"Why yes, Ma'am, if you would be so kind." She walked back to the bed and handed the cup to Jonathan after putting the cream and sugar in, and he immediately took a sip. "Mmmm. You make the absolute best coffee there is, Gloria."

"These were coffee beans that Margaret and Bob brought back from their trip to Costa Rica. We got them in the mail yesterday. I already had a cup this morning. It is good, isn't it?"

"I'll say."

"Oh, I almost forgot," Gloria said. "Give me a minute." Quicker than she came in, she was out the door again. Jonathan didn't know what to make of this, so he simply waited, staring at the door. Less than a minute later, Gloria came back into the room, carrying the morning newspaper. "I went down to the gate and got it while the bacon was cooking. I thought you could just lie here, eat your breakfast, and read the paper."

"Come on over here," Jonathan said.

Gloria made her way onto the bed and cuddled up next to him. He put one arm around her and said, "Thanks."

"You're welcome. I just wanted you to enjoy this morning. I know that it is getting harder for you to get out of bed in the morning and that it takes you a while to get going, so I thought you could stretch a bit while you're lying here."

"Gloria, do you know what I admire most about you?"

"What?"

"You have got to be the most selfless person I know."

"Oh," she said, waving her hand to dismiss the thought. "There are so many who are truly selfless. I just want to make you happy."

"Well, I appreciate it very much. You know, our whole lives, you have been like that. I appreciate how you have dedicated your life to helping me. You have always done such a terrific job. I love you, you know?"

"I know. You have always made sure that I knew, ever since before we got married." She squeezed tighter around Jonathan's chest.

They both lay there for a few minutes, two old lovebirds enjoying the sun and the quiet of a Saturday morning together before Gloria got up again and began to leave. "I have to make a quick run to the grocery store. You enjoy your breakfast and the peace and quiet. And skip over the bad news in the paper. It never does anybody any good." Jonathan chuckled and Gloria disappeared around the corner and down the hall.

July 4

J ONATHAN AND GLORIA and Scott and Jennifer found themselves together on a yacht in New York Harbor for the Fourth of July. Martin Hart, one of the senior partners at Scott's law firm, also happened to be an old friend of Jonathan's, and so Hart decided it would be fun to have the four of them out on the boat to see the annual fireworks display. The yacht was a sleek, white and blue, 75-foot Hatteras, so there was plenty of room for six.

As the sun set, the six of them dined on the lower back deck, enjoying the warm weather, the water, the food, and each other. As usual, the fireworks were spectacular, and the Blakes basked in the time together with their friends and Scott and Jennifer. When the night was almost over and the group was on the way back to the marina, Jonathan found himself alone with Scott on the upper of the two back decks. Jennifer and Gloria were in the galley helping Mrs. Hart clean up the dishes from dinner and put them away before docking.

"So, how goes the battle at work?" Jonathan asked.

Scott looked around. "Well, with my boss driving the boat and in such close proximity, I would say that the battle goes well." They both laughed. "Actually," Scott continued, "It is going very well. I'm feeling challenged. I'm enjoying myself, and I feel like I'm making a significant contribution."

"How is it going with Jennifer?" Jonathan asked, looking out over the water.

Scott immediately felt defensive. Here was his father-in-law asking about his marriage to his daughter. It seemed to him like it could only go one direction, especially given the stormy track record he and Jennifer had compiled thus far. Things were changing, though, and he felt good about it. He decided that he had nothing to hide. He and Jennifer were doing their best, and they seemed to have taken a turn for the better.

"Well, as a matter of fact, things are going quite well on that front as well."

"They are?" Jonathan sounded surprised and was embarrassed that he sounded so. "I mean, that's good."

"Look, Mr. Blake. I know that you know that things have been tough between Jennifer and me at times, and that has surely caused concern for you, but things are turning around for us. We have been getting along very well lately."

"Oh, how so?" Jonathan was now leaning against the railing, facing Scott.

"Well, for one, Jennifer seems to be much more forgiving lately. She used to hold things against me, almost like she was punishing me so to speak. But now she is letting go of things more quickly."

"That's good, isn't it?"

"That is very good."

"You know, Scott, women are interesting. Even strong women like Jennifer, who seem like they are so self-sufficient, still need to feel like they are important, like they are cared for, like they matter to someone. They need to feel special. I suspect that is something that would go a long way in developing your relationship with Jennifer. She seems so strong, and don't get me wrong, she is, but she needs to be special to you. She needs to be the center of your universe, and, frankly, I think she should be."

"I know, I'm trying."

"I believe that you are trying, Scott. You'll get it. It takes a while sometimes. I have had a hard time of it myself over the years. I hate to sound proud, but you think you're busy. My schedule was about as busy as they get in this old world, but one always has to make time for those who mean the most."

"Yeah, you're right."

Jonathan thought he'd lighten the mood of the conversation. "Any grandkids on the way?"

Scott laughed. "No, not any that I know of, but you'll be the first to know, I promise."

"Okay, I'm going to hold you to that."

Jennifer came back out onto the deck. "What are you two talking about out here?" she asked.

"Oh, just stuff," Scott said.

"Yeah, guy stuff," Jonathan added. Jennifer decided not to pursue it. Soon, all six were up on the bridge for the final leg into the marina.

When they were back in the slip and were heading to their cars, they thanked their hosts, Martin and Carol Hart, who were spending the night on the boat. When they reached their cars, Jonathan let Gloria into her side of their car, and Scott did the same for Jennifer in theirs. Then, with neither of the women able to hear, Jonathan looked across the roof of his car and called to Scott.

"Scott."

"Yes?"

"Keep up the good work. You make my daughter happy."

Scott smiled. "Thanks, Mr. Blake. I will."

Jonathan winked and got into his car for the drive home to Three Lakes.

July 8

I T HAD BEEN almost four months since Jonathan found out that he would die. He had alternately rejoiced in the pleasures of everyday life, which he no longer took for granted, and the extraordinary events like his anniversary. Through it all, he experienced the pain of knowing that all of these events were set against the backdrop of his own demise. The onset of even greater pain that was still tolerable but almost constant now also reminded him daily that he was dying. Jonathan was by now regularly taking pain relievers to help him in the more painful times. He was still able to walk all right, but sitting down, like getting up in the morning, could sometimes be a chore.

In spite of all of this, Jonathan was looking forward to playing host to Samantha and William's wedding and reception. The wedding was too big for their local church, which only sat about 150 people, so the Blakes had the wedding in their ballroom. There were 250 guests coming. Obviously, the wedding could have been a thousand people or more had they chosen to, but William and Samantha decided to keep it relatively manageable by inviting William's family, the Blake family, friends from college and high school, and of course, there was an allotment to Jonathan and Gloria for some of their friends and business associates. The reception would be held on the back terraces and lawns.

Jonathan always loved a good party where he could help everyone else to enjoy the day. The sit-down dinner was catered by a company in Parsippany, one that Gloria had heard about from a friend. Even now, they were busy readying the meal to be eaten in a few hours.

Samantha and her bridesmaids were in the two bedrooms of the guest wing, which had been converted for the day into the women's dressing rooms, preparing for the ceremony, which would begin in about a half-hour. The men were using Michael and Thomas's rooms. Samantha was a stunningly beautiful bride. Her medium-length, dark-brown hair cascaded down around her neck and contrasted fantastically with the bright white dress she wore. Samantha was naturally beautiful, and so she wore just a touch of makeup, the truth being that she didn't need much. There was not so much as a hint of nervousness, which is not usually the case with the bride-to-be so close to the wedding. No, she was quite assured and as calm as she could be.

Gloria approached her. "Well, honey, are you ready for this?"

"Sure," she replied. "It's all coming together today. Thanks for all of your hard work in making this happen. I appreciate it very much." Gloria and Samantha faced each other, holding both hands.

"You're welcome, Darling."

The next 20 minutes were filled with a bride and 5 bridesmaids all making sure that their hair was done just right and that all other considerations were taken care of. About 10 minutes before the wedding, Gloria asked the bridesmaids and the personal attendant to allow Jonathan and Gloria some time alone with Samantha. They gladly obliged. When the last young woman had left the room, Jonathan, who had been waiting outside the door, came into the room. His eyes caught his youngest daughter all dressed in her white wedding dress, and he was noticeably moved. She was so beautiful. Gloria could tell how much these few minutes would mean to them, so she was smiling broadly.

Jonathan stepped into the room and stopped. "Wow," he said.

"Oh, Dad."

"Samantha," Jonathan said, walking closer to her. "You are truly a vision of beauty. William is quite a lucky man." Samantha blushed. "Are you all ready?"

"Yes, Dad, I sure am," Samantha said, beaming.

"Good. Your mother and I just wanted to have a few minutes with you before the wedding. Once the wedding starts, I'm sure we won't have any time to speak alone with you." He paused. "You know, Samantha, your mother and I love you very much. And we are very, very proud of you. We have also come to love William as a son. He is a fine young man. You know that you will always be able to count on us to help in any way that we can."

"Thanks, Dad."

Jonathan reached into his pocket and produced a small, wrapped box. "You know, we've made some adjustments to our relationship over the past few months. We've spent more time talking and getting to know each other better. I have enjoyed that very much."

"I have too, Dad," Samantha said, reaching out for her father's hand.

Jonathan took her hand. "I hope we can continue after you get married."

"We will."

"Well, here is a present from me to you, to celebrate the change in our relationship and also to celebrate your new life with William." Even Gloria didn't know about the gift.

Samantha took the gift and unwrapped it, then opened the box. In it was a gold tennis bracelet with alternating diamonds and emeralds.

"Oh, Dad, it's beautiful!" Samantha exclaimed.

"I thought it would go well with your dress," Jonathan replied. Samantha handed the bracelet to Gloria, who helped her to put it on Samantha's right wrist. It really was gorgeous. Samantha gave her father a huge hug.

"Thanks, Dad," she said.

"You are very welcome, my love." Jonathan turned to leave. "It's time for me to go. I'll let you two girls have some time together, and then I'll see you when I get to walk you up the aisle." Jonathan stopped and turned back to Samantha just as he reached for the door handle. "You know, I've made one change in the ceremony."

"Oh? What's that, Dad?"

"This giving away business. I don't like that, so I'm just putting you out on loan. William can be married to you, but you will always be my little girl, even if I can't still bounce you on my knee." Jonathan smiled his big smile and left the room.

Gloria hugged Samantha tightly, and they spent a few more minutes talking before it was time for the ceremony.

Once the guests had been seated, and the family as well, Reverend Wilton led William and his groomsmen to the front of the ballroom. There they stood, Reverend Wilton in his black ministerial robe, and William and his groomsmen in black tie. A handsome group, to say the least.

One by one, the bridesmaids made their way down the aisle, walking in their teal bridesmaid dresses to "Jesu, Joy of Man's Desiring." The guests watched and anticipated the moment when Samantha would arrive on Jonathan's arm. When the last bridesmaid took her place, there were a few more seconds of music, then the end. It was timed perfectly, just as planned.

A few moments for dramatic effect and the double doors into the ballroom came bursting open to reveal Jonathan and his Samantha. Both of them smiled as the congregation looked on. The pianist began "Wedding March," and Reverend Wilton motioned for everyone to stand. Jonathan and Samantha began their walk down the aisle. They walked slowly, methodically, and smiled at as many people as they could. These were their friends, their family, and they were special for being here.

When they arrived at the altar that had been prepared for the wedding, Reverend Wilton asked the traditional question. "Who gives this woman to be wed to this man?"

"Her mother and I," said Jonathan. Jonathan then shook William's hand, kissed Samantha on the cheek, whispered in her ear that he loved her, and sat down next to Gloria.

After welcoming the guests and saying a short prayer for the service, Reverend Wilton stepped to one side and allowed the speaker for the day to come to the front and center. A friend of William's from seminary had been asked by him to give the message, the charge to the couple, and he relished the opportunity. His name was Anthony Barton, and he was adequately prepared.

"It has been two centuries since the great New England preacher Jonathan Edwards put the fear of God into the hearts of his listeners when he preached his famous sermon, 'Sinners in the Hands of an Angry God.' On a much smaller scale, this is perhaps the most fearful time of the ceremony for William and Samantha, as they are now, by being gracious enough to give me the pulpit, a bride and groom in the hands of a friend who has a colossal propensity for practical jokes. They have shown the truest of faith in me, though, to allow me these few short words, not knowing what those words will be. In deference to the significance of these moments, I will forgo anything unsuitable and will instead give some thoughts on the character of the kind of marriage relationship that will endure.

"The following is a story that I recently read: Years ago in a little village, the city council was meeting in an effort to curtail expenses when they noticed a relatively small amount allocated to someone called the 'Keeper of the Springs.' A frugal man on the council asked, 'Why are we paying this fee? What does this Keeper of the Springs do?' Another member of the council said, 'I'm not sure, but I think there is an old mountain man who stays up in the mountains and cleans out all the springs and all the little creeks up there which flow into the river that fills the reservoir and provides our drinking water.' They all agreed, 'That's a ridiculous fee to pay somebody we never see. We don't even know if he does his job, so let's just cut that out of the budget.' They voted unanimously no longer to employ the strange mountain man who supposedly kept all the springs clean at the headwaters before they flowed into the river that provided water for the people to drink.

"During the first year after terminating the Keeper of the Springs, people began to notice that the water wasn't quite as sparkling as before, but, of course, 'sparkle' wasn't all that important. During the second year, the people noticed that the water had changed color, and some even mentioned that there had been more infirmity that year than in past years. During the third year, the pollution in the water was readily visible. Even with the purification process, the water in their reservoir simply was not clean. That same year, an epidemic broke out in the village that cost many people their lives. Authorities and chemists were brought in to test the drinking water, and they discovered contamination. When they traced the contamination back to its source, they discovered, at huge expense, that the waters there in the mountain had become polluted because no one had been routinely cleaning out the springs. The city council met again and agreed, 'Let's go find the old Keeper of the Springs and re-employ him because we can't live in this village without him.'"

Anthony continued, "The merging of two distinct, separate lives into one is always, to use an understatement, a dynamic situation. Because of this, marriage should not be entered into lightly but with sober judgment. This is so because, as two people come together to pledge their lives one to another, all of the potential for either a salubrious future or for a loathsome existence are innately there for the making. Yes, the union of two lives has marvelous potential to accomplish great feats and to provide unsurpassed pleasure for both the participants and their descendants, but it also has the awesome potential to destroy many lives as well.

"The merging of two lives increases exponentially the possibilities for the individuals involved. The scriptures tell us that one person can put a thousand to flight, but two can put ten thousand to flight. Two people can bring together with immense potency all of their high-minded hopes, all of their youthful dreams, all of their physical, emotional, spiritual, and character strengths, indeed, all of the good of which they are capable. Together, they have the prodigious possibility of synergizing their respective strengths, and their potential for excellence is virtually boundless. With this, the memories at the end of their lives together will provide them with the joy of having been part of raising healthy, whole children, being committed and responsible members of society, as well as thousands of other heartwarming and rewarding experiences.

"On the other hand, it is also veritable to say that there are many unions that have ultimately destroyed countless lives. The individuals involved end up, at best, caustically annoying each other, and, at worst, you can imagine. Tragically, it is often children who bear the brunt of the injurious situations created in an unfit marriage.

"The joining together of male and female can turn in either direction. Why is this? What makes the difference between the marriage made in heaven, the one that glorifies seemingly everything that comes in its path, and the marriage that starts with the power and excitement of exploding Fourth of July fireworks, filled with visions of grandeur, yet somewhere along the line derails and becomes a ruinous force, ending with the hearts of hurting family and friends strewn out behind its destructive wake?

"What is the difference? Perhaps 'Who is the difference?' is the more appropriate question. The difference is the Keeper of the Springs. The monumental difference is God. Without one to purify us, the individual soul remains in its contaminated state. It is innate to every human being that our natural course, left to ourselves, leads us to the sin of selfishness that weaves its deceptive fiber through every area of our lives. G.K. Chesterton once rightly said, 'The doctrine of original sin is the only philosophy empirically validated by 3,500 years of human history.' I would add that this original sin even has the audacity to bare its teeth within the confines of what is intended to be 'holy' matrimony.

"And so, without a Keeper of the Springs, the water we bring to our newly established community is contaminated at best.

Contaminated with the ugliness of the desire of personal determination, individual gain, and selfish glory.

"But with a Keeper of the Springs—what a glorious opportunity! In the same way that the water in the story of the Keeper of the Springs supplied the community life-giving refreshment, so, too, does the purity of the individual life serving God bring to the marriage life-giving refreshment.

"As God Himself purifies the hearts of the bride and groom, they are enabled to treat one another the way they were intended to. Personal sacrifice is bestowed, rather than service demanded. Freedom reigns instead of the sinister and insidious jealousies that lead to the desire to control found in all too many marriages today. Compassionate tenderness replaces raging anger. Selfless humility effectually eliminates the kind of pride that can destroy a relationship. In short, through the beauty of two lives depriving themselves of their personal goals and giving themselves over to a commitment to the greater union, the wonders of this life and of their God are discovered together and enjoyed beyond their wildest imaginations.

"Let me say that the idealism and altruistic feelings of these moments at the altar, with hundreds of friends and relatives watching on, need not be lost, yet we must temper those feelings with a dose of honesty and remind ourselves that it is much easier to love and to cherish when your marriage is for richer rather than for poorer, when for better than for worse, in health, rather than sickness. But the truth be known, a marriage made in heaven must still be lived on earth, and 'for poorer,' 'for worse,' and 'in sickness' are normal parts of human existence, and every marriage inevitably travels their wearisome path, even if only for a short period of time.

"It is indeed easier to forsake the Keeper of the Springs when life is progressing well, but my challenge to you this day is to not be like the leaders of that city council; do not send away nor ignore the Keeper of the Springs.

"William and Samantha, you are going to have many times when you will be tempted to draw from your own reservoir rather than from the waters kept clear by the Keeper of the Springs. My challenge is to you to always spend time with God in order to draw your strength from Him, to be able to treat one another as you should.

"Now, here is a verse that should govern every moment between you two, and if it does, you will have a blessed marriage. Ephesians 4:32 says, 'Be ye kind to one another, tenderhearted, forgiving one another, even as God, for Christ's sake hath forgiven you.'

"Now may our Lord Jesus Christ Himself and God our Father, who loved us and by His grace gave us eternal encouragement and good hope, encourage your hearts and strengthen you in every good deed and word. Amen."

Anthony sat down, and Reverend Wilton gave the vows to the couple. They were the traditional vows.

"Do you, William, take Samantha to be your lawfully wedded wife, to have and to hold, to love and to cherish, from this day forward, for better or for worse, for richer or for poorer, in sickness and in health, 'til death do you part?"

"I do," William replied.

"And do you, Samantha, take William to be your lawfully wedded husband, to have and to hold, to love and to cherish, from this day forward, for better or for worse, for richer or for poorer, in sickness and in health, 'til death do you part?"

"I do," Samantha said with confidence as she looked at William and beamed.

After the vows, the couple exchanged rings and lit a unity candle. Another friend from college sang a song, then Reverend Wilton prayed and allowed the groom to kiss his bride. Then came the introduction of the new couple.

"Ladies and gentlemen, it is my great privilege to introduce Mr. and Mrs. William Moore." The crowd gave them a standing ovation as they exited the room, followed by the bridesmaids and groomsmen. When all in the wedding party had exited the room, Reverend Wilton gave the guests instructions.

"There will be a receiving line as you exit out to the back terrace. While you wait in line, there will be champagne and sparkling cider and appetizers served. Dinner will be in about 45 minutes. Please, all of you, enjoy this special occasion."

By the time the guests had gone through the receiving line and had found their seats, it was close to 5 o'clock, and dinner was ready to be served. Unlike the anniversary party, this reception was in the open air, not tents. The weather was absolutely magnificent. No wind, 78 degrees, which was unusually cool for a July in New Jersey, but that worked out well. The tables were set with fine china above white tablecloths, around lovely floral arrangements filled with a myriad of colors. The meal consisted of salad, chicken or beef, and pasta, vegetables, and dessert. All in all, it was an elegant reception.

Shortly after the guests had eaten dinner, the best man, Eric Jackson, rose to give the customary first toast. "Ladies and gentlemen, my name is Eric Jackson, and I am the best man here today, so it is my distinct privilege to offer a toast to William and Samantha. Would you please raise your glasses with me?" He then turned to William and Samantha, who were seated to his right. Lifting his glass to them, he toasted, "To William and Samantha: May God take this day and use it as a stepping stone to many years of love, joy, and happiness. May you be filled with faith in hard times and gratitude in times of plenty. May you also enjoy the blessings of many children to fill your home with the warmth that comes from hearing the sounds of pattering feet. May you live long lives, filled continually with the same love and passion that you feel for one another here today. And when it comes time to say goodbye to one another at the end of your lives, may you know deep in your hearts that you were for one another all that you could be, that you spurred the other on to be their very best, and that you were a source to one another for strength in all things. To William and Samantha: All of God's best to you!"

The guests clinked their glasses together. Just before the last line of the toast, Jonathan and Gloria had turned to look at one another.

Michael also turned briefly to see his mother and father looking at each other. He knew that they would be able to say those things to each other. They had always been all they could be for the other, they made each other their best, and they were a source of strength for each other in all things. Now the final months of Jonathan's life would give them the opportunity to live those characteristics out in the hardest of times.

The clinking of glasses snapped Michael, Gloria, and Jonathan back to the reception. They each turned to those around them and touched glasses softly, then drank the sparkling cider that filled them.

Albert Manning rose next and raised his glass as well. "A toast to the bride and groom," he said. "Spencer Michael Free said in 'The Human Touch':

> 'Tis the human touch
> in this world that counts,
> The touch of your hand and mine,
> Which means far more
> to the fainting heart
> Than shelter and bread and wine.
> For shelter is gone when the night is o'er,
> And bread lasts only a day,
> But the touch of the hand
> And the sound of the voice
> Sing on in the soul always.'

"William and Samantha, may you always be close enough to remember that all of the earthly possessions one can store are but rubbish to burn, not to cherish, and that the far greater prize is to always be able to touch one another in the tender ways that you do now, proving your love to burn in endless passion and bliss. This is the reward of the married life."

Again, the guests raised their glasses to the toast. "To William and Samantha!"

After the toasts, there was music and dancing in the ballroom, which had had the chairs removed to make room for the dancing. The music was more of the contemporary genre, so the younger crowd stayed to dance and enjoy the grounds of Three Lakes and the setting sun that gleamed down upon it. The older guests separated to talk, most of the women to the various rooms of the mansion, the men to the terraces, some enjoying the smell of fine cigars to mark the occasion. Everyone basked in the opportunity to rejoice with William and Samantha on their special day.

After the guests had dispersed around the estate, Jonathan decided to make a quick phone call he had forgotten to make the day before to an associate in California. He walked to his office to make the call.

When Jonathan walked through the door and into his study, he found William and Reverend Wilton sitting by the window talking. "What are you two doing in here?" Jonathan asked. "You're supposed to be out enjoying yourself, especially you, William; this is your day. What are you doing, solving all the world's problems?"

"Oh, we just got to talking and decided to come in here where it's a little quieter," William replied. "I suppose you're right, though; I should join my lovely bride. I'll let you two finish solving the world's problems." With that, William got up and left the room, leaving Jonathan and Reverend Wilton alone.

"I really want to say thanks for performing the wedding, Reverend Wilton. It means so much to have you here, since you did Gloria's and mine."

"Jonathan," Reverend Wilton responded, "I wouldn't miss this for the world. I love your family very much. It was an honor to be involved."

Jonathan changed the subject. "You know, Reverend Wilton, I'm glad we have a little time together. I have something I want to talk to you about." Jonathan's face took on a serious demeanor.

"I hope what I'm about to speak about can be completely confidential, at least for now."

"Of course, Jonathan, what is it?"

"Well," Jonathan paused and looked inside for the right words and then decided the straight attempt would be the best, "I'm sick, Reverend Wilton. I have terminal cancer. I found out a couple of months ago. They said then that I had about a year at the most to live. That would put my funeral somewhere in March or April, if I even make it that long."

"I am so sorry, Jonathan." Reverend Wilton said, reaching out to touch Jonathan's arm.

"I'm sorry too," Jonathan said. "It just doesn't seem fair. Why? Life isn't supposed to end like this. Where has all the time gone? What about Gloria and I spending our retirement years together traveling? This ending just seems so, so… dark. It's morbid. I'm only 57…" Jonathan's voice trailed off.

Reverend Wilton rubbed the bridge of his nose, thinking before he finally spoke. "Jonathan, I have always known you to be a man that wants his conversation to the point. I'm terribly sorry to hear about this, but the reality is that death is a part of life. It is not fun, and it is nothing to look forward to. But we must come to grips with the fact that we all pass through those dark doors someday. Some of us have a short stay here, some as short as a couple of years. Others, God allows 100 years or more. Most last somewhere in the middle. It isn't when we die but how we live and how we die that matters most. It probably will not be much consolation to you, but I think you have lived well, Jonathan, very well. Now, it is your turn to make that passage. It is dark behind that veil, but once through, you shall see the Light of Glory. There is a poem I memorized for funerals many years ago that talks of this. Would you like to hear it? You have heard it before, I'm sure."

Jonathan agreed.

"It is Henry Wadsworth Longfellow's 'The Rainy Day.'" Reverend Wilton took Jonathan Blake's hands in his and began.

'The day is cold, and dark, and dreary;
It rains, and the wind is never weary;
The vine still clings to the moldering wall,
But at every gust the dead leaves fall,
And the day is dark and dreary.

'My life is cold, and dark, and dreary;
It rains, and the wind is never weary;
My thoughts still cling to the moldering Past,
"But the hopes of youth fall thick in the blast,
And the days are dark and dreary.

'Be still, sad heart! and cease repining;
Behind the clouds the sun is still shining;
Thy fate is the common fate of all,
Into each life some rain must fall,
Some days must be dark and dreary.'

Reverend Wilton looked at Jonathan. "Jonathan, look at me."

Jonathan raised his head. His eyes met his pastor's. Reverend Wilton continued. "Your day is dark and dreary, I am sure. But behind the clouds, the sun is shining. When you pass on from this life, you will pass through those clouds and the God who you have served so faithfully these 57 years will meet you, my friend. He will greet you with a smile on His face, and His words to you will be, 'Another of my children has come home.'"

Just then, Gloria came through the door. "Here you are. I've been looking for you. What are you two doing in here when there's a great celebration going on outside?"

"I must confess, Gloria," Reverend Wilton said. "I was in here first with William, and Jonathan came to ask us the same question."

"I just told Reverend Wilton about my cancer, Gloria."

Gloria frowned and walked over to Jonathan. "Well, now he knows, and we have a lot of guests here and a wonderful moment to enjoy." She reached out and took Jonathan's hand and pulled him up. Reverend Wilton stood, too. Gloria wasn't annoyed. She just wasn't about to allow Jonathan to think about something so terrible on what should be a momentous day.

"She's right, Jonathan," the Reverend agreed.

"She's always right, I'm afraid," Jonathan retorted as they moved for the door.

Reverend Wilton put his hand on Jonathan's shoulder as they went through the door. "You go and enjoy yourself and your family and friends. I'll get in touch with you, and we can talk at a later time." Jonathan thanked him as he and Gloria turned toward the ballroom. Reverend Wilton made his way to the sun on the back terrace.

The rest of the day was indeed a celebration. The guests stayed for quite some time, well into the evening. Around 8 o'clock, a limousine arrived to take William and Samantha away for their honeymoon. They would stay in New York City tonight and then go on to Bermuda tomorrow around noon.

As they left, Jonathan spoke with Samantha one more time. Stopping her as she went out the front door, he leaned forward to speak closely to her. "Have a wonderful time, dear. Your mother and I are very proud of you." Turning to William, he shook his hand firmly. "Young man, she's yours now. Take good care of her."

"I will," William said with a broad smile on his face. With that, William and Samantha got in the back of the car and were whisked away.

July 12

J ONATHAN AND GLORIA had been on Martha's Vineyard for two days now. It was Jonathan's idea to get away from New Jersey for a week after the wedding so as to provide a respite for Gloria and himself from all of the activity that had encompassed the past few months. The Vineyard had been a restful place for Jonathan and Gloria over the years. At first, they simply rented small homes in the summer for them and their family to enjoy for vacations. Eventually, they purchased a home there so they could enjoy it at their leisure year-round. It wasn't extravagant as some homes go on the island, but it was indeed a charming place, and Gloria had poured much effort into making it so over the years.

They had flown in on Monday, having taken Sunday to sleep in and relax from the day before. The weather was beautiful, and Jonathan looked forward to quiet dinners and long, relaxing walks on the beach with Gloria. Gloria loved to dine out at the quaint little restaurants on the isle, while Jonathan found nothing as glorious as a simple dinner out and a walk on the beach as the sun set. This is exactly what Jonathan had in mind for this evening.

After a late meal, Jonathan led Gloria down the beach, hand in hand. They wondered aloud how Samantha and William were doing, wondering if they were enjoying themselves on their honeymoon. They talked about everything really, except Jonathan's illness. That was one thing Gloria had always appreciated about Jonathan. They seemed to be able to talk endlessly to one another about almost any topic. The waves crashed to the shore as they made their way back to their home that overlooked the beach. Suddenly, Jonathan stopped about a quarter-mile from the house.

"Let's just sit here for a while and watch the sun set," Jonathan suggested.

"All right," Gloria said, kicking her sandals off and sitting down in the warm sand. A few dozen or so other vacationers and retirees walked the beach as well, but it didn't seem crowded. Jonathan sat close to his wife. The sun was still about 30 minutes from setting, but the sky was already turning a bit reddish orange.

"I love sunsets," Jonathan said.

"I do too."

"I especially like sunsets with you at my side," Jonathan said, leaning over and kissing Gloria softly on the cheek. There they sat, in love, as though on their own honeymoon. Jonathan and Gloria loved to watch people. They particularly enjoyed watching people who were on their vacations. At home, people always looked so hurried, so bothered. On vacation, they seemed so overjoyed. Everything took on a sense of peace. People's faces were so bright and carefree on vacation. Together they sat and watched the many people, some couples, some families, as they walked past.

They hadn't been saying much as they watched. After a while, Jonathan looked at Gloria out of the corner of his eye. There were tears in her eyes. "I hope those are tears of joy, overwhelmed with the pleasure of being here with me," Jonathan said, wrapping his arm around Gloria.

"No," Gloria responded, "They are definitely not tears of joy."

"What's the matter, dear? What could possibly be wrong? It's a beautiful night. You're here with me. What's the matter?"

The repressed emotions of the past few months burst forth like an opened dam as Gloria began weeping. Jonathan was a little embarrassed at first, looking around to see if anyone was noticing. They weren't. "Gloria? Gloria, what is the matter?"

"I just can't take it anymore," she said between sobs, almost pushing the words out. "I love being here, but I simply can't take the thought that you are going to be gone so soon. You're here now, and you still seem to be in good health and all, but you won't be here anymore. Jonathan, I can't live without you." Her head was in her hands, and she was weeping uncontrollably. Jonathan pulled her tighter with his right arm and took her head in his left hand.

"Dear. Why all this so suddenly?"

"It isn't 'so suddenly,' Jonathan," she said, briefly looking at him. "It has been months and months of buried emotion, not being able to tell anyone. It has been months of smiling and behaving as though nothing is wrong so that others can enjoy their lives and events. All the while, I'm trapped in a living nightmare. It has been horrible, Jonathan. Simply horrible."

"Oh, Gloria, I am so sorry. I didn't know that you were hurting so terribly. I just assumed…" He didn't know what he had assumed, actually.

"It has just been so hard, Jonathan."

"What has been so hard?"

"Pretending that everything was okay. Jonathan, you are going to be dead soon." The words shocked them both. "I'm sorry, Jonathan. I didn't mean to be so harsh."

Jonathan looked out into the water. "It's all right, honey. It's true. I will be dead soon." Both were quiet. It didn't make sense. Jonathan was still in pretty good health. Day by day, it didn't seem like he was dying. Sick, yes. But dying seemed so far off. Yet, in their minds, they knew it was coming. Jonathan tried to make peace with it. Gloria had worried and pained herself endlessly, silently.

"Jonathan, how am I going to come up here without you? How will I walk these beaches alone? How will I ever watch another sunset without you?" Jonathan didn't answer immediately. He knew that he would probably feel the same way if it were Gloria who was dying.

"I don't know," he finally replied. "I don't know."

There wasn't much else to talk about tonight. They realized the futility of it all. There were so many unanswered questions. So many painful situations lie ahead, mainly for Gloria. Gloria eventually regained most of her composure. They waited until they couldn't see any more of the sun, which had dropped fully below the horizon, then they got up and walked home.

As they got into bed that evening, Gloria rolled close to Jonathan. "I'm sorry, Jonathan."

"Whatever are you sorry for?"

"For losing it on the beach."

"You have absolutely nothing to be sorry for, Gloria. Nothing at all."

"I should have better control over myself."

"Gloria, if anybody should be sorry, it's me. I should never have made you wait so long before telling anyone and talking about it. We should have just told people as soon as we knew."

"No, we needed to keep it to ourselves. It did make sense to do it that way. Besides, it will be over soon. Now we can begin to let everyone know."

"Yes, I suppose," Jonathan said.

"I love you, Jonathan."

"I love you very much, Gloria." They each rolled over to their own side of the bed to go to sleep. Gloria mulled over the idea of selling this house when Jonathan was gone.

The rest of the week was generally leisurely and uneventful. Both Jonathan and Gloria tried not to broach the subject of death. It just took so much energy to do so. Instead, they tried simply to enjoy themselves, and they did as best they could.

After church on Sunday, they ate out for brunch, shut the house up, and flew home to face the daunting task of telling the children about Jonathan's cancer.

July 23

CHURCH HAD BEEN good that morning. It was again a lovely New Jersey summer day. The temperature would push up toward 85 later in the day, but it wasn't particularly humid as it could often be. New Vernon Presbyterian church is a small white church in the old style. They had left the doors open during church, and every now and then, a cool breeze swept through the congregation. The songs were inspiring, and the sermon was practical. All in all, just the perfect start to the summer weekend day. The rest of the family was going to go out together for brunch, but Jennifer had told Scott that she didn't want to. She said that she wanted to go home and finish a book that she had been reading, lie in the hammock in the backyard, and take a nap. There was one other task she wanted to do.

When they got home, Jennifer went upstairs to their bedroom and then to her dresser. There she pulled out a plain, white, number-10 envelope that had come in the mail earlier in the week. Scott was down watching baseball in the living room, a soda in one hand, a bag of chips in his lap, and the remote control in the other hand. One leg was draped over the side of the chair. The Mets were losing. Jennifer sat down on the edge of the bed and inhaled deeply. The moment of truth had come.

She tore the edge of the envelope along one side. She blew into the open end and pulled out the letter. It was addressed to her. She read swiftly through the one-paragraph letter and felt like laughing and crying at the same time—tears of joy. Now, how to tell Scott.

"Scott, can you come up here for a moment?"

"I'm watching the game, honey," he yelled from downstairs.

"It's important," she called out.

"Come and tell me then."

"Obstinate beast," she said as she got up to go downstairs, only half-jokingly. Jennifer quickly ran down the stairs and went into the living room. Scott's eyes remained fixed on the screen before him. Jennifer walked right to the set and turned it off.

"Hey," Scott protested.

"If you want to, you can turn it right back on. Right now, however, Mister Pro-baseball Fanatic, I want your undivided attention." She sat in his lap. "Remember a couple of months ago when our relationship took a turn for the better?"

"Uh, well, I don't know if I remember the exact moment."

"Do you remember coming home after Mom and Dad's wedding anniversary?"

Scott thought for a moment, then got a smile on his face. "Yes, as a matter of fact, I do." He wrapped his arms around her and pulled her close.

"Don't get any ideas, buster," she said. "I've got some news. We really did change our life that night." She left the thought out there to hang for a while.

"I don't get it," Scott said.

"You don't, Dad?" she asked.

All of a sudden, it all came together for Scott. "You have got to be kidding me."

"Nope."

"You mean?"

"Yes, I do," she said matter-of-factly.

Scott picked Jennifer up and whirled her around the living room. They both laughed out loud and danced for close to five minutes. Jennifer was indeed pregnant. The first Blake grandchild was on the way. The two lovebirds spent the rest of the day cuddling and cooing with and to one another. They talked about names, whether it would be a boy or a girl, and how to tell their folks. They decided that they would tell the rest of Jennifer's family this Wednesday night when they would all be having dinner together at Three Lakes.

July 25

JONATHAN WAS OUT on the back terrace when he heard the phone ring. He made his way back inside the house, hoping to get to the phone before the answering machine picked up. He picked up the receiver just as the fifth ring ended. The answering machine had started but quickly shut off.

"Hello?"

"Jonathan. This is Charles."

"Hello, Reverend Wilton. To what do I owe this honor?"

"Well, I simply wanted to call and see how you are doing. Frankly, you caught me off guard there at the wedding. I haven't stopped thinking of you and Gloria since then."

"You are too kind. I'm doing okay. Getting sicker, though. I can tell that my body is deteriorating, so I'm frustrated by that. I just try to take each day as it comes, enjoy it, and live life. That's about all I can do, right?"

"I do want to encourage you to do something, though, Jonathan."

"What is that?"

"Prayer."

"I do plenty of that, Reverend Wilton. In fact, I think I've prayed more in the last couple of months than in the two years before that combined. I've certainly asked to have this dreaded cancer taken away if at all possible."

"That would be tremendous if it happened, Jonathan, but I want to remind you of something C.S. Lewis used to say. He said that he prayed, not to change God, but to see himself changed. Jonathan, you are entering a time, and you well may be significantly into it, wherein you are going to ask the most basic and yet deeply profound questions of your life. You are going to ask them of God. That's prayer. And I want to encourage you to ask those questions with the goal of seeing yourself changed as you embrace the answers."

"I've never thought of it that way before."

"I don't think many of us have, Jonathan. Most of us, especially when confronted with something so final as our own death, seem to demand of God that He answer to us, as though all of existence answers to us. We do better to seek to learn and understand a greater will for our lives."

"That's a good word. Thank you."

"Be strong, Jonathan, and know that from now on, you may call me any time, day or night, and I will do anything for you and your family. You just let me know."

"I will."

"Splendid. Have a good day."

"I will, and thank you again, Reverend Wilton."

"Goodbye, Jonathan."

"Goodbye."

Jonathan returned the phone to its cradle and headed back out to the terrace. He had a lot of thinking to do. Reverend Wilton was right. Most people do become extremely selfish when faced with their own death. It's to be expected, he supposed. But he knew that there was more to be gained through learning from his situation, from changing, rather than simply questioning all of the time.

He sat down on the chair out on the terrace. He began to think of the children. He would be telling them tonight. He thought about Samantha. She was married now, only Thomas was left, and he certainly wouldn't see that. He had had a few good interactions with her lately. She seemed now to be responding well to him. The relationship between the two of them was still a little uncomfortable at times, as they really didn't have much in common to talk about. Jonathan thought long and hard of ways to connect, but it seemed like it was always a stretch. Just the effort made a difference, though.

He thought of Scott and Jennifer. He worried about them, actually. Although he did see a change in them both lately, and they had both assured him separately that things were on the road to recovery. He just wished there were an older couple who could take them under their wing and encourage them. A couple who had gone through some tough times would be best. He knew that Gloria would be encouraging to Jennifer, but Jennifer had the capacity to be overbearing when confronted. Jonathan could handle her, but he wondered about Gloria. And who would be close with Scott? Michael could, he supposed, but still, Jennifer would always be Michael's older and, in her mind, wiser sister.

As he thought longer, he could only dream of how his family would turn out. He assumed that the kids were all close and that they would be a strength to one another. He just wondered whether or not they would rely on one another. Michael and Patty would be all right. No worries there. If there was ever a laid-back, straight arrow, Michael was it, and Patty was about as amiable as they come. They would surely have their ups and downs, as do all couples, but they would sail through because neither one of them got particularly perturbed by the other's downfalls.

Young Thomas. There was the worry. He seemed to have his head on his shoulders, but he was still somewhat impressionable. The world wasn't the same as it was when Jonathan went to Princeton and started out in business. Values have changed. Ethics are different. Morality has altogether shifted. All of the ground rules seemed to be out the window, and there were many who liked it that way and played by the rules they made up as they went along. Jonathan was concerned that some young lady might find Thomas's wealth more attractive than Thomas himself. It had been the case with the other three that some who dated them had an eye on something in addition to romance, so Jonathan and Gloria always kept a close eye on the attitudes displayed by those who dated their children. How would he talk to Thomas about that? He would have to find the right time and just do it. Jonathan looked at his watch. It was time for the nightly news, so he went inside to find out what went on in the world today.

July 26

JONATHAN ALWAYS LOVED a formal family dinner. Nothing brought greater satisfaction to Jonathan's heart than a table filled with good food surrounded by his family to partake of it together. Ever since about 1980, when Jennifer was in the middle of her teenage years and Michael was starting them himself, the family seemed to have always been going in opposite directions. So, from time to time, Jonathan called for a formal family dinner. Everyone would come together at least a few hours before the meal and simply stay together, catching up, helping with the meal, and spending precious time together. For many families, this would be difficult, but for the Blakes, it was rather easy. They, excluding the every-now-and-then family squabble, genuinely liked each other's company.

To tell his family of his impending death, Jonathan called again for a formal family dinner. Since these happened with some regularity, once or twice per year, no one suspected anything out of the ordinary. Jonathan knew, though, and he was looking forward to tonight with great trepidation. In fact, this night would be a mix of emotions. There would be the pleasure of being with his family, there would be the release of telling those who cared about him, letting go of his secret, and there would be a sense of sober finality. To him, it was as though finally telling his children would seal the fact of his death.

The whole family was gathered together in the formal living room, drinking coffee and tea by 5 o'clock. Everyone had taken off of work early in order to make it to the dinner. Gloria entered the room and announced that dinner would be ready at 6:30, so everyone was free to do as they pleased until then, though she would appreciate any help in the kitchen she might receive.

Jennifer and Samantha quickly followed their mother into the kitchen to help prepare the meal, and Jonathan excused himself to his study for some phone calls. That left Michael and Thomas, the two brothers, and Scott and William, the two brothers-in-law, to themselves in the living room.

"Shouldn't you go help in the kitchen?" Scott teased Thomas.

"Only if you'll let me borrow your apron, honey," Thomas quickly retorted.

Michael interrupted. "Okay, you two girls, stop your bickering. Billy-boy and I want to challenge you to a game of pool. That is, if you feel up to the match."

The words were barely out of Michael's mouth when Scott and Thomas were making their way past him on the couch on their way to the billiards room.

"You two are gluttons for punishment. If you remember correctly, we beat you quite handily the last time we played together," Thomas said as he headed out the door. Thomas was the most eager, mostly because he rarely lost a game.

William stood and began to leave, following Michael. "What have you gotten me into again?" he asked with feigned disbelief.

"Pass me the baster, will you?" Gloria asked Samantha. Samantha handed her mother the baster and went back to making the salad on the working end of the island in the middle of the kitchen. Jennifer was behind them at the counter, busily working on cleaning and preparing the asparagus.

"I hope I got the potatoes in early enough," Gloria said to no one in particular.

"They'll be fine, mother," Jennifer assured her.

After a few moments of silence, except for the sound of knife blades against the cutting board and the sound of the oven opening and closing while Gloria basted the turkey, Jennifer spoke.

"So, is there anything special on the agenda for tonight?"

Gloria paused, looked up, and wondered what to say. Finally, she settled on, "Oh, I'm sure there will be important things to talk about. There always are." From down the hall, they could hear the loud antics of the men playing. Gloria realized this provided the opportunity to change the subject. "It sure sounds like the boys are having fun," she said.

Jonathan had escaped into his study for a moment. He figured he could get a few phone calls in before dinner. "Jim Butler, this is Jonathan Blake." Jonathan was leaning back in his easy chair, his feet on the ottoman, the phone in his right hand, his weekly cigar in the left. "I'm finally returning your call."

Jim Butler owned three newspapers in Arizona and was attempting to increase his empire by adding a few in the San Diego area. He had never met Jonathan Blake but had heard of him and was able to get in touch with him through a mutual friend, a newspaper baron in the Midwest.

"Well, thank you, Mr. Blake. I have a few questions I wanted to ask you about this deal I'm trying to put together out in San Diego. Do you have some time?"

"Sure, Jim, I have a half-hour or so before I sit down for dinner with my family. If I can't help in that time, we can talk again at a later time. The only rule I have is that you call me Jonathan, not Mr. Blake. Deal?"

"That's great, Jonathan. I appreciate it. Now, I was wondering..."

"It's dinner time!" Gloria's shouts resonated through the house. She dispatched Samantha to tell the four boys and Jennifer to tell Jonathan. She knew she had to start 5 or 10 minutes before she actually wanted to eat just to make sure everyone got to the table on time.

The table was elegantly set, and the sun shone brightly through the western bank of windows in the formal dining room. The beautiful pastels of the tablecloth, runner, and napkins added to the beauty of the second-generation summer place settings, passed down from Edgar and Charlotte, and the crystal water goblets.

Dinner was turkey, twice-baked potatoes, asparagus, corn, salad, and fresh-baked bread. Apple pie would top off the meal for dessert.

"Everybody, take a seat," Gloria said.

After everyone had done so, all eyes turned to William. Jonathan asked the question everyone knew was coming. As the minister in the family, it was more often than not that he was asked to say grace before meals.

"William, would you do the honors?" Jonathan asked.

"I'm sorry, Mr. Blake, but I'm off duty. I only work Sundays, you know, and…"

Jonathan interrupted. "Thanks, William." With that, everyone bowed their heads and William blessed their meal.

"Thank you, Heavenly Father, for this meal which we can have and enjoy together. Thank you for our family and for our health. I pray that you would continue to pour out Your blessing on us and enable us to use Your blessing responsibly to help others who are less fortunate. Please bless this time together tonight. Amen."

Everyone around the table joined in with their own "amens," and the table suddenly became a flurry of activity, each person intent on filling their plate and enabling others to do the same. Mozart came from the speakers in the room. The family enjoyed their time together, talking, among other things, about the latest pool match, the family vacation later on in the year, work, new investment opportunities, as well as all the normal catching up that needed to be done.

Finally, somewhere between dinner and dessert, when everyone was sitting talking, Jonathan decided to wade into deeper waters. He was just about to speak when Jennifer began. "Well, Scott and I have an announcement that you all need to know about." Everyone looked at each other. The way she had said it, no one knew if it was bad news or good news that was coming. Michael thought the worst—that Jennifer and Scott were getting divorced or something.

"Well, you all need to know because it will affect you to a great degree…" She paused for dramatic effect.

"Go ahead, Jennifer," Jonathan urged her.

"Okay, I suppose you will want to hear it straight." Michael was now convinced it was something bad. Others were beginning to think the same. "Scott and I are going to… have a baby!" She said the last part half-shouting. She knew that they were all probably expecting something else.

After a brief pause to let the announcement sink in, the table erupted in joyful celebration. Jonathan and Gloria smiled at the prospect of their first grandchild and gave their congratulations. Samantha and Patty were particularly joyous. Michael bemoaned that he was sure Patty would want one now, too.

Jonathan got up and moved to Jennifer and hugged her. "That is wonderful, Darling," he said. He moved to Scott. "Congratulations," he said as he hugged him around the neck. Jonathan went back to his seat, and the questions began. When did they find out? Did they know whether it's a boy or a girl? When is Jennifer due? The typical questions new mothers-to-be are asked.

After a few minutes, Gloria announced that this would call for a party, and they just happened to have some apple pie to celebrate with. She excused herself from the room. "Jonathan, would you help me?" she asked as they left.

Jonathan got up and followed her into the kitchen. They began cutting pie and placing the pieces on the plates. Jonathan put some whipping cream on each. "What are you going to do?" Gloria asked.

"About what?"

"About telling the children."

"I don't know. This definitely throws a wrench in the plan. I certainly don't want to spoil Scott and Jennifer's night." Jonathan shrugged his shoulders. "What do you think?"

"We could wait until after dessert and just tell them. You could explain that you felt like you had to tell them soon and that you had planned on it tonight. I don't think that they'll mind. They are going to want to know." Jonathan's body was showing more and more signs of deterioration, and it would only be a matter of time before the kids would at least notice that. There really wasn't another time in the near future to tell the whole family together. They decided to tell them tonight.

"That was the best apple pie you have ever made," William said to Gloria.

"Thank you, William."

The rest of the family added their compliments as well. Jonathan was pouring more coffee around the table. When he had finished, he sat down and stirred his own coffee. "You know," Jonathan began. "I would like to talk to you all about something myself. I have an announcement of my own, though it isn't one I really rejoice in." He paused and looked down into his coffee cup. He was searching for the right words.

"What is it, Dad?" Jennifer asked.

Jonathan looked up again. He slowly panned the table, looking into each of the kids' eyes. It was finally time to own up to his own mortality. "As you know, I was sick early on this year." Patty immediately got a sick feeling of her own in her stomach. She sensed what was coming, without the specifics. Though Michael had known for a while, he hadn't told Patty. "And so, I went to see Dr. Kidman. He checked me out and decided that I needed to see a specialist. So, he went with me into Manhattan to see someone, another doctor. In fact, he is world-renowned for his specialty. After an exhaustive set of tests, I was told that I have cancer." The word crashed heavily on the children when he said it. "I really can't even remember the name. It's six or seven syllables long. The worst part, for me and for all of us really, is that the cancer has spread and is spreading, and it is inoperable." There was quiet all around the table as the news sunk in. Still, a few didn't get what was meant.

Samantha finally broke the silence. "So… what does that all mean, Dad? Are you saying that you're dying?"

"Yes, Samantha. I'm dying." Those words caused even greater shock in everyone at the table.

"The doctors say that I have about a year to live. Well, actually, it was a year as of a few months ago. Now it would be about eight months. They really just don't know. They said it could be six months, it could be two years, though they severely doubt I would be able to live that long.

"I could have chosen to have treatment, but they said that it really wouldn't help. In fact, it would just cost thousands of dollars—well, hundreds of thousands, really, and it would just make me sick on top of the sickness the cancer would give me." Again, silence.

"I'm sorry, Jennifer and Scott, for saying this tonight," Jonathan said. "I hate to put a damper on your wonderful news."

Scott shook his head. "No, that's fine. We need to know." He was speaking to Jonathan but looking down into his plate.

Jonathan wanted to try and make the best of the situation. "I know that this is terribly difficult. This is life, though. We need to make the most of our remaining time together. We will have Thanksgiving, our vacation together, Christmas… There are still many good times left. Let's make them the best they can be." Still, everyone sat speechless.

Gloria finally decided the evening should come to an end. "Look, we all have a lot to think about. You will all be numb for a few days. It's getting late, so let's clean up and call it an evening."

"That's a good idea," William said. "We'll help you get all of this into the kitchen." Everyone began getting up from the table, slowly clearing their setting as they did. For the next 15 minutes, the family cleared the table, talked infrequently, and the children got ready to go. A half-hour after Jonathan told them, his family, except for Gloria, and Thomas, who was in his bedroom already, was gone.

Jonathan now sat in the living room, sipping some decaffeinated coffee. Gloria came and sat next to him on the couch. For 20 minutes, they didn't say anything. Instead, there they sat, wondering how their lives would progress for the next six months. Then they talked briefly before Jonathan suggested they go upstairs to bed. "It's been a long night," he said. "We should get some sleep." Gloria rubbed Jonathan's thigh and agreed. They got up, held each other's hands, and walked to their bedroom together.

A few more minutes, and they were in bed. Gloria snuggled up to Jonathan. "I love you," she said before kissing him.

"I love you, too."

And they went to sleep.

July 27, 3:30 p.m.

T HE CLUTTERED KITCHEN was a little coffee shop that Jonathan frequented, located about 15 minutes from Three Lakes. There he sat patiently, waiting for Albert Manning to meet him for a cup of coffee. Jonathan was still exhausted from the night before when he told the children about his illness.

"More coffee?" the waitress asked, already pouring the drink into Jonathan's half-empty cup.

"Sure," Jonathan responded. After the waitress was through filling his cup, he added the customary creamer and sugar. When he was done, he again picked up the *Wall Street Journal* to look over the day's financial picture. Even with his great wealth, Jonathan kept a picture of where all of his stocks were and what they were doing. Not that he could skip a month and be ready for the poor house, but he wanted to keep abreast and make changes where need be. After getting out of the day-to-day operations of the newspaper business, this was his work.

"Bad day on the stock market yesterday. You're probably only worth half the total value of New Jersey business production!" Jonathan laughed as he put down his newspaper. The familiar voice signaled that his friend, Albert, had arrived.

"Hello, Albert," Jonathan said as he rose and shook Albert's hand.

"Hello to you, Jonathan."

The two sat down, and Albert said, "I hope you don't mind, I ended up missing lunch, so I'm going to eat. A sort of half-lunch, half-dinner meal."

"Not at all," Jonathan said.

"I'm sure Gloria has already made you an exquisite lunch, or I would ask you to join me."

"Well, if you call a ham and cheese sandwich an exquisite lunch, I guess that's what I had. What made you miss lunch?"

"Oh, I had a meeting with CNBC about a talk show they want me to host. It lasted from 9 a.m. until about a half-hour ago. They wanted me to stay, but I was tired and hungry, and I wanted out. So, here I am. I can't believe they didn't have any food at that meeting. Cheapskates. It probably tells me about what I'll get paid." Albert laughed as he finished and perused the menu.

Jonathan laughed, too, as he said, "Ah, the pains of an American icon. I feel so very sorry for you."

"Also, I figured you were buying so... I hope they have a New York steak special."

"Go ahead, I'll buy," Jonathan said.

Just then, the waitress reappeared. "Can I take your order?"

"Yes," Albert started, "I will have your French onion soup, a turkey sandwich with yellow, not brown, mustard, and an iced tea, please."

"Is that it?" the waitress asked, looking at Jonathan.

"Nothing but coffee for me," Jonathan said.

"I'll have some coffee when I'm done with my meal," Albert added.

"Coming right up," the waitress said as she wheeled around and headed for the kitchen.

"So, Jonathan, I've been meaning to ask: How are you feeling?"

Jonathan was startled. "Why do you ask?"

"Well, I've noticed you're getting thinner. And your face is a little ashen lately. Is everything okay?" Albert took a sip of water while waiting for the reply.

Jonathan's heart began to speed up. He had planned on telling Albert about his sickness this afternoon, and Jonathan had planned on doing it his way and when he wanted to. Now, he was wondering how he would regain control of the direction of the conversation. He paused for a moment, looking out the window behind Albert. He realized there was no way to control this conversation, the same way there is no way to control this life he was handed.

"It is interesting you ask, Albert," Jonathan said, refocusing on his best friend's face. "I have been sick."

"I thought so. I should have been a doctor." The waitress set Albert's tea in front of him. He began to add some sweetener, eager to take a large drink. He continued, "No, doctors don't make enough. I couldn't afford the pay cut. So, what is it?" Albert was still being his brash self, not realizing how serious the conversation was about to turn.

"It's cancer."

Albert stopped stirring his tea and looked up, his eyes wider than Jonathan had ever seen them. "Cancer? What kind of cancer? Is it treatable?" Albert was overwhelmed.

"Albert, I can't ever remember the name of it. It isn't treatable, though. The doctors have given me until spring at the most."

"I don't know what to say," Albert said.

"Now that's the first time I have ever heard the great Albert Manning say that!" Jonathan exclaimed in mock surprise.

"Don't!" Albert said suddenly, raising his voice and showing an edge of anger. "Don't joke around about this," he finished, lowering his voice again.

Jonathan was surprised at Albert's response, as he was with Michael's. There was silence as they sat, not knowing what to say next. Albert looked down at his plate. After a few moments, the waitress reappeared and set before Albert his soup and sandwich.

"French onion soup, a turkey sandwich with yellow, not brown, mustard. Anything else?"

"No, thank you," Albert responded. The waitress disappeared into the kitchen.

Albert looked down at his food, then back at Jonathan. Finally, he decided to think more about Jonathan than his own pain. "I'm sorry about snapping, Jonathan, forgive me. I'm just so… stunned. So, how are you feeling?" he asked Jonathan. "I mean, physically as well as emotionally."

"Oh, I have been better physically. The medication I'm on keeps me tired and a little queasy at times. Emotionally, it's a mixed bag." Jonathan's eyes teared up a bit.

"I can imagine," Albert said.

"This whole thing has caused me to think a lot about the meaning of life. It amazes me that we think so little about an event that we are all sure to experience someday. Death is always in the back of your mind; you see relatives die and so forth, but, like fools, we believe it will never happen to us. Then when the doctor says, 'nine months to a year,' all of a sudden, you start realizing that death will happen."

The waitress came back, not understanding what she was interrupting. "How's everything?"

Jonathan looked up. "Fine," he said.

She left again, and Jonathan took another sip of coffee and continued. "Then all of the emotions hit. You're angry because you're so young. Albert, I always thought I'd live to be 90. You ask God why you have to be the one who goes early. You feel a sense of injustice. I wish that I was less sure that this cancer would get me. I could get into a fight for life if the chance was even 10 percent that I could win this battle, but they tell me it isn't so.

"You get sad because you will miss your family. I can't imagine being without Gloria. I wish I could see the kids have kids, not to mention great-grandkids. By the way, Jennifer and Scott are pregnant." Jonathan mentioned the pregnancy just as a sidelight, then continued on.

"I've seen a lot of the world, but there is so much else I wanted to do and so many places I wanted to see…" Jonathan's voice trailed off.

After about 30 seconds, Jonathan finished. "I just feel robbed, I guess."

Albert reached out and touched his dear friend's hand. "I'm sorry," he said. He held his hand in place for a moment and then brought it back to his side. Never before had these two friends experienced this level of friendship and empathy. All the years of sharing experiences, and it came to one of them dying to realize how much they loved each other.

"Is there anything I can do for you?" Albert asked.

"Well, there is, actually. Nothing official, but I would ask that you keep tabs on Gloria and the kids. Especially Michael. I'm giving him rein of all the assets, and I have the utmost confidence in him, but he is only 29, and he could probably use some good advice and encouragement from time to time. I know he respects you and would appreciate it. Would you do that for me?"

Albert agreed, "Yes, Jonathan, of course."

"Look, I don't want to talk too much more about this right now. I told Gloria and the kids last night, and that took a lot of energy. I try to limit the amount of discussion about death to a small fragment of my time. We can talk about it more later. I'm not going to die tomorrow. That is, if that's all right with you."

"Oh, of course," Albert said.

The two finished with some conversation about the stock market, Albert's new TV opportunity, and their favorite subject— fishing. These are the times Jonathan relished, time with Albert just spent talking. Then, soon enough, they were on their separate ways.

July 28

G LORIA'S SISTER MARGARET had just set one bag of the groceries that she had carried in from the car down on the counter when the phone rang. At first, she thought about ignoring it and letting the answering machine pick it up, but then she had an odd feeling that she should answer it. She set the other bag down, glanced over her shoulder at the open car door outside, the rest of the groceries on the front seat, and then moved to pick up the phone.

"Hello?"

"Hi, Margaret, this is Gloria."

"Oh, hi, Gloria. It's been a while since I've talked to you. Say, can I call you right back? I'm right in the middle of bringing the groceries in."

"Sure. I'm at home."

"Great. Thanks. Just five minutes."

"Okay, bye."

"Bye."

Gloria hung up the phone and plopped into the chair in her office. She began to think of Jonathan. She needed to tell Margaret about him. She had decided along with Jonathan to hold off on telling everyone, but now she needed to get the task done. It was hard to tell how Margaret would handle the news. She would be sad, of course. Sad for Gloria. She would be supportive, Gloria figured. There wasn't much anyone could do for her, she knew, except maybe pity her and try to encourage her at the same time. She picked up the latest issue of *Architectural Digest* and began to leaf through it. She was nervous. Soon the phone rang.

"Hello?" Gloria answered.

"Hi, Gloria, I'm done. I had to get some of the frozen things in before we settled in for a talk. So, how's it going?"

"Well, that's what I wanted to call you about, Margaret. It isn't going very well at all."

"Gloria, what's wrong?"

Gloria began to cry slightly. "It's Jonathan."

"Jonathan? What is it?"

"Oh, I wanted to tell you earlier, but we decided to wait until now to tell everybody. Jonathan has terminal cancer and isn't expected to live through the winter. We found out early this spring."

Now Margaret began crying herself. "Gloria, I am so sorry." She wanted to say more, but she couldn't find the words to say. They both sat on the phone for about half a minute, just crying together. Finally, Margaret asked, "Is there anything I can do?"

"No. There is nothing anyone can do. That is what is so frustrating. We are just waiting and hoping that he hangs onto his physical health as long as possible. And then, when that starts to deteriorate, we'll hold out hope for him to live as long as possible. They said that it could progress fast or slow but that they gave him about a year to live, and that was five months ago about."

"How is he doing?"

"Right now, he is still getting around. He's getting slower, though. I don't even know if he's realized it. I have, but I wouldn't say anything. He's walking slower. He has pretty intense pain at times. It's hard for him to get up in the morning."

"Is he on any medications?"

"Yes. Dr. Kidman has been wonderful through this whole ordeal. He keeps up with Jonathan and makes sure that he has the appropriate prescriptions. Some of the medications make him nauseous, though. That is tough on him when he has to vomit."

"Would you like me to come up or anything?"

"No, Margaret. I don't think there is anything you can do. It is just up to us to wait and enjoy the time we have. I guess, if anything, you can pray for me and the kids to have the strength to make it through this."

"How have the kids reacted? Have you told them?"

"Oh yes, we've told them. We told them at a dinner the other night. Michael has known for some time, though."

"I imagine they are terribly upset."

"Yes, they are pretty shaken up. The other thing I need to tell you, which made for a roller coaster evening, is that right before we told the kids, Scott and Jennifer told us all that they are pregnant."

"They are! That is wonderful. When are they due?"

"Some time at the end of February or early March. We're hoping that Jonathan lives that long."

"Gloria, I don't know what to say."

"There really is nothing to say, Margaret. I just need you to be there if I need you. Right now, we're doing fine, just in shock."

"You know that anything I can do, I will."

"Thanks, Margaret. Look, I need to get going, but I wanted to tell you."

"Okay, I'll let you go. Call whenever you need to, day or night."

"Thanks. Goodbye."

"Bye, Gloria."

Margaret hung up and immediately called Bob at work.

July 29

JONATHAN WAS LYING on the couch in his study, reading a novel, when Samantha opened the door.

"Dad?" Jonathan looked back over the armrest, lifting himself up a bit to see.

"Yes? Samantha?"

"Yes, it's me. Can I talk to you for a minute?"

"Well, sure, come in and sit down." He put the bookmark back in between his pages and set the book on the floor next to the couch. Samantha crossed the office and sat at the front edge of the chair facing the sofa. She put her hands on her knees, obviously nervous. Jonathan swung his feet to the floor and sat up.

"What can I do for you?" Jonathan asked.

"How are you feeling?" she asked, ignoring the question.

"Oh, at the moment, I'm okay. I'm feeling worse than a month ago, but I can still get around."

Quiet filled the room. Jonathan figured Samantha had something on her mind, so he decided to wait. She looked down at her hands. "So, Dad, did finding out you were dying make you come to me to fix our relationship?"

"I wouldn't say that it made me. It was certainly the catalyst. I found out one afternoon and came in here after the appointment. Your mother was gone, and I started looking at those pictures."

He pointed at the wall. "I saw your picture, and it just hit me. You had realized it years ago, starting when you were but a little girl. I realized it the day I found out I was going to die. The sad thing is that everybody knows they are going to die, and still, they just go about their business. Most people, then, just die fast. They never get a chance to say goodbye. They never get a chance to restore a relationship like you and I have. They never get a chance to say to someone that they are sorry."

Samantha was quiet again. "Is that the answer you were looking for?" Jonathan asked.

"It's the answer I was hoping for," she replied.

"I really do love you and care for you, you know," he said.

"I know." She got up and went over to Jonathan, where she bent over and pecked him on the cheek. "Thanks, Dad. I love ya." Then she bounded out of the room, forgetting to close the door behind her.

"If you love me, shut the door behind you!" he yelled to her. A few seconds later, the door shut.

August 21

ABOUT THE TIME they were getting ready for bed, Jonathan, who had been feeling sick all day, collapsed while walking up the stairs. He had just about made it to the 10th step when he lost his footing and began to fall. The glass of lemonade he was carrying cascaded down the steps and then shattered on the floor below. Jonathan reached out to catch himself. He didn't quite get a grip, though, and he fell down about three or four stairs, but not any further because he didn't have enough momentum.

Gloria heard the glass shatter and also heard Jonathan gasp loudly and then the thud of him hitting the stairs. She came running. Finding Jonathan lying there in a heap shocked her. He was still conscious but barely. He was terribly sick and extremely weak. Gloria immediately went to the phone and called Dr. Kidman, who in turn called the ambulance.

For the next 15 minutes, Gloria kept a cool, wet cloth on Jonathan, whom she had helped move to the bottom of the stairs. She kept talking to him while he tried to remain conscious. Soon the doorbell rang. It was the ambulance. Dr. Kidman was minutes behind.

After checking all of Jonathan's vital statistics and checking him over thoroughly, the medics and Dr. Kidman decided that the primary problem was that Jonathan was sick with a viral infection but was worse because his body was fighting another disease as well. Topping it off, Jonathan had been eating less, which had robbed him of needed nourishment and was leaving him weaker than before. Dr. Kidman decided to keep Jonathan home and prescribe some more medication.

The ambulance crew carried Jonathan up to his bed and laid him there. Gloria was still scared, even after the assurances of the doctors, so she began calling the children. Soon they were all on their way to Three Lakes, thinking that they were probably going home to say their last goodbyes to their father. Michael and Patty arrived first, then Jennifer and Scott, then Samantha and William. Thomas was on vacation with a friend and his family, so Gloria was unable to get a hold of him.

The panicked children all wanted to see their father, of course, so they went up to his bedroom. The children gathered around the bed, but Jonathan was asleep. They waited for a half-hour and then decided that he was probably going to sleep through the night. Besides, by this time, Michael had asked enough questions of Gloria to realize that this particular event wasn't life-threatening. They all gathered down in the living room, fretting together for a while and then, slowly, they left for their own homes. As they did, they realized that this was a false alarm but that soon the real call would come.

Jonathan recovered most of the way in the next week, regaining much of his strength, but he was definitely deteriorating, becoming weaker overall, walking slower, and remembering less. Gloria knew that autumn was coming and that the cold weather would take an even greater toll on Jonathan. She could only pray that God would grant him a few extra months. At other times, as she saw him getting more and more sickly, she secretly hoped that Jonathan would go quickly, sparing him of a drawn-out, painful death.

AUTUMN

September 2

I T WAS ABOUT 7 o'clock the evening before Thomas was to go to Princeton for the year, and he was upstairs just finishing his packing. Gloria and a friend had gone to dinner together, and then they were going to go to a local nursery to look at some plants for the friend's home. So, Jonathan and Thomas were at Three Lakes alone. Jonathan was down in his office, looking over his stock portfolio and trying to make decisions on some trades for the coming week. He was actually tempted to give up working on his stock accounts when he realized that it was pretty meaningless for him to do so since he would be gone soon enough; but he kept himself going knowing that he had to get things situated as best he could for Gloria and the children. Besides, having worked in the publishing business for his whole life, he really hadn't invested in the stock market a whole lot while he was working. He invested a little in some publishing companies, basically because he had a good idea where most of the companies were going and what they would be accomplishing in the near future. He never traded on inside information, though he could have many times because every now and then, another CEO would let something slip or tip Jonathan off to something they were doing or were about to do. Jonathan stuck to his intuition and the articles he read in the magazines and papers. This did him well enough. Having received the multi-hundred-million-dollar purchase price for his business two years ago, he knew it was most prudent to invest in stocks, in addition to having cash, money markets, and bonds. He spent maybe 20 hours a week on his portfolio and had done reasonably well the past two years, up about 47 percent on the portion he had in the market.

Upstairs, Thomas wandered back and forth between his bedroom and his bathroom, packing his shaving kit and deciding which things to bring with him to school. Many things he decided to just leave at home, knowing that he could always make the hour drive back to Three Lakes if he thought that he really needed them. He decided on his clothes, his computer, a few furnishings, the basics of college life.

Gloria had told him that he could take some silverware and kitchen things that she had left over and were dispensable. She had cleaned out one of the pantries and left the things Thomas could take on the counter yesterday. About a year ago, Thomas had taken up drinking coffee, even if it was what Michael called "children's coffee"—so loaded with cream and sugar that it tasted more like hot chocolate than coffee. Gloria had an old drip coffee maker that she had recently replaced, and Thomas decided he would take it with him. He made his way out of the bedroom and down the hall toward the stairs. As he came down the stairs, he hit the creaking step that Jonathan had been promising to get fixed for the last six months. Jonathan was making his way back from getting something to drink in the kitchen and heard the step creak. He met Thomas at the bottom of the stairs.

"How's the packing going?" Jonathan asked.

"Pretty good," said Thomas. "I'm just on my way to raid all of Mom's old kitchen utensils and stuff. She's giving me the old coffee maker and some hot-water, soup-maker gadget she says she never uses. I thought it might be good for making those instant noodles in case I get hungry while I'm studying late at night."

"I know you," Jonathan said with a wry smile. "You'll be hungry most of the time, not just late at night."

Jonathan moved closer to Thomas and put his arm around him, directing him toward his office. "Come with me, I want to talk to you a bit, and then I have something to give you. Let's go in my office."

"Sure, Dad, what do you want to talk about?" Thomas asked.

"Oh, school, I guess," Jonathan said.

They went into Jonathan's office, and they sat in the two chairs by the window, semi-facing each other.

"You know, Thomas, Princeton is a tradition in this family. You did wonderfully at Delbarton, and I hope you will do as well at Princeton."

"Well, I'll do my best, Dad."

"I know you will, Thomas," Jonathan assured him. "You have a good head on your shoulders." There was an awkward silence. Thomas could tell Jonathan wanted to say something.

"Are you nervous at all?" Jonathan asked.

"No, not really. I think I'll pick it up okay. There are a couple of other guys from Delbarton going. They aren't really close friends or anything, though. It's Mike Porter, Danny Cerrelli, and a couple of other guys. I'm sure we'll hang out at first, at least until we make new friends. I hope my roommate will be somebody I can hang out with. We'll see, I guess."

"Yes, you'll make new friends soon enough," Jonathan said. "What kinds of classes do you think you would like to take this year?"

"Well, the basic requirements, I guess," Thomas said. "I'll probably get the chance to take a few electives. I don't know. Maybe I'll try some business classes, Global Economics, or something. I'd also like to take some courses on foreign cultures, someplace where I could take a trip to study abroad. I'll have to see what's available, though. I suppose for freshmen, the pickings can be pretty slim by the time all the upperclassmen get through with their choices."

"It will be interesting to see what you get," Jonathan said. "Maybe you can even combine some foreign culture classes with your economics classes. I'm sure they are available. So many economies are so intertwined nowadays."

There was again awkward silence. Jonathan didn't really know how to talk to Thomas sometimes. He had felt like that with the other children, but as they left their teenage years, he was able to converse better with them. He always had an insecurity that maybe he was boring them or not able to speak their "language." He had always attempted to keep connected with the kids, playing games with them, talking, taking them on trips, going to their sporting and school events. He wanted them to be able to come to him or Gloria in the case of an emergency or problem. Though it was hard at times relating to the kids, he knew that keeping the relationship intact would encourage them to approach Jonathan or Gloria if something went wrong. Fortunately for the Blake family, up until this point, their lives had been virtually free of any significant problems.

Jonathan slapped his knees and began to get up. "Well, I bought you a present the other day." Jonathan walked across his office, bumping his leg on the ottoman as he walked by it. "Ouch. Darn thing," he said, continuing to his desk drawer. When he got to the desk, he pulled the top right drawer open. He removed a small gift box and shut the drawer again.

As he made his way back to Thomas, he began explaining. "You know, the night before I went to Princeton, your grandpa pulled me right here into this office and gave me a gift. I still have it, in fact. This isn't exactly like the one that I got, but it's the same idea anyway. This one is actually a little nicer." He handed Thomas the box and sat back down. Jonathan watched excitedly as Thomas peeled back the wrapping paper and began to open the box. Inside was a beautiful, stainless-steel Rolex watch. Jonathan had decided to spend the extra, a total of $2,800, and buy Thomas a Rolex—it would last him the rest of his life. He had decided, though, that the gold Rolexes were out of the question, being too ostentatious, especially for an 18-year-old.

"Wow, Dad, it's beautiful," Thomas said. "Thank you."

"You're welcome," Jonathan replied. As Thomas took it out of the box to try it on, Jonathan informed him that he had already had the band sized. Thomas hooked the clasp around his wrist. The watch fit perfectly.

"Now you probably won't need another watch as long as you live," Jonathan said.

"Yeah, it's great," said Thomas.

"You don't have to take it off now, but you'll notice that I had it engraved on the back. A little message from me to you," Jonathan explained. Thomas nodded. "Now, give me a hug," Jonathan said. The two stood up and embraced each other. Jonathan held Thomas tightly. "You are a great young man," Jonathan told him. "All right, you better get to finishing your packing." Thomas walked to the door then turned back to his father, who was just sitting down to his desk to return to work.

"Dad?" Thomas said.

"Yes, Son?"

"Thanks again. I really like it."

"My pleasure, Thomas," Jonathan said.

Thomas went to the kitchen and picked out some of the things he wanted to take to school but left most of what Gloria had left him right on the counter. Gloria would take the rest to the Market Street Mission in Morristown sometime this week. When he got back to his room, Thomas placed the kitchen items in the half-full duffel bag on his bed. He then went to the chair by his window and sat down. He unclasped the new watch and looked at the engraving on the back.

To my youngest child, Thomas. To your success and happiness in life. I love you, Dad. 9/2/95

It was a gift Thomas would not only wear but cherish for the rest of his life.

September 3, Afternoon

IT WAS MOVE-IN day for Thomas, the day when every young student has no choice but to move out of the safe home that they had lived in for 18 years and to strike out on their own to be responsible, at least to some degree, for him or herself. While Thomas was young and came from a wealthy home, this day, he was much like everyone else who was arriving at Princeton for the first time. Today was the day that he would step outside of Jonathan and Gloria's protective hand and begin to strive for himself, to take responsibility for himself. And Thomas was ready.

Thomas Blake was a strong yet quiet boy, not at all the typical youngest child. Everyone who knew him loved Thomas. He was the boy many middle-aged women dreamed would be brought home by their daughter. He had been and was a responsible boy. He was tentative about the move out of his folk's house yet knew that the time had come. He was ready to grow as an individual, to make his mark, and begin being known as Thomas Blake, not Jonathan Blake's youngest child, as he had been known mostly these past 18 years. Yes, those who were familiar with the Blake name, and there were many, would eventually put things together and ask the inevitable question of whether or not he was the son of the publisher. He, however, wanted those questions to be staved off for as long as possible. He wanted to stand on his own.

Thomas had looked forward to this day all summer, and it had finally arrived. He had contemplated living at home for the first semester, what with Jonathan's illness and all, but decided to move into the dormitory with everyone else, knowing that he was only about an hour from home if he needed to go quickly. Perhaps next semester, he would move home for the final months of his father's life. He had the same regrets that the others in his family had. His life had moved to the next stage, and there was sadness in his heart. Yes, he wanted to leave adolescence and become a young man, taking care of himself and making his own decisions, but he also wanted to remain at home to be his father's son. Unlike many his age, Thomas recognized this dichotomy and allowed himself to feel it rather than arrogantly running headlong into his own delusion of self-capacity.

Thomas was excited to be out of Delbarton for the one reason that, while he believed it provided him with such an excellent education, he wanted to go to school with some young ladies. There had always been the dances arranged between Delbarton and other all-girls schools, but Thomas never connected for long with someone of the opposite sex. He now wanted to change that. He was excited to learn alongside the young women, to experience life with them, and, if the opportunity provided itself, he was ready, he felt, to venture into love. After all, it was during college so many years ago that a young Jonathan Blake had courted and won his Gloria. Perhaps fate would provide as well for Thomas.

Gloria and Jonathan had held a going-away brunch for Thomas, the whole family arriving around 10 a.m. after the 8:30 service at New Vernon Presbyterian had concluded. Gloria hadn't wanted to cook that morning, so she hired a Far Hills caterer to arrive around 7:30 and begin the preparations for brunch. Gloria had arranged about 20 pictures of Thomas at varying stages growing up on a table near where they ate. The family spent their time reminiscing about Thomas's youth and giving their prognosis for his future. Michael and Patty guessed that Thomas would become a physician, Jennifer and Scott placed their guess at a teacher, William and Samantha thought that a small business was in Thomas's future, and of course, Jonathan and Gloria gave the standard parental answer of Thomas doing well whatever he placed his hand at.

After brunch, Michael and Scott helped Thomas bring the few boxes he had down to the foyer. Out in the driveway sat Jonathan's BMW that he had brought around from the garage a few minutes after brunch. Jonathan and Gloria would follow Thomas down to Princeton. The boys loaded the back of the Jeep and placed a few things in the passenger's seat. Jonathan and Gloria got in the front seats of their car. The rest of the family stood on the front porch, waving goodbye to their little brother.

The drive from Far Hills to Princeton was an easy one, about an hour's drive straight south down Route 206. It was a beautiful fall day, the colors in the trees just beginning to change, the leaves preparing to eventually fall to the ground. Jonathan set the cruise control at 50 miles per hour, and he and Gloria took in the beauty of the surroundings. Thomas followed behind them, wondering why his Dad was driving so slowly. In the depths of his heart, Jonathan realized he was doing something he had been trying to do a lot of lately, prolonging the inevitable. He secretly hoped that if he drove slowly enough, he would be able to squeeze something, he didn't know exactly what, out of the experience. Perhaps he thought that if he drove slowly enough, they wouldn't ever get to Princeton, and he wouldn't have to see his last child off into adulthood.

"I wonder if he's excited about all this," Gloria wondered aloud. She wasn't excited. She could see where many of her friends got their excitement, knowing they would soon be spending their time not caring for children anymore but with the love of their youth. Nothing but them and their husbands. Gloria didn't have that luxury. She knew that this was another huge detour on the road her life had been traveling not even one year ago. She didn't have much to look forward to but to send her last child out of the house and make preparations for her husband to die. There would be many good times in the next few months, she knew. That is, if Jonathan lived through the winter. She hoped to herself that Jonathan would live to see the birth of Jennifer's child. They never spoke of that situation, though.

"Yeah, he is. I think it will be good for him. He's looking forward to making new friends." Jonathan replied. The rest of the drive was dominated by silence, punctuated with small talk. Each spent the time enjoying the time together, looking at the colorful foliage. They held hands and listened to Chopin.

When they got down to Princeton, there was the usual 15-to-20-minute hunt for the correct dorm. When they found it, they took all of Thomas's things to the second floor, Room 212, and placed the belongings on one of the beds.

Obviously, from the lack of additional luggage and belongings, Thomas's roommate had yet to arrive. The resident assistant came into the room to welcome the Blakes and to see if he could answer any questions. He informed them that there would be a student initiation for the dorm that night at 7 and a simultaneous event for the parents. Jonathan and Gloria helped Thomas place his things where they would go for the time being.

By dinnertime, there was still no sign of Thomas's roommate, so the Blakes decided to go for dinner. They went to the Nassau Inn, a favorite of Jonathan and Gloria's. After dinner, they took a walk through the campus, Jonathan and Gloria excitedly showing Thomas all of the places they had frequented when Gloria visited the campus and noticing a few of the new buildings that had gone up since Jonathan had graduated. Times had definitely changed.

At 7 o'clock, Thomas went to his meeting, his parents to theirs. They met back at the room afterward and finally were able to meet the young man who would be his roommate. His name was Sam Connell. He was from Vermont, where his father and mother both worked in a factory. They didn't have the money to send Sam to Princeton, but Sam had the brains and the good fortune to have a high school principal who had attended Princeton and starred on the basketball team some 15 years ago. He went to bat for Sam and helped him get an academic scholarship. The Connells were already in the room when the Blakes came back from their orientation.

"Well, hello," said Jonathan Blake, extending his hand toward Mel Connell.

"How are you? I'm Jonathan Blake. This is my wife Gloria and our son Thomas. I guess you two will be rooming together this year," he said, nodding at Sam.

"Hi there, I'm Mel Connell. This is my wife Sharon and our son Sam," Mel replied. Everyone greeted one another with handshakes. "Say," Mel continued, "Jonathan Blake. That sounds familiar. Have we met before?"

"Do you read the *Montpelier Ledger*?" Jonathan asked.

"Yeah, we get it at the house."

"Until about two years ago, I owned it," Jonathan explained.

"Of course, I remember," Sharon jumped in. "You sold a bunch of newspapers all at once. I read about it."

"That's us," Jonathan said. "A little more time on our hands since I sold out."

Sharon continued, "I also remember a very nice editorial you wrote about five years ago when the unions were having trouble. You talked about patience and unity. It helped bring a little calm there. It was good." Sharon was smiling. She liked the Blakes even though she had barely met them.

Sam asked Thomas to help him carry up a few more things. The Connells said that they were going to have to get going back to Vermont—work tomorrow and all. The next 15 minutes saw all of the boy's things up to the room, and the Connells saying goodbye to the Blakes. Jonathan glanced at his watch and mentioned that it was indeed time for him and Gloria to be heading home as well.

"I'll walk you down to the car," Thomas said.

Jonathan, Gloria, and Thomas got to the car in the parking lot in a short time. The sun had set, but it was still light out. Jonathan opened Gloria's door. Thomas gave her a hug and said thanks for all she had done, told her that he loved her and that he would call soon. Gloria began to cry small tears. Jonathan embraced his youngest son. He held him tightly.

"I love you," Jonathan whispered into Thomas's ear. "Make me proud."

"I love you, too, Dad. I will. Thanks."

Jonathan turned and walked around the car. He got in, started the engine, and pulled out of the parking lot. Thomas stood, his hands in his pockets, and watched as his father and mother drove away, his mother sitting in the passenger seat crying. Thomas stood there for a good five minutes, letting the thoughts of what was happening, the change that was taking place, set in.

Gloria sat in the car sobbing all the way back to Three Lakes. Jonathan, knowing better than to talk or try to talk Gloria out of her feelings, simply laid his right hand on Gloria's knee and drove. Gloria knew it was a good thing in the greater scheme of life that Thomas was growing up and moving out on his own, but she despised the fact that the whole life she knew for so many years was shifting, like sand with a wave overcoming it, under her feet.

September 3, Evening

AFTER A BUSY day of arriving, getting acquainted, seeing the campus, and finally getting unpacked, Thomas and Sam began to unwind and get ready for bed. It was finally dark out. The window to the dorm room was cracked open and let in a cool breeze, taking a slight edge off of the muggy feel the weather had tonight, as it had most of the summer.

Thomas was just putting the last of his socks in his drawer when Sam began to inquire about the Blake family. Sam flopped down on his bed and asked, "So tell me a little about your family. Your parents seem cool."

"Yeah, they are. I have two older sisters and an older brother."

"You like 'em?"

"Oh, yeah, we get along great. I'm closest to my sister Samantha. She and I are the most alike. I like my brother Michael. We usually go fishing together and stuff. My sister Jennifer and I talk and get along all right, but we don't have a lot in common." Thomas sat down in a chair and took another drink of a soda he had opened earlier. "What about you? You have brothers and sisters?"

"Nope. I'm the only one. My mom and dad are great. They both work in a factory. Not a lot of money in our house, but they have always worked hard to get me stuff and open up opportunities for me. My mom's the typical mom, I guess. Dad is Mister

Proud around the neighborhood. You know, 'My kid's going to Princeton,' and all. It's embarrassing, but I understand. He's giving me a chance to go somewhere and do something he didn't. What about you? My folks seemed like they had heard of your mom and dad. Are they famous or something? I've never heard of them, but that doesn't mean much."

"Well, my dad owned a bunch of newspapers. I guess he was famous in that world. I don't know if I ever would have heard of him if he wasn't my dad." Sam laughed at that.

"So, you must have a lot of money?"

"I don't. My dad does."

Quiet again. Sam was thinking. "What's it like having a lot of money?"

"I don't know. I think it's a lot like everybody else except we had more money. I guess you have a bigger house, fancier vacations, a newer car, but it doesn't stop life from happening to you." Thomas started to get teary-eyed. "You know, everybody admires my dad… but he's gonna die."

"What do you mean, 'he's gonna die'?"

"He's got cancer. He's gonna die."

"When? He didn't look that bad to me."

"He looks lots worse than he did a year ago. They gave him 'til next April, maximum. Who knows when he'll die, though."

Sam didn't really know what to say next. He hadn't known anybody who had died. All of his relatives, grandmas and grandpas included, were still alive. He just sort of sat there. Finally, Thomas saved Sam from his uncomfortable state.

"Look, you don't need to hear about my problems. I'll keep quiet."

"No, that's all right. I just don't know what to say, really. I can't imagine my dad dying. I mean, I know it's going to happen someday. Hopefully it won't be anytime soon."

"Well, you'll see my dad die before yours does. We'll have plenty of time to talk about this later. After all, you're my roommate now, and you'll hear all about it sooner or later. Right now," Thomas said as he got up and began to strip down for bed, "I'm tired. Tomorrow is going to be busy, so we better get some sleep."

"Yeah, good idea," Sam concurred. They both threw their clothes on the floor, as teenage boys do. When they were in bed, Sam, whose bed was next to the switch, leaned up and turned out the light.

"Another day, another dollar," said Sam in the dark.

"Huh?" replied Thomas.

"Nothing. Just something my dad said every night after work."

"Whatever." In minutes, they were both asleep.

September 10

G LORIA PEERED AT the ceiling momentarily, then turned her head to look at her alarm clock: 2:15 a.m. She had woken up just seconds before, one of those times when a person is wide awake instantaneously. There was a slight draft in the room. She could feel it with her left hand that hung slightly over the edge of the bed just outside of the comforter. The room wasn't too dark because of the full moon that perched itself what seemed like right outside the window to Jonathan and Gloria's bedroom. It was quiet in the room except for the pendulum swinging back and forth in the clock that stood in the corner.

Lying motionless in bed and looking out the window past the alarm clock on her nightstand, Gloria took in the beauty of the moon. It was exceptionally white tonight. She could clearly make out the shadows of the valleys on the surface.

Gloria had taken an astronomy class at Drew and was fascinated by it. Throughout the years, she would read an occasional article about the celestial objects seen at night. What always struck her most was their age. Millions of years pass by, and they are still there. They outlast everyone on earth who looks up at their beauty and wonders what's out there. People come and go, but hanging out there in the sky, like so many far-away lanterns, they continue burning brightly, forever.

Hearing his sleeping breaths, her thoughts turned to Jonathan. Soon, surely within a year, he would be gone, and she would be sleeping here alone. The moon and the stars would still be there in their places. She and the kids would still be here. Then, with time, it would be her turn, and the stars would remain after she had passed on, too. Then her children, and their children. Her heart was beating fast as she lay there, confronting death in her mind and realizing she would someday lose her final confrontation.

Life seems so futile, she thought. *What is it all about? You grow up, full of dreams, you marry, have children, with luck and hard work, you make a living and enjoy some extras, see your grandchildren, play some golf, and lie on the beach—and then you die. No ifs, ands, or buts. You die.*

Suddenly, she stopped herself from thinking this way. She realized that it did her no good except to work her into a cold sweat. She knew she had to accept death's reality and dwell on the positive things that make up the joys of life. Soon she was thinking about Jonathan again. A smile came over her face as she thought of their lives together. Then a tear. He made her so happy. He always went out of his way to make her a better person. He always supported her in the endeavors that she undertook. He always treated her so patiently and tenderly. She knew that she was the center of his universe. She thought about how he had been a wonderful husband and caring father.

At that moment, Jonathan rolled over, his foot brushing her calf. She knew she wouldn't be able to go back to sleep any time soon, so Gloria decided to get up and go downstairs for a while. A little reading sometimes helped her become tired again. She carefully folded the comforter and sheets back to allow herself out of the bed without waking Jonathan. Against the corner next to the window was a small brass hook where she kept her robe. She slipped it on, along with the slippers that sat on the floor beneath it, and headed toward the door. Jonathan and Gloria always left the door slightly ajar out of habit from when the children were little, just in case one of the little ones called. Now that the kids were grown, it didn't make logical sense, but sometimes habits die hard.

Down the stairs she went, and she headed toward her office. Gloria's office was nothing like Jonathan's. His was dark; hers was light. Everything was white and light oak color. She didn't want the rustic look in her office. There was a gas fireplace on one wall, and Gloria turned it on as soon as she entered. Sitting down in one of two easy chairs that adorned her office sitting area, she reached out and tugged on the chain to turn on the reading lamp that stood on the floor between the two chairs. She had planned on reading some, but now that she was in her office, her thoughts again turned to Jonathan. She wondered how he really felt about dying. It was hard enough for her, yet a year from now, God willing, at least she would still be here, and Jonathan would not. It was he who peered through the black door of death, knowing he must go through it alone, no one else to accompany him. He seemed to be taking it well, but she wondered what really went on inside the recesses of his heart. She wondered if he had any regrets, any dreams left unfulfilled. She wondered if he was completely happy with having had her for a wife. She wondered if she had communicated to him just how much she really loved him. As she was thinking this, she had an idea. She wanted to write Jonathan a letter. One that would tell him all of the things she wanted to.

She quickly arose and went to her desk. Opening the top right drawer, she removed her stationery. After she closed that, she opened the middle drawer and took out a pen. Then she went over toward the window and pulled out a footstool from behind a planter. She kept it there, out of sight and out of the way but accessible when she wanted to put her feet up while sitting in her chair by the fireplace. Paper and pen in one hand and the footstool in the other, she made her way back to her chair. She was surprised to find herself almost a little excited to put these thoughts down on paper for Jonathan to read. She drew her knees up in front of her, placed the stationery on her lap, and began, pausing from time to time to think of what to write next.

Dear Jonathan,

My dearest, precious Jon. How shall I begin? I wish that I didn't have to write this letter. I wish that circumstances were such that I could tell you these things over and over again in the coming years as we live out our lives together. But God has other plans... As I sit here, my mind is filled with so many fond memories. You have brought me nothing but joy in the 38 years since we met. I want to share some of those times with you and tell you how profoundly they and you have affected me and made me a better person.

I remember the first time I saw you. I was down visiting Martin for the weekend, and you and Albert were walking in front of Firestone Library. Martin pointed you two out and said he wanted to introduce me to you. Albert was so funny, as he still is. But you! You were so intelligent, so tall, and strong, and handsome. I said to myself, "I would like to be married to a man like that." I determined then and there, after meeting you that first time, that I would be visiting Martin more often.

I remember our first date. You were pretty shy back then, at least around girls. I remember how it took you three minutes just to say the words to ask me out. Do you remember where we went? That little ice cream parlor on Palmer Square. I even remember what you had—peppermint. I remember because I thought to myself how you must march to a different drummer, ordering something other than chocolate or vanilla. I loved you for always choosing to be different than the rest.

You always seemed to see things and do things differently. I have watched you, admired you, and stood by you as you have always done what was right, regardless of what others would think. Thank you for being an example that way to me and especially to the children. Your life may end young, Jonathan, but those kinds of character traits will live on through our children and then theirs.

Before I knew it, we were standing at the altar there at the New Vernon Presbyterian Church. What a marvelous day it was. All of our family was there, the sun was shining, and I was being married to the greatest man on earth. (Do you remember how young Reverend Wilton was? How young we were, for that matter!) Mom and Dad were so proud. Edgar and Charlotte were, too. I wish they were all still around. They would be so proud of you, Jonathan. They would delight in how their son has grown up to be a leader in the community and how he has helped so many people. They would be proud of the children that you and I have raised. And it all started in that little church 35 years ago. You were stunningly handsome, as you still are, but a younger version!

I remember our wedding night. I was a terribly nervous schoolgirl. I didn't know what to expect. Before that day, I always looked up to you for caring more about others than yourself, but I think deep down, I wondered if it was really entirely authentic. I have never told you this before, Jonathan, but you proved yourself to me that night. I was so nervous, and yet you were so patient with me. That meant so much to me and showed me that you truly were more concerned with me than with your own needs and desires. I can honestly say that I have seen that same selflessness in you ever since then. You always are willing to forgo personal gain for the betterment of those around you. I think this is why God has blessed your life so, Jonathan.

The bulk of our life has been spent building. We built our family. We built our business. You are a good builder. It was so tough many of those years. I am sure many people have thought through the years that life was always easy here at Three Lakes. If they only knew! Thank you for being such a hard worker and a good provider, Jonathan. I know that I have said this many times before, but I want you to know now more than ever how much I appreciated your hard work through those building years, even though they were tough at times.

I remember when we finally sold the business. You and I went out that night and celebrated with a quiet meal and a movie. People would be surprised. You had just become one of the richest men in the country, and there was no party to celebrate yourself. You were satisfied with just me and a quiet night spent together. I appreciated that. I looked eagerly toward the rest of our lives together. I looked forward to sleeping in until 10 a.m. after so many years of early-rising mornings. We have had a few late sleeps these past two years but certainly not enough. I looked forward to traveling more together. I simply looked forward to anything that included time together with you!

I love you, Jonathan. I am going to miss you greatly. You may think I am silly for saying this, but I want you to know that I will never marry again. No one could ever compare to you. You have been the greatest blessing in my life, and I could never replace you. Thank you for committing your life to me. Thank you for loving me. Thank you for making me a better person by always challenging me to grow intellectually, relationally, and spiritually.

I don't know how to end this letter...

I love you, Jonathan. You mean the world to me. We will all be at a loss when you are gone.

Your love,

Gloria

Gloria folded the letter and placed it in its envelope. She now just had to find an appropriate time to give it to Jonathan. By the time she had finished writing the letter, she was beginning to feel a little sleepy again. The warmth of the fire was getting to her. She stuck the letter in the top drawer of her desk under some papers and read from a magazine for about 10 minutes before heading back up to bed.

October 20

I T WAS THE first chilly Friday night of the fall, and both Jennifer and Scott had cleared their busy schedules to spend the evening together, so they decided to build a fire and sit beside it and catch up with each other. Scott had brought in the wood and gotten the paper and kindling together to start a vigorous fire. By the time it was really burning, Jennifer had made some hot chocolate for them to drink. They pulled the ottoman close to the fire and leaned up against it, looking into the orange and red flames. They each sipped slowly from their drinks.

"I love a hot fire on a chilly night," Jennifer declared.

"I love a hot fire on a chilly night cuddled up next to you," Scott answered.

"You are one smooth talker, Scott Rogers." They giggled.

"It's nice to finally relax and unwind. This has been a bear of a week," Scott said.

"Yeah, I feel like I've been running constantly from one meeting to another."

"Thanks for being so patient with me. I appreciate it."

"No problem. I know that you must have to be so patient with me, too. It works both ways." Jennifer was trying to be more patient and forgiving with Scott. There were a couple of points this past week where Scott had made her angry, but she decided to overlook them. It made all of the difference in the world. They weren't big things, things that she needed to talk to him about. They were instead the little petty things that she used to get upset about and that eventually ruined her day and caused her and Scott to blow up into an argument that neither enjoyed.

"You seem to be a lot more patient with me lately," he said.

"I'm trying."

"Well, I think it's great. I try to honor that by not forcing you to have to be patient with me."

Jennifer changed the subject. "I heard you on the phone with Dad tonight. What did he have to say?"

"Nothing really. Just finding out how the week was. I would have gotten you, but I thought you were busy."

"That's okay. I'll talk to him tomorrow. I have to call Mom anyway. I wonder how he's doing?"

"He sounded fine on the phone."

"I saw him this week, and he didn't look very well."

"What do you mean?"

"Sunken face. He was pale. I don't know. He just wasn't the same old Dad I have always known. He wasn't full of the usual energy and vigor."

"The cancer is taking its toll, slowly but surely."

"Yeah."

The conversation stopped for a couple of minutes. They both sipped from their mugs and enjoyed the warmth of the fire.

"Thought of any names for the baby?" Jennifer asked.

"Well, we've pretty much decided on 'Jonathan' for a boy, right?"

"That's what I would like."

"Me too. So that's settled. Girls' names, though... I kind of like the name 'Alexis.' What do you think?"

"You want the truth?"

"Okay, Alexis is out. How about 'Jennifer'?"

"One per household, please."

"No to 'Jennifer.' Then the only other one that strikes me is 'Bertha.'"

"Scott, be serious," she said, jabbing him in the ribs. He quickly raised his mug to keep it from spilling.

"Okay, the only other one I like is 'Leslie'?"

"Oh, brother. Let's pray that it's a boy."

"I like those names!"

"I have veto power."

"We'll keep thinking."

Scott and Jennifer sat there in front of the fire all evening, getting up only for more wood, more hot chocolate, and to finally go to bed. Indeed, as they both thought to themselves, their marriage was improving. Talking was easier. Forgiving was easier. Serving one another was easier. It was timely, as the baby was only months away and getting closer with every day.

October 29

I T WAS 7 O'CLOCK on a cold and windy Sunday night. Fall was beginning its metamorphosis into winter. The winds were blowing stronger with each day, the night temperatures dipping colder and colder as well. There would be snow soon.

Jonathan had started a fire that afternoon, and he was just getting ready to enjoy it, settling into his favorite chair to watch *60 Minutes*. When there wasn't something else more important going on, *60 Minutes* was a Sunday night ritual in the Blake household. Just as the familiar tick, tick, tick of the clock at the beginning of the show began, the phone started to ring. Jonathan started to get up, then decided that Gloria would answer it, probably before he could get to the phone anyway. He picked up his cup of coffee and brought it to his lips for a sip. The warmth felt good to his bones, still chilled from the afternoon outdoors.

A moment later, Gloria called. "Jonathan, the phone is for you."

"Who is it?" he asked.

"It's Will Douglas."

"I'll take it in here," he said loudly enough for her to hear.

Jonathan set his cup down and got up from the chair. As he walked over to the phone, he wondered why Will Douglas, the governor of New Jersey, was calling him, especially on a Sunday night. Will Douglas's and Jonathan Blake's lives had crossed for many years, yet they were never much more than acquaintances. They had both gone to Delbarton, though Will was a year younger than Jonathan. Will's father was a banker, owning six banks in Northern New Jersey, a couple of which were fairly large in terms of deposits. Will had grown up with the same privileges of wealth that Jonathan had. They both went to Princeton, but as far as Jonathan could remember, they hadn't ever done anything together there. They would casually say "hello" as they passed each other crossing campus or would discuss the latest news from Delbarton if they saw each other in the library, but they weren't friends per se.

After college, Will, who had majored in history, went straight into politics. Jonathan thought that Will's father, who was never a politician but was heavily involved with politics, may have nudged, even pushed him in that direction. He had been a representative to the State House, then a senator. He ran for the U.S. Senate and lost, then came back a few years later and won a trip to the Governor's Mansion. He was in his third term, and Jonathan thought he was doing all right for the state. Jonathan was never taken with any brilliance on Will's part but endorsed him nonetheless in his campaigns, primarily because their political philosophy was the same, give or take a few issues.

Jonathan picked up the phone. "Hello?"

"Yes, Jonathan, this is Will Douglas calling. I hope I didn't catch you at a bad time. Do you have a few minutes?"

"Sure, the *60 Minutes* gang can wait. Besides, Andy Rooney isn't on for another 55 minutes. What can I do for you, Will?"

"Well, Jonathan," Will began, "I'll get straight to the point. I was at a dinner party last night and Albert Manning was there. We were sort of off by ourselves later in the evening, and I asked about you. He told me, in confidence, of course, about the cancer. I'm so sorry to hear that, Jonathan. Is there anything at all that I can do?"

"This is very kind of you, Will, but no, I'm afraid there is nothing anyone can do. They offered me some treatment as soon as they found out about the cancer, but they told me that it would be of no benefit. They gave me up to a year to live. So… I'm trying to live these last few months the best I can."

There was a moment of silence. Will really didn't know what to say. He was surprised at the relative calm with which Jonathan seemed to be taking this. "A person must just feel helpless," he said. "I'm sorry, Jonathan. You know, our paths have crossed many times for many years, and though we never did anything socially together, I have always admired you. You have done a tremendous amount of good for this region. You know how us politicos generally despise the press. I can say, though, that your papers were always fair, and I believe they led the way in many trying instances. You are a very good man, Jonathan, and I wanted you to hear that from me personally."

"I appreciate that greatly, Will. You will never know how much. It is difficult for our family, this ordeal, but I try to enjoy family and remember that I have done my best, and I do believe that Gloria and I have been helpful to our community." Jonathan paused, then finished. "I guess that's all a man can do."

"You have done it well, Jonathan. I'll let you get back to your evening. Remember, Jonathan, if there is anything, anything at all that I can do for you, please do not hesitate to call."

"Thank you very much, Will. That is a generous offer, and I'll keep it in mind."

"I'll be seeing you, Jonathan. And you can be assured that I will keep this to myself. Have a good evening."

"You too, Will. Thanks for calling." Jonathan set the phone down and sat there for a moment. It was odd that Albert had told Will about the cancer. Jonathan hadn't really thought much about other people knowing. He had told his family and Albert. He hadn't really thought about telling anyone else. What was he supposed to do, take out an advertisement in the newspaper? Will said he wouldn't tell anyone, and Jonathan believed him, but he decided he wouldn't be terribly upset if Will did tell anyone. It seemed to Jonathan that the rumor mill must be the way most people find out that other people have a terminal disease. This way seemed as good as any other for people to find out.

November 12

THOMAS AND SAM were at the Ivy Club on Prospect Street, eating alone together for their Sunday night meal. Two other friends were going to join them but had to study for an exam in the morning. It had been a while since the two roommates had had a chance to connect. They had no classes together, so they were usually going in opposite directions. They also hadn't become particularly close. Each of them had become friends with others. Still, they would usually chat some before going to bed, and every couple of weeks, they would eat dinner or lunch together. They were just about through with dessert when Sam brought up Jonathan.

"How's your dad doing? I haven't heard you talk about him for a few weeks."

"Oh, he's not doing well. I haven't seen or talked to him for a couple of weeks, but my mom says that he is quickly deteriorating. She says that it is sad. My dad used to be so strong, and now, I guess, it's different."

"That's too bad. When are you going to see him again?"

"I'm going to try to get home a couple of times before we go on our family vacation the first week of December. If not, I'll spend a week with him then. I should be able to get home at least once, though."

"You're going to miss him a lot."

"Yeah. I sure am."

"I can't even imagine my dad dying."

"I still can't imagine my dad dying, and he is. That's the difference between you and me. Your dad is going to live, and mine will be dead in a few months." Thomas wasn't trying to extract pity. He was just stating the obvious, as much as he hated to.

Sam put down his spoon after eating the last bite of his ice cream. "Let's get out of here," he said.

"Sure," responded Thomas, "where do you want to go?"

"Let's go to the library. I have to pick up some books. Then we can go back to the room."

"I actually have to find a magazine article for a class Tuesday, so I may stay there after you head back." They left the Ivy Club and headed for Firestone Library.

Along the way, they met different groups of students, and they would occasionally stop and talk. Thomas was much like any other freshman at Princeton. He had all of the same concerns as the others. Except one. But even that he kept closely to himself. Not many people knew what was going on in his life. Only Sam and his closest friends had any clue as to the gravity of his father's situation. He couldn't imagine what he would tell people or why he needed to for that matter. There was nothing they could do for him. The few who did know did their best to encourage him and keep a listening ear in case he wanted to talk. He never seemed to need to, though. He never seemed to need to break down and cry like others might. Time would tell how this would affect Thomas in the long run.

Finally, he and Sam arrived at the library. Sam went to the books while Thomas headed to the periodicals. "I'll see you later on at the room," Sam said.

"Yeah, I'll see you later."

November 15

WILLIAM AND SAMANTHA lived in Chatham in a small little house they bought together a week before they got married. Samantha had moved in before the wedding, and William joined her there after the honeymoon. It was a quaint, tiny house. Samantha had enough money that her mother and father had given her for estate tax reasons throughout the years, but she and William had decided to start with a house they would have started with had they been in the circumstances of others their age. Besides, they figured it would be an example to those in their church that sometimes less is more. It was just the two of them, and they were busy most of the time anyway and out of the house, so they didn't need anything bigger.

This was one evening they had to themselves. The Wednesday night church meetings had been canceled for the couple of weeks prior to Thanksgiving, so they decided to stay home together. They were both sitting in the living room. William was lying on the couch, wrapped up in a comforter, reading the current issue of *Reader's Digest*; Samantha was sitting in the love seat to the left of the couch, working on a cross-stitch she was wanting to finish before Christmas. Classical music was playing softly in the background. William finished an article and put the magazine down to look at his bride.

"What are you doing over there?" he asked.

"Oh, just trying to make some headway on this cross-stitch."

"What are you thinking about?"

Her eyes watered up a little bit. "Nothing really," she said.

"Thoughts of nothing don't generally make a girl cry," William said as he took the comforter off and made his way over to sit next to Samantha. "What's the matter, Honey?"

Samantha put the cross-stitch down on the table. "I'm just thinking about Dad."

"Yeah, I know what you mean. I've been thinking a lot about him, too. Have you talked to him at all?"

"A little," Samantha said. "I don't really know what to say. We've had the conversations about getting to know each other better, and he and I talk more than ever, but not a whole lot about him dying. He has always been so strong. I've always looked up in awe at him. I feel like talking to him would be admitting that he was weak or something. I don't know. That doesn't make much sense, does it?"

"No, I don't think that you would be saying he is weak, Samantha. I hate to say it because it sounds so cold, and you know I love your dad as much as anyone in your family, but everybody dies, and this is just his time."

"You're right; it does sound cold," Samantha said. "It isn't his 'time.' It can't be. There is too much time left for him to live. He's only, what, 57? He and my mom are just at the point where they can really start doing things together. And what about the grandchildren? We don't even know if he'll live long enough to see Jennifer and Scott's baby."

There really wasn't much else to say, and William wasn't about to sit and argue with Samantha's feelings. Here she was, about to lose the man who gave her her very life, who provided for her in every area, and she was dreading it, as would he if he were in the same situation.

"I know, Samantha. I'm sorry. I should be more sensitive to your feelings. I am just as broken up about this as you are. The whole situation is horrible. I guess I just... I just try to keep going. I can't stop living. I mean, that's the hard thing about anytime someone close dies. They stop, and you can't. It's like riding on a train with someone, and they fall off. You look back as long as you can, but the train keeps moving. Life doesn't afford the luxury of staying in one moment in time."

"I know," Samantha said. "That's what hurts, I guess. Dad will stop being around, and I'll have to live without him influencing me, shaping me, us... For the first time in my life, to use your analogy, I'll be riding that train alone."

"Well, you won't be alone, Samantha. Your mom, me, the rest of the family will all still be here."

"I know, I didn't mean that. I just mean that I'm so used to Dad's imprint on my life, even though I didn't feel particularly close to him, and in a few months, it won't be there."

William pulled Samantha closer and hugged her.

November 23

NORTHERN NEW JERSEY got its first touch of snow in early November, and by Thanksgiving, there was a foot of snow covering the grounds of Three Lakes. Three Lakes, the carefully groomed and manicured estate, was beautiful during each of the seasons, but during winter, with a blanket of snow on the ground wrapping the mansion in its chilly splendor, it was wonderful to see. There wasn't a cloud in the sky, and the bright sun shone down on the Blake home, reflecting off of the glistening snow. Looking up at the house from the drive, it appeared as though thousands of diamonds were strewn out across the yard. The evergreen branches all hung low from the weight of the slumbering snow. The branches of the other trees all stood bare, like ice-covered bones, stark reminders of what happens to much of the earth when fall comes. The lakes on the grounds were frozen over, though not thick enough to skate on yet. Three stories above the ground, the giant chimney serving the main fireplace billowed out large plumes of smoke from the fire Michael had stoked earlier in the day.

Upstairs in the bedroom that they used when they were at Three Lakes, Scott and Jennifer were waking from a nap. The sun was shining brightly through the window and went directly onto both of their faces. Jennifer woke up first and gazed at her sleeping husband. She thought to herself how much Scott had changed since her folks' anniversary and especially since they had found out they were going to have a child. He had become less selfish, she thought.

Scott began to stir as Jennifer kept looking at him. He rolled over to see if Jennifer was still asleep and instead found her staring right at him.

"Hi," she said.

"Hi. What time is it?" Scott asked, blinking his eyes.

Jennifer looked past Scott to the clock on her old desk. It was the same desk she had used to do all of her high school homework. Gloria had purchased it for her when she went into the ninth grade so she would have a bigger desk than the one she had been using, presumably for the loads of homework high school would bring her way.

"It is 2:47. We got in a pretty good nap. What time did we go to sleep, 1?"

"Yeah, about that," Scott said, now rubbing his eyes to wake up. "Did you sleep the whole time?" he asked.

"Oh, I fell asleep pretty quickly. It felt good to get a nap in. The afternoon will be busy, and dinner and dessert will take until 9 or so. So, we won't get home until 9:30 or even later. I'm glad I'll be rested. Carrying this baby around is starting to get tiresome. I get worn out so fast." Jennifer was starting to feel the weight, literally, of carrying a child. She was pretty big for the stage she was at.

"Anything I can do to help you out, make it any easier?" Scott asked.

"You can just continue to be your great, terrific self," Jennifer said as she pulled herself closer to Scott and wrapped her arms around his neck. "You do know that I think you're terrific, don't you?"

"Well, I try," Scott said with a smile on his face.

"I'm serious," Jennifer continued. "I have really seen a change in you, Scott Rogers." She paused. "And I appreciate it very much." She pressed her face closer to his and kissed him squarely on the mouth. After a few minutes of affection, they arose and went downstairs to get on with the day's activities.

The rest of the afternoon was spent with the women in and out of the kitchen preparing the evening meal, and the men in the TV room, watching football, taking a break occasionally to play a game or two of pool. Everyone enjoyed just hanging out at home. Surprisingly, the phone didn't ring all afternoon, which in and of itself was a miracle, so the family enjoyed their time together uninterrupted.

Shortly before it was time to eat, Jonathan had excused himself from the TV room and had gone into his office. He reached his head out and yelled down the hall to where Michael was playing pool. "Michael, may I have a moment with you?" he yelled. Jonathan wanted to have a talk with Michael about the estate plans he was arranging to take care of Gloria and the other children when he was gone.

Michael came quickly down the hall. "Sure, Dad, what's up?"

Jonathan, standing in the door to the office, motioned his hand toward Michael and led him in. "Come in and sit down. I want to talk to you about a few things. It will only take about 10 minutes."

Michael entered and slowly moved across the office, noticing a stack of paper on his dad's desk. He made his way around the desk and sat down in one of the chairs by the window; his father came behind him and sat in the other. "Michael," Jonathan began, "I need to talk to you about the estate."

"Three Lakes?" Michael asked.

"No, sorry, I mean my financial estate. It has taken me a lot of time and effort to arrange things, unless I want the government to get more than the rest of you, so I have been making some arrangements that I need to let you in on."

Jonathan and Gloria had already begun a few years ago to give the maximum amount allowed under federal gift laws to their children. That meant that, already, each child and their spouse, if they were married, had received $20,000 per year. This seems like a lot of money to some, but compared to what they were about to receive, it was merely a pittance. There had been stipulations on the money they received, however. First of all, they were encouraged to give 10 percent of the amount away to charity. Jonathan and Gloria had always held charity in high regard, and they wanted to encourage the children to do the same. Secondly, they allowed the kids to spend 20 percent on themselves for things that they needed, first, and things they wanted, second. Lastly, they were required to save or invest the remaining 70 percent for at least five years. This encouraged them to learn about investing and not spend their money haphazardly.

In spite of their previous openness about money, Michael shifted uneasily in his chair. "Why do I need to be let in on any of that? I really don't think we need to talk about this, Dad."

"Michael, we do because the papers are being drawn up, and there's three times as much as you see on the desk there, leaving you, my son, in control of virtually everything."

Michael went wide-eyed in shock and began to respond. "Dad, I..." Michael never in a thousand years even assumed that he would have a say in Jonathan's estate matters, let alone be left in control of his multi-hundred-million-dollar legacy.

Jonathan sensed Michael's shock and said, "Stop being so nervous and listen." Jonathan thought to himself that he was glad that Michael was a little anxious. This meant that he would take this job with a full understanding of the responsibility involved. "In a nutshell, here's the plan the estate and tax lawyers, in cooperation with the accountants, are drawing up. Your mother will keep $20 million in cash and securities. She will have another $25 million placed in an income-producing trust. Jennifer, Samantha, and Thomas will each receive $10 million dollars in an income-producing trust, with a cap of $200,000 available per year until the year 2005. This way, they will grow into their wealth. After 2005, they will receive all of the income produced if they choose, or they can leave it to add to the principal. In 2010, all funds will be available to them to use at their discretion."

"And me?" Michael asked, not asking out of greed but merely to understand.

"You will have the same amount in trust as the others, with the same conditions. In addition to this, there are some donations I want to make. Ten million dollars will go to Delbarton, $10 million to the American Cancer Society, $5 million to the Market Street Mission in Morristown, and $25 million will go to Princeton for the founding of a school of Conservative Journalistic Studies."

Jonathan chuckled. "They'll love that one. The remainder will be placed into a trust to provide for the descendants of future generations. Estate taxes will take a chunk, though the lawyers have helped me shield a lot of it through these trusts. You will be in charge of investing and distributing the money. When your mother passes on, everything she has, including the trust, will go into the other trust and be passed along. I think that's about it, minus the legalese. Any questions?"

Michael had significant questions and felt as though they needed to be asked and answered now. "Dad, I am honored and all, but I sincerely question the idea of leaving me in charge. I appreciate the thought, but this is way out of my league."

"Why?" Jonathan asked. "You were top of your class at Princeton. You know more about money than I do. And above all, you're family. I want family in charge, not some lawyer."

"But what if I mess it all up?"

"First of all, even if you lost half of it, which you won't, the other kids will get more than they need, and I will have donated significant amounts to the charities I believe in. But here, let me give you the only guidelines I'd like you to follow. First, keep your mother informed and defer to her if she feels strongly about something, even if it's not the smartest financial thing to do. She and I earned the money together, and she has the final say about it if she wants. Even if she were to make a mistake, which she won't, she has earned the right to blow it all if that were the case. I don't think she'll bother much, though. She trusts you as much as I do, and she's already signed off on this plan.

"Next, and hear me, Michael, once I die, there is nothing I can do to change anything. It will all be up to you. The way I look at it is this. I have spent 29 years pouring my life and values into you. You are a fine young man. I love you dearly, and I trust you as much as anyone else on earth. You have great integrity. Do what is right; be fair, equitable, and honest. And, of course, be very charitable. Keep the other children informed. Ask for their input if you like. In fact, that would be a very good idea. If you do these things, everything else will take care of itself."

"I don't know, Dad, it seems like too much responsibility to put into my hands," Michael argued.

"Michael, you may not understand my thinking on this, but do you remember about six years ago when your mother and I went to Florida for the weekend, and we asked Patty and you to take care of Samantha and Thomas?"

"Yes."

"Well, I learned something about you that weekend. You probably won't even remember this. It may seem like a small thing, but I peered into the character of your soul when I got back from that weekend. I gave you $100 for the weekend, in case you needed or wanted some cash for dinner, movies, or whatever. Your mom left you another $100 on the counter, though I didn't know it until we got to Florida. Here's a 23-year-old kid with $200 to burn and parents wealthy enough to not notice it if he did. Do you remember how much you spent that weekend? Do you remember what you did with the money that was left over?"

"Well, I don't remember how much I spent, and I suppose I gave the rest back. What are you getting at?"

"Michael, you spent $28.48. Do you know how I know that? Because on the kitchen counter when we got home was an envelope with $171.52 in it." There was a pause as Jonathan smiled and raised his eyebrows, waiting for Michael to catch on. "Now, do you see what I'm getting at?"

"Ummm, no, Dad, I don't," Michael said, in a slightly exaggerated way, hinting to his dad to make the point.

"Michael, first of all, you had $200 with our full permission to spend it, and you didn't. Second of all, you put 52 cents in change in that envelope. You wouldn't even keep 52 cents that wasn't your money. I really saw then, Michael, what a fine, honest young man you are. You'll handle this estate just fine."

"Well," Michael responded, trying to take another tactic, "what about the other kids? Won't they be upset or jealous or something?"

"I figured you would ask that question. First of all, the two girls won't care. You know that. And Thomas couldn't possibly expect that I would put an 18-year-old in charge. That leaves Scott and William. Scott is a good lawyer, but he doesn't know a lot about portfolio management, and William will be happy because he'll be the richest minister in the whole United States, save for a few TV evangelists.

"Michael, you're the only logical choice. And you're the only one capable. Besides, you can hire some advisors. I'll give you some names, but I want you in charge. There's no way around it, Pal, it's gonna be your baby, and you'll do fine."

At that moment, Jonathan and Michael heard Gloria call from the foyer. "Jonathan and Michael. Come on in for dinner."

Michael was still hesitant but accepting. "Well, okay, but we need to still talk some more about this."

"That's fine, Son, we will. We also have some papers for you to sign. They will be ready in the next week or so."

"All right."

Jonathan was glad that he had been able to begin the process with Michael. He put his arm around his oldest son, pulled him tight, and led him into the foyer toward the dining room.

This Thanksgiving dinner was the same as many the family had enjoyed over the years, but in ways, it was quite different. The thought had settled in with everyone that this would surely be the last Thanksgiving Jonathan would sit at his place at the head of the Blake family table. The meal was standard Thanksgiving fare: turkey, mashed and sweet potatoes, corn, beans, cranberries, bread, and the other staples. Dessert would be fresh pumpkin pie with homemade whipped cream.

Jonathan sat at one end of the table in his usual place, his body looking smaller in his chair than it ever had before. Jonathan had lost 20 pounds and a little bit of his hair as well. His walk was producing more of a shuffled look, too, though it wasn't extremely pronounced yet. It would be soon, though.

As he sat, he took it all in. Scott and Michael talked about a company in White Plains that would be going public on Monday. William and Samantha sat helping each other get cranberries to their plates without spilling the large bowl on themselves. And Patty and Jennifer talked about the vacation to Florida that Jonathan was taking the family on in two weeks, while Thomas scooped from the bowl he was holding and declared to his mother for all to hear, "These potatoes look awesome, Mom!"

Jonathan smiled at his family in action, his elbows on the table, his hands folded together, and his chin resting on his knuckles. Patty noticed him first and asked, "What are you so happy about, Dad?" The rest of the family turned and looked at Jonathan.

Thomas also asked, "Yeah, Dad. What's the big grin for?"

"Oh, I'm just watching all of you, realizing it's Thanksgiving, and… just how thankful I am right now."

"What are you thankful for, Jonathan?" Gloria asked.

"I'll make you all a deal," Jonathan responded, sitting up straight. "I'll tell you what I'm thankful for in each of you if you will, in turn, tell the rest of us what you are thankful for." Jonathan had wanted to focus this Thanksgiving meal around this anyway, and now he had his opening.

William spoke. "I think I can say on behalf of the rest of the family that we are willing to enter into that agreement. Perhaps we can get Scott to go to your office and quickly draw up the pertinent documents."

"Pipe down over there," Scott said from the other side of the table.

Samantha urged her father on. "Okay, Dad, it's a deal. You start."

"All right," he started, "I'll begin with the youngest and work my way up. First of all, I'm thankful for Thomas because of his dashing good looks—he looks like his father, you know. And also that he is doing so well in school, carrying on the Blake Princeton tradition. I had nightmares about a year ago that he would break that tradition and go to some second-class school like Brown, or, heaven forbid, that he really sell out and choose Harvard." The rest of the family laughed.

"For Samantha, I am thankful that she has turned out to be such a bright and cheerful young woman. She reminds me a lot of Gloria at that age. No one brightens a room with joy the way Samantha does, wouldn't you all agree?"

All at the table agreed, William verbally. "I would heartily agree!" he said.

"This brings me to William. William, I am thankful for you because I know you to be a young man of integrity. I know you could have chosen to be anything in the world you would have wanted, yet you chose to go into the ministry to help people and chase down all of us wandering sheep." His eyes looked directly at William's, and he concluded, "I admire you for that."

By now, no one was eating; no dishes were being passed. The whole family sat at rapt attention. Jonathan turned his attention to Patty. "Patricia. I remember when Michael first brought you home to meet us. Three Lakes can be a pretty intimidating place for the first-time visitor, yet you seemed so at ease while you were here. You talked so freely and spoke so intelligently. I was very impressed. Still to this day, you can converse with anyone and make them feel so at ease, like they are the only one in the world, that they are truly important. That is a wonderful gift."

Patty began to get teary. She had always loved Jonathan and Gloria, and Jonathan's words of praise meant so much to her.

The table was still quiet as the dying family patriarch continued to bless his children with praise. He turned to his oldest son. "Michael. You are my firstborn son. There is always a special place in a father's heart for a firstborn son. Michael, I am thankful for the kind of man you are. You are kind and generous. You are trustworthy to the utmost degree. You are committed to what is right, and you do not veer from that path. I am thankful that I can know without a doubt that when I am gone, you will carry on as the leader of this family."

Scott fidgeted a bit in his chair as Jonathan turned to him. "Scott, you have had large shoes to fill since the day I met you. Jennifer is my first child. She is also a daughter. Combine those two facts, and you came into this situation on the short end of the stick. I was fiercely protective of Jennifer, and I thought no man was good enough for her. I have come to realize the strength of your personality, though. You are strong. You are combative at times, but given your dose of humility, combativeness is a strong character trait. You have a brilliant mind for law and seek justice at any cost. You have great discernment of truth and work to make it prevail. You are a man I am proud to have my first daughter married to and my first grandchild born to.

"Jennifer. You are a beautiful woman—and full of spunk. You have a confidence that shines through. It is always clear what you think because you are ever willing to share your opinion. It is always well thought out and cogently presented. But you have a characteristic that isn't found in many people, let alone people with great confidence, and that is that you are a terrific listener. I have seen you time and again listen intently to a person, seeking to understand them and the issues of their mind and heart. I am thankful for that."

Jonathan then turned to his wife of 35 years. He gazed across the table at her. He then took his napkin from his lap and placed it by his plate, pushed his chair from the table, arose, and walked slowly around the table toward Gloria.

When he reached the side of her chair, he knelt beside her. All of the children leaned forward in their chairs to see and listen. "I am above all thankful for my wife, Gloria, whom God gave to be my partner those many years ago. I am thankful that she has steadfastly stood by me all of these years as I pursued my dreams. She has been the strength of our relationship and of our family. I am thankful for her intelligence. I am thankful for her bright wit. I am thankful for her discernment in tough situations. I am thankful for her peace, her inner strength. I am thankful for her servanthood. I am thankful for her patience. Above all, I am thankful for her love. She loves me, even with all of my faults, and that is something I'm not so sure many could do."

Jonathan arose and turned again for his seat. Everyone sensed that he was not quite through yet. He arrived back at his place at the table and lifted his glass of wine toward Gloria. As he looked around the table, each child lifted their glass as well. The passing of the torch would be done tonight. "To my beautiful bride and the mother of this home, Three Lakes, Gloria—to God, I am thankful for you."

The children said in unison, "To Mom!" They clinked their glasses and drank a toast to their mother. Gloria's face was a swell of tears. She dabbed at her eyes with her napkin.

"I do have one more person I am thankful for," Jonathan interrupted. "We must remember that Thanksgiving is not just about being thankful for people, though that is good in its own right and entirely justified. I believe that it is imperative that we always remember and acknowledge our God. For it is He who has bestowed us these lives we have, and it is by His good hand that we are able to enjoy them. I am thankful for God's graciousness in my life, and though it is a painful process, I know that He is in control, and I look forward to seeing Him in His time."

The table turned increasingly quiet as Jonathan spoke. By the time he had finished, everyone had turned and was looking only at their plate. They knew that what Jonathan had said was true. An unplanned moment of silence took place before Jonathan ended it. "Well, my family, this food is going to get cold if we don't eat it soon, so let's get it moving again."

The rest of the dinner was joyful. Jonathan had set the mood for the perfect Thanksgiving. After dinner, Jonathan reminded the others present that part of his deal was that they would have to share one thing that they were thankful for. Each child and Gloria took their turn. They ate dessert, and when they were done, they retired to the various rooms of the house to relax and enjoy the evening.

Just before leaving to go home, Michael went into the living room where Thomas and Samantha were playing a game of chess. William looked on from the side. Patty was in Gloria's office, leafing through some decorating books with Jennifer.

"Who's winning?" Michael asked.

"I am," Samantha beamed. "Another few minutes, and I'll have him in checkmate."

"Not so fast," Thomas grumbled under his breath, never taking his eye from the board.

"Where is everybody?" William asked Michael.

"Oh, Dad and Mom went to bed, Patty and Jennifer are in Mom's office looking through magazines. Jennifer is still looking for decorating ideas for her house. I don't know where Scott is."

William stood up and suggested to Michael that they go find Scott. "Okay," Michael agreed.

They wandered out of the living room and down the hall. "Maybe he's in the library," William said.

"Let's look," Michael replied.

William and Michael turned into the library, and sure enough, there sat Scott, in the complete darkness, his chair turned to look out the window. The moon was bright enough that night to look out the window and see the faint form of the landscape. It was also bright enough that when Michael and William came into the room, they could see Scott's outline against the window.

"Hey, what's going on in here?" Michael asked.

Scott turned and looked back over the top of the chair, then turned himself once again to the window.

"Oh nothing, just looking out the window thinking," Scott said, staring out the window.

"Mind if we join you?" Michael asked.

"No, not at all. Pull up a couple of chairs."

Michael and William walked across the room, grabbed two chairs, sat them on either side of Scott, and sat down, both of them looking out the window as well. "It's a gorgeous night," Michael said. The others agreed.

"Everything all right?" William asked Scott.

"Sure, everything's fine," Scott said.

"You don't sound too convincing," Michael added.

"Oh, it's just normal stress. I've got a lot on my mind right now."

Prying a little deeper, Michael asked, "Such as?"

"Do you guys think much about dying?" Scott asked.

There was a moment of pause. William spoke first. "Well, I have spent a lot of time thinking about dying in the past, both personally and professionally. After all, it's when people realize for the final time that they really are going to die that they are apt to turn to God. Being a pastor, I see that with some regularity. And," William turned to look at Michael to make sure he didn't say anything to hurt him, "what, with Jonathan going to die soon and all, I have thought about it a lot from that perspective."

Michael winced inside. Here they were talking about his father's death, and it hadn't even happened yet. He looked straight ahead out the window. He really didn't want to talk about this much. It was hard enough to have to accept it inwardly, let alone talk about it. He and Patty had hardly talked about it between the two of them.

William wasn't going to let Michael go without answering. "Michael?"

Michael sighed deeply. "Yes, I do think about it. What is that passage from the Bible, 'You are a mist that appears for a little while and then vanishes'? I think about that sometimes. It all seems so futile. Dad really shouldn't be going so soon, but such is the nature of life." They all sat quietly, none of them saying anything for a few minutes.

Michael broke the silence. "His turn now, our turn soon enough. I guess we shouldn't feel too much pity for him. Someday, our kids will be sitting here in these chairs talking about us the same way we are talking about Dad." Again, quiet.

Minutes later, "Why do you ask all this, Scott? What are you thinking about?" Michael asked.

"Well, Jennifer hasn't been taking this too well. I don't suppose any of us are, especially you kids. It is a lot of pressure. She just lies in bed sometimes wondering if it's really true. Now that Jonathan is deteriorating physically, she knows that it's going to happen. I don't know how to treat her. I don't know what to say. I certainly don't have any answers to her questions. I believe in God, I believe in Christ, I believe that there is a heaven, a better place than this world where we go when we die. I just don't understand the process. I have no explanation as to why this all happens and why some really rotten people who never do anything for anybody live to be 105, and why great people like Jonathan die when they're 60. Then there is the question of babies who die, and I don't even want to get into that one. I just pray that our baby is healthy, so we don't have to go through that. I don't know how some parents make it."

There was again a hush over the room. It was as if each was placing thoughts out into the air to be contemplated quietly then built upon by the next person's thoughts. They were finding that, in all reality, they were all thinking the same things. They all had the same questions.

After a few moments, William got up from his seat and turned on a table lamp. He went over to the bookshelf where the Bibles were kept and brought one back to his seat. "There is a passage that deals with the same thing you are, or we are. This is a question men and women have wrestled with for thousands of years."

He turned to the book of Ecclesiastes and began to read chapter eight, verses 14 and 15. "There is something else meaningless that occurs on earth: righteous men who get what the wicked deserve and wicked men who get what the righteous deserve. This too is meaningless. So I commend the enjoyment of life, because nothing is better for a man under the sun than to eat and drink and be glad. Then joy will accompany him in his work all the days of life God has given him under the sun."

William shut the Bible and continued. "The New Testament says much the same thing. It says that God causes the sun to rise on the evil and the good, and He sends rain on the righteous and the unrighteous. I guess the reality is that bad things happen to us all, and sometimes it happens to good people before it happens to bad people. Why? I don't know that. That is the mystery of life."

They all sat in the dark, quiet room for a few moments, pondering what William had said. Shortly, Michael spoke. "I guess that's why I try not to think about death much. I know intellectually that it's going to happen, but emotionally, I don't want to deal with it. You know the old saying, 'The unexamined life isn't worth living'? Well, as far as I'm concerned, the overexamined life isn't worth living either. There is too much life here to live, to enjoy."

"But what do you do when it hits you right in the face? When it steps right up and says, 'Sorry, but you have to deal with me right now'?" Scott asked Michael.

"Then I guess you deal with it like we're dealing with this situation now. But it can't paralyze us," Michael responded. "I mean, I wake up in the middle of the night, and I get angry and sad and all of that. Don't get me wrong. It's just that I still have to go to work and live with Patty and all of the other things that go on."

"I guess you're right," Scott said.

"Look, we are going to be dealing with this for the rest of our lives. We are all going to die. Probably Mom will be next, but who knows, it might be you, Scott, or me, or William. Over the next 50 years, we are going to go through this over and over. In the meantime, there is a lot of life and joy to live. There will be lots of good times to keep us going through the hard times."

Just then, Patty walked through the door. "Oh, here you are," she said to Michael. "I'm ready to go home if you are."

Michael got up and said, "Sure, let's go." He turned to William and Scott as he walked away and said, "Let's talk some more about this later if you want, but I have to get some sleep tonight."

William and Scott both rose as well. They both said that they had to get their wives and get home, too. Scott said to Michael as he left, "Thanks, Michael."

Michael stopped at the door and turned to Scott. "No problem. Besides, William's the one who had all the wisdom tonight."

Scott turned to William, "Yeah, thanks to you, too. I appreciate it. Thanks for hunting me down tonight. I needed to talk, not sit here all by myself."

"No problem," William said as they both headed for the library door.

December 4

"WELL, ARE YOU excited about the trip?" Patty asked Michael. Tomorrow they were leaving on the family vacation that Jonathan had been planning all year. Patty was packing clothes into her suitcase, while Michael lay on the floor doing sit-ups.

"Yeah," he said in between the up and down movement. "I think it will be really fun. I can't wait to get out of this weather. I could use some sun."

"Me too," said Patty as she folded her swimming suit and placed it on the right side of her quickly filling suitcase.

Michael got up and lay on the bed. "One hundred sit-ups a day keeps the flab away—at least I hope so."

"You don't have an extra ounce on you. Besides, flab hardly runs in your family." Patty moved the suitcase, still open, onto the floor. "I'll put the final stuff in tomorrow." She lay down on the bed next to Michael. Both lay on their backs facing the ceiling.

"Are you still worried about managing the trusts your dad set up?" she asked.

"No, I suppose not. I've been meeting with those advisors Dad has. And I guess my philosophy of investing is such that I don't think I could blow it if I tried."

"What philosophy is that?"

"I'll leave most of it exactly where Dad has it right now. Then as I need to, I'll diversify even more. You know, for as much money as he has tied up in the markets, he really doesn't own a broad enough portfolio. I'll keep it in safe investments: big companies with proven track records. I'll keep it safe until the other kids get control over theirs. If they want to risk it, then they can."

"That's it?"

"Yes. That's it. I may put a little in some riskier, small-cap stocks. Technology is surely a place where one could venture with some risk capital. Not much, though. I feel like the name of the game for me is 'preservation of funds.'"

"Sounds smart to me. Look, your dad would never have chosen you unless he had the utmost confidence in you, right?"

"You're right. I'm not worried. It will be all right. I still would prefer to have Dad around for the next 30 years. Fact is, I would give up every penny, even live in a trailer in Iowa, if I could guarantee that he would live until he's 90."

"You and he sure have a special relationship."

"Yeah, we sure do."

"What's your favorite memory of you and him growing up?" Patty asked.

"Boy, that would be hard. Give me a minute." They lay there, Michael thinking of all the fun things he and Jonathan had done together. Finally, Patty feigned impatience.

"C'mon, you have to have one."

"Here's one that keeps coming back to me." Michael laughed as he thought of it. "I don't know if I've ever told you about this or not. I was about... oh, about 10, I guess. I got it in my mind that I wanted to make a car out of plywood. It was going to be a kind of go-cart without the motor."

"How was it going to run?" Patty interrupted, slightly smirking at Michael's crazy idea.

"It ran on gravity."

"Gravity?"

"Yes, Patty, down a hill?"

"Oh, gravity, yes."

"Would you like me to finish the story?"

"By all means, I would love to hear the story to its completion."

"So, I con Dad into going into town to buy a couple of sheets of plywood. We bring it home and start planning and cutting. Then we get the hand-turned drill out. I bet it took us two days to get that thing done. Then we had to attach wheels to it. We dismantled an old red wagon for its wheels. Then we put those on. I can't even remember how. We rigged up the steering with two ropes attached to the front wheels. Then we drove it."

"We?"

"I drove it."

"Where?"

"Right down our driveway." Michael laughed again.

"What's so funny?"

"Well, Dad just got me going without thinking about how I would stop. About halfway down, I realized that brakes didn't come standard in this model, so I ended up having to run it straight into the lake down by the gate. Dad was so embarrassed and scared that he never let me ride it again. That's all I got, one ride."

"That's the fondest memory you have of your youth?"

"Okay, so it's not the fondest. But it is one of the funniest. Besides, it is a fond memory. I think of all the time Dad took helping me build that contraption. That took a lot of patience, I'm sure."

Michael was still smiling at the ceiling when Patty broke in with, "You'll have to keep thinking of fond memories, and I'll ask you again in a couple of days." Michael grabbed his pillow and playfully hit Patty between the eyes.

"Let's go to bed so we're rested up for this big trip tomorrow. And I'll think of a more 'fond' fond memory for you."

"It sounds like a deal."

They each changed into their pajamas, and within 30 minutes, they were asleep, dreaming of the sun to come.

December 5

J ONATHAN HAD RENTED an airport limousine to pick up the entire family at 5 o'clock at Three Lakes for their family vacation. He knew that this would certainly be their last, and so he wanted to do it extravagantly. This trip would be something special that the entire family would remember for the rest of their lives.

As the limo pulled into Newark International, Michael noticed that they were going a direction they hadn't gone before. "Hey Dad, aren't we flying Northwest? We're missing the terminal."

"No," Jonathan responded. We're taking a different airline this time."

"Which one?" Jennifer asked.

"You'll see," Jonathan said with a twinkle in his eye.

A few more minutes, and the limousine passed through the security gates and pulled up to a private hangar. The two massive doors were pulled wide open to reveal a sleek Citation X sitting inside atop the slick, polished hangar floor. The car pulled into the hangar next to the plane and came to a stop. Everyone got out of the car wide-eyed.

"We're going in this?" Thomas asked.

Jonathan explained. "Well, gang, I wanted to make this trip memorable. You know that I'm on the board of World Alliance Publishing, right? And their CEO, Bill Kraft, has been a friend from many moons ago, so WAP owed me one, and so did Bill, and they have generously provided their plane to us for the trip to Captiva."

At this point, the pilot came around to their side of the aircraft and welcomed them to his plane. "Glad you all made it. It's pretty cold out here, so why don't you board, and I think we can be out of here in about 20 minutes."

"Sounds like a plan," Jonathan said, and the family boarded for their trip to Southwest Regional Airport in Fort Myers, Fla. The flight took about three hours, but the fun of being in such a luxurious airplane kept everyone excited and talking about the plane, yes, but also about the trip and what they would do when they arrived.

When they did arrive at the airport, it was about 8:20 p.m. Eastern Standard Time. They picked up their luggage from the luggage compartment, and by the side of the hangar were two custom vans. The two vans would take them on the 45-minute trip to their house on Captiva. The weather was a warm 65 degrees, and a slight breeze blew from the north.

"Okay, Dad, so how are we doing this?" Michael asked.

"Well, let's see. How about you and Patty, Gloria and me in one van, and Scott and Jennifer, Samantha and William in the other? Oh, and Thomas. Thomas, take your pick: Which van do you want to go in?"

"I'll go with the young, hip crowd," Thomas said.

The family piled into the vans and began their way. Soon they were crossing the causeway onto Sanibel Island, the island just south of Captiva. There is no direct car access to Captiva, so those staying there must drive across Sanibel. The van drivers both pointed out to their passengers the wildlife preserve on Sanibel, "Ding Darling," as it is called, after a Pulitzer Prize-winning conservationist who lived on the island. Sanibel Island is a 12-mile-long island covered with mangrove trees, shallow bays, and white sandy beaches. Some have said that there are two kinds of people on Sanibel: the professional environmentalists and the amateur ones. That is probably why it is still such a relatively unspoiled place to visit.

Captiva is much the same, only smaller and a little more exclusive. Captiva is the home for the rich and not particularly famous, save a few has-been actors and actresses. Multi-million-dollar estates line the beaches, and there is a large resort at the north end.

When the vans arrived at the estate the Blakes were renting, the drivers both opened the doors and helped everyone out. The men gathered around the back of the vans and began carrying the suitcases up to the front door. Jonathan paid both of the drivers and tipped them well. "Thanks for the rides, guys," Jonathan said as they climbed back into their vans. "We'll see you when you come to pick us up."

"Have a good one," one of the drivers said as he shut his door.

The Blakes got all settled into their rooms and walked around the estate, making plans for the week. When they were done, they relaxed in the living room and played cards before bed.

"Who wants to go grocery shopping with me tomorrow morning?" Gloria asked. Patty and Samantha volunteered. Scott won the card games.

December 7

CAPTIVA ISLAND, JUST north of Sanibel Island in the Gulf of Mexico off the coast of Fort Myers, is a tiny reclusive island with a small population and beautiful beaches. December is still before the big rush of snowbirds and tourists hits, so the Blakes didn't have to battle the crowds much but could enjoy themselves amid the warmth of the weather that gave them some respite, be it temporarily, from the bitter cold of the harsh Northeast winter. The house they were staying in was 6,000 square feet, with five bedrooms, five baths, with a rec room, swimming pool, and tennis court. Along with the rental came the use of the owner's minivan for getting around the island. The Blakes would have to cram in, but they wouldn't be going a whole lot of places, mainly just the occasional dinner out.

It was 10 a.m., and most of the family was out by the pool or on the beach, starting early on their quest to get a tan to show off back home. Michael and Patty were out playing tennis, though. Jonathan went outside to the pool to find Thomas.

When he got to the veranda by the pool, he noticed that Thomas wasn't there.

"Where's Thomas?" he asked.

Gloria answered, "I don't know. I thought he was going to join us, but he never got down here. We girls are just reading and talking about what we should do for dinner tonight. How about the Bubble Room? It would be fun." The Bubble Room is a wildly popular restaurant on Captiva known for its great food and unusual decor, which could be described as "wonderfully tacky," as well as the waitstaff, who introduce themselves as "Bubble Scouts." It is a must for those visiting Captiva to eat at least one meal there.

"Sure, the Bubble Room is fine for me, but we'll have to go early to beat the crowd. Just let me know what you decide. I'm going to find Thomas." Jonathan turned and began to make his way slowly back into the house to see if he could find Thomas.

Young Thomas was the one child that Jonathan worried most about. The other kids seemed to be grounded, out of college and all, beginning families and holding down jobs. Jonathan had a lot of faith in Thomas and knew that Gloria would look after him, as would Michael and the other kids, but he also knew that this was a tough world, one with many changing values and ethics. Jonathan hoped and prayed that Thomas wouldn't drift from the proper direction. This is one reason he wanted to spend some considerable time with Thomas here in Captiva, so he could make sure that Thomas was told how much he was loved by his father, and so there could be some final fatherly advice and encouragement. Jonathan knew that it would be a tough row to hoe for all of the kids but thought it would be especially difficult for young Thomas, still in the impressionable stage of life.

"Thomas?" he called as he entered the back of the house, into the kitchen. "Thomas!" He yelled again. From upstairs, he could faintly hear the return yell of his youngest boy. Slowly, he moved around the island in the kitchen and through the living room to go to the foot of the stairs where he could be heard and hear better. "Thomas, what are you doing?"

"I'm just reading a bit, Dad. I have to keep up on my assignments for school, you know."

"Can you take a break for a while? I'd like to talk to you." Jonathan asked.

Thomas put down his book and rolled off his bed, slowing only long enough to slip on his sandals. He then came out of his door, shutting it behind him after turning out the light.

"Sure, Dad. What do you want to know?" Thomas said, ever the 19-year-old.

"Oh," Jonathan replied, "are you in the wisdom-dispensing mode? What can you tell me that you have learned at Princeton that I didn't learn there?"

"Well, since you graduated, we discovered something called electricity," Thomas joked.

"Yes. And the-what-do-you-call-it? The automobile. Yes." Jonathan and Thomas laughed together.

"Let's go for a walk on the beach, Thomas," Jonathan suggested.

"All right," Thomas said, "but let me get my hat first. I'll meet you out by the pool."

Thomas wheeled and ran back up the stairs to get his hat to shade the south Florida sun. Jonathan walked back out to the poolside. There he arrived just as Gloria was hanging up the phone. "Jonathan, we decided to go the Bubble Room about 5:30. Is that okay?"

"Sure," Jonathan said, "we'll have to leave around 5:20 then. Thomas and I are going for a walk on the beach. We'll be gone a half-hour or so, I guess. Maybe we'll find some shells for you."

Thomas just then came out of the back door and walked to the pool. "Ready to go, Dad," Thomas said.

"Okay, I am too."

Jonathan and Thomas began down the walkway that would take them to the beach. Jonathan walked slower and slower as the disease that would one day claim his life continued to smother his mobility. Thomas and the rest of the family recognized and accepted this, knowing that it was part of the process and would only get worse. In a few minutes, they had made the 100-foot walk down the wooden ramp that led from the back yard of the house to the beach.

Sanibel and Captiva Islands are world renowned for their white sandy beaches, littered with literally millions of shells. The beaches are made for walking on, with the many who do routinely performing the "Sanibel Stoop," bending over to collect yet another shell. Jonathan and Thomas turned left, south, on the beach, back toward the small bridge from Sanibel to Captiva. Thomas walked slowly, knowing that walking was becoming difficult for his dad, and that he would need to go cautiously, especially in the sand.

As father and son walked on the beach, 23 dolphins swam in the water, about 25 feet off the shore. The weather was warm, about 75 degrees. The wind blew slightly, brushing Jonathan's hair back and forth as it shifted directions. Jonathan should have brought a hat as Thomas had to shade himself. Instead, he squinted. As they walked, they noticed the houses along the beach. At one time, they would have been right on the waterfront, but with the beach renovation the island has been doing lately, they now sat back a good hundred feet. They were mainly large homes, though some smaller homes dotted the island, a throwback to a time when the rich didn't necessarily build extravagant, large homes. About a quarter of a mile down the beach, there were two wooden chairs sitting back from the beach a bit just in front of a house.

"Let's sit here for a while. I need a rest," Jonathan said, pointing to the chairs and obviously out of breath.

"Are you sure? Won't the owners get mad?" Thomas asked.

"No. This is Cal Peter's house. He's a doctor I know from Hackensack. He won't mind, especially since they aren't here." Jonathan smiled. They both sat down in the chairs. They sat and watched the small waves lap at the sand and shells.

"Dad?" Thomas said after a few minutes.

"Yes, Son."

"Can I ask you a question?"

"Sure," Jonathan said.

"Are you scared?"

"About what exactly?"

"About dying."

"You know, at first I was really scared, at least after I got over being numb. Now, I get scared sometimes. Fear of the unknown more than anything. But all in all, I really believe that God will be there to meet me on the other side. While it's all by faith, from everything I've ever studied, there are great reasons to believe that. I take a lot of comfort in my faith in God, Thomas."

"What do you feel, then?"

"The one thing I feel more than anything is regret. I regret that I won't be able to see you or the other kids anymore. I'm not the most perfect man in the world, but I often wonder why lesser men, criminals, others, why they get to live, enjoy life, see their grandkids, go on vacation, enjoy their wife… regret. That's what I feel most, Thomas." Jonathan sat for a moment, staring into the crashing waves, then asked, "What do you feel about all of this?"

"I feel mad," Thomas said, digging a stick into the sand below him.

"Mad at me?"

"No, just mad."

"Mad at God?"

"No. Oh, I suppose He could stop it if he wanted, but I know deep down that everybody dies, and it isn't His fault. I'm just mad at nothing. Mad at the situation. I sometimes think, 'Why does my dad have to die?'"

"I'm sorry, Son."

"It isn't your fault, Dad. It's just Life 101, as Albert would say. I just don't like it very much, that's all. I've thought and thought about it, and there's just no sense to it at all. It makes me mad. Mad that I can't do anything."

Jonathan and Thomas sat in those weathered chairs for a good hour. They talked more about how they were feeling, what the next few months might bring, Jonathan's hopes for Thomas in regard to school and his life, and, oddly enough, what they thought heaven might be like. It would be the final time that Jonathan and Thomas really had a chance to talk, just the two of them alone. They finished their business as best as they could, and then they walked south a little bit more before returning back to the house. As they approached the house on the walk from the beach, Jonathan reached out and hugged Thomas with one arm around his neck. "Thanks for being such a fine young man, Thomas. It makes me feel good to know that I don't have to worry for your mother about you after I'm gone. I appreciate that, you know?"

"I know, Dad. Thanks."

They came to the pool, where most of the kids and Gloria were still sunbathing. "How was the walk?" Gloria asked.

"Fantastic," Jonathan said. "We're going to change into our swimming suits and come lie by the pool with you."

The Blake family spent the rest of their time on Captiva lounging around the pool, taking walks on the beach, going out for dinner, playing games, and renting movies to watch in the evenings. This would be the last vacation of Jonathan Blake's life. It wasn't too eventful, but it was fulfilling, and that was just what he had desired. There was plenty of time with his family, plenty of chances to connect with each of the kids. His mobility was waning, and the pain increasing day by day, so when it came time for them to leave, he knew he was going home to begin the final leg of his journey to death's dark door. Physically, it would only get worse from here on out.

WINTER

December 24

"WELL! LET'S GET some help cleaning up the table for your mother, and then we can go open some presents." Jonathan and the family were finishing their delectable Christmas Eve dinner of ham and other goodies. It was 8 o'clock. Everyone had gathered at Three Lakes around 4 that afternoon to be with one another and help put the finishing touches on their dinner for the evening, as well as to finish wrapping the rest of their presents. As might be expected, the boys were the worst in the wrapping detail. Thomas was the most flagrant offender, having not wrapped one present yet. Yes, they were purchased, but they were still in his room, put off being wrapped until the last minute. Thomas knew that he could get away with wrapping just one present before tonight's opening of presents.

The Blake tradition was set in stone. Every Christmas Eve, the family would gather together for a ham dinner, and then they would retire to the living room to sit around the tree and enjoy coffee and dessert while Jonathan read the Christmas story from the Bible. While Jonathan and his family enjoyed enormous wealth, and the presents sometimes reflected that wealth, Jonathan never wanted Christmas to be remembered or looked forward to for the presents or the material aspect of the holiday that so often embodies Christmas in today's society. Jonathan wanted his children to remember Christmas the way it should be remembered: a time where family enjoys and celebrates one another and where they together celebrate the good news that God sent His Son into the world. No matter what evil prevailed in their world, no matter what monumental challenges faced them day by day, there was hope because of Christmas. He wanted his children to get that message, and he and Gloria had always accomplished that task in the lives of their children. One way they did that was to set aside time to read the Christmas story.

After the reading of the Christmas story, each member of the family would be allowed to open one present each. The remainder of the presents would be saved until the next morning. Each person could pick any present to open, but if they picked the best one, someone, mostly Jonathan or Gloria, would usually step in and encourage them to open another instead, saving the better present for the following morning. After opening all of the presents, the family would just sit by the fire together and talk. Sometimes they would talk about the past, sometimes the talk turned to the future, but they always made the Christmas Eve "fireside chat," as the family called it, one that was meaningful and enriching.

After their time talking, they would each go to their rooms for a restless time of sleep, anticipating the excitement of the next morning. As little ones, the Blake children would usually go upstairs and then gather in Michael's room to contemplate what each thought of their Christmas Eve gifts and to wonder aloud with each other about what tomorrow morning might bring for each.

Eventually, they would tire and make their way to their individual rooms, though on more than one occasion, the Blake children ended up all falling asleep in Michael's room. When morning would come, whoever woke up first would then excitedly wake up the others. Since the children had grown up, this tradition of waking the others had given way to the more civilized tradition of allowing everyone to wake up on their own. Jonathan and Gloria were especially appreciative of this.

As the Blake family went about cleaning up from the meal they had just eaten together, Gloria fast finishing up the final preparations for dessert, it was beginning to snow. There had been snow on the ground for some time now. Occasionally, the weather would warm and melt it off of the roadways, but a little snow stayed on the ground, creating a thin white blanket that embraced the estate.

Tonight, it was snowing quite hard. The snow was piling up quickly on the ground and the roads. Pine trees were gathering so much snow on their branches that they were beginning to sag under the weight. Inside the Blake home, the cold of the snow gave way to the warmth of the family. The large windows of the home gave precious views of the snow-covered terrain of Three Lakes. A fire was being started by Michael in the living room that would soon be raging away.

Soon the whole family had gathered in the spacious living room. The room had hardwood floors, which would have been cold but that most of the floor was covered with large rugs. Gloria had elegantly decorated the room and had done quite well in creating a smaller sitting space in the room for gatherings of 6 to 10 people. She had arranged couches, love seats, and chairs in a semi-circle around the large fireplace. In the middle was a huge coffee table, decked at Christmas time with a large, brown wicker team of reindeer pulling a sleigh.

Everyone was taking their seats. Thomas was the last to arrive, having gone up to his room to get his one present wrapped. Jonathan and Gloria were on the couch, Samantha and William in the love seat, and Michael in the chair with Patty next to him, seated on the floor. Jennifer and Scott sat in individual chairs across the coffee table from Jonathan and Gloria. Thomas had traditionally been the "runner," the one who, at Gloria's direction, brought the gifts to each person. Each had a hot drink in their hand, and a few were beginning to dig into the cookies and slices of pie and cake that Gloria had placed on the coffee table around the reindeer. The chandelier was turned to just above low, and the fire was picking up, crackling as each bit of sap came in contact with the flames. The room was beginning to warm. Everyone was settling in.

"Well, another Christmas," Samantha said, "they seem to go so fast."

"Yeah, it doesn't seem like too long ago that we were all just kids," Michael added.

"Ha." Jennifer laughed.

"What's so funny?" Samantha asked.

"Oh, I was just thinking. Do you remember those one-piece pajamas that Mom found for us? The kind that 2-year-olds wear, but Mom found in sizes for us when we were all over 10? The kind that have feet in them and zip up the front?"

Everyone laughed aloud as Gloria defended her actions. "Now those were cute pajamas, and at least I never forced you to wear them out in public or put them on our Christmas card. Say all you want about those pajamas, but I thought they were great."

Jonathan agreed. "I thought they were great, too!"

"You're just saying that to get in Mom's good graces," Michael said. "You know those things were hideous. They were all sort of these offbeat colors if I remember right."

"Now, that's just not true," Jonathan chided Michael. "Those pajamas were very practical. Besides, I liked Thomas's burnt-orange pair."

"They were practical all right," Thomas said, "a practical joke. You know, people might have been concerned about your parenting had they known that you forced your children to dress like that. This very well might be something we could hold over your heads."

Samantha chimed in. "Hey, we could go on a talk show. Children who were made to dress like clowns—on the next Oprah." Everyone laughed.

Michael turned the conversation. "Well, on a more serious note. Merry Christmas, everyone."

"Merry Christmas," they all said.

"Can you make a toast with coffee?" Scott asked Jonathan.

"Sure, what do you want to toast?" Jonathan replied.

Scott stood up and held his coffee in the air. "I would like to make a toast to the Blake family. Thank you so much for allowing me to be a part of it. To Jonathan and Gloria, a toast to you for being so welcoming and such great parents. To the kids of the family, I look forward to the many days we have to look forward to together." He turned and looked at Jennifer. "And to my most beautiful bride—you are the best thing that ever happened to me. Thank you for being such a terrific life partner. And finally, a toast to the last Christmas before Jennifer and I become parents. Next Christmas, there will be another pair of feet padding around this place."

Everyone clinked their mugs together. Mostly they were all happy about how well Jennifer and Scott were getting along. The past few months had been very good to Jennifer and Scott. Their commitment to one another to renew their marriage at Jonathan and Gloria's wedding anniversary was lasting. Now with the baby on the way and due in less than a few months, they were getting along better than ever. The pregnancy was drawing them together, and Scott was spending less time at the office, devoting quite a bit more attention to Jennifer, his behavior toward her at times even bordering on doting. Jennifer herself was becoming less biting in her attitude toward Scott, and she was giving him much more room for mistakes. This made it easier on the whole family, as there were fewer times of awkwardness at family gatherings. They were all happy for Scott and Jennifer.

"Any other toasts?" Gloria asked.

"Here's to me getting really awesome presents this year!" Thomas said to laughter.

"Don't worry," Jonathan said, "I got you the biggest and best bag of coal I could find."

Gloria gave some perspective. "Now you boys, that's not what Christmas is all about. Scott knows what he's doing with his toast." She turned and smiled at her son-in-law. He graciously smiled back.

"Well, it's time to read the Christmas story then," Jonathan said. He picked up the Bible that he had brought in earlier from his office and turned to the Gospel of Luke to read the Christmas story. After turning there, he looked around the room to be sure that all were ready, and he began:

In those days Caesar Augustus issued a decree that a census should be taken of the entire Roman world. (This was the first census that took place while Quirinius was governor of Syria.) And everyone went to his own town to register. So Joseph also went up from the town of Nazareth in Galilee to Judea, to Bethlehem the town of David, because he belonged to the house and line of David. He went there to register with Mary, who was pledged to be married to him and was expecting a child. While they were there, the time came for the baby to be born, and she gave birth to her firstborn, a son. She wrapped him in cloths and placed him in a manger, because there was no room for them in the inn. And there were shepherds living out in the fields nearby, keeping watch over their flocks at night. An angel of the Lord appeared to them, and the glory of the Lord shone around them, and they were terrified. But the angel said to them, "Do not be afraid. I bring you good news of great joy that will be for all the people. Today in the town of David a Savior has been born to you; he is Christ the Lord. This will be a sign to you: You will find a baby wrapped in cloths and lying in a manger." Suddenly a great company of the heavenly host appeared with the angel, praising God and saying, "Glory to God in the highest, and on earth peace to men on whom his favor rests." When the angels had left them and gone into heaven, the shepherds said to one another, "Let's go to Bethlehem and see this thing that has happened, which the Lord has told us about." So they hurried off and found Mary and Joseph, and the baby, who was lying in the manger. When they had seen him, they spread the word concerning what had been told them about this child, and all who heard it were amazed at what the shepherds said to them. But Mary treasured up all these things and pondered them in her heart. The shepherds returned, glorifying and praising God for all the things they had heard and seen, which were just as they had been told.

After Jonathan had finished the passage, Jennifer said, "You know, we've been reading that passage for years, and it seems like every year it touches me differently. There were times when I was a kid it seemed almost silly to me, what with just wanting to get to the presents and all, and I wondered how a story from 2,000 years ago could possibly have any relevance to me today in New Jersey. But most of the time, and especially tonight, it has really drawn me back to the simple realities of this life. The simple truths that govern us. I forget those too often…" Her voice drifted off. Everyone nodded to themselves knowingly. No one said anything for a few moments. Mostly, everyone looked at their feet. Jonathan realized again that this would be the last time for him to read the gospel story on Christmas Eve. The thought shocked him. It made his heart race, and he wanted to freeze this moment in time. He was tempted to pick up the Bible and read it all over again. He wanted it all to stay here forever. This is what his life had been all about, and he knew it was slipping away.

It was obvious others were thinking about things as well. After a few moments, Gloria realized what was taking place, so she quickly moved the family on to the next stage of the evening. Normally, the idea had been to get the children thinking about the significance of the day; this time, however, she knew that the message had gotten across quickly and powerfully, but that there needed to be a change in the atmosphere, or this evening would end up sad and not the joyous occasion that it was supposed to be and had been so many times over the years.

The family took about an hour to allow everyone to open their one present. They would open a present, then pass it around, talk about it, get some more dessert and coffee, then start with the next person. There were the usual gifts brothers and sisters give to one another. Small, practical, and convenient gifts. The shining moment of the night, though, came after all the gifts had been given and everyone had thought they were through for the night. Gloria got up from the sofa.

"Hold on for one moment, everyone; there is one more gift to give," she said as she walked over to a long buffet standing against the wall. She reached into the third drawer from the top left and pulled out a package. Everyone wondered what the gift was and who it was for. Everyone had already opened one gift, so it was anybody's guess as to who would be the recipient of this one.

"This is a very special gift for a very special person," Gloria said as she came back around the end of the couch and sat down. "This gift is for Jonathan from all of us."

By now, everyone was confused that it was from all of them together because Gloria was the only one who knew what the gift was. Jonathan beamed a giant smile. Gloria handed the package to Jonathan. He smiled and turned to the rest of the family.

"This is special," he said to all. They all smiled in return, pretending to know what they had given him.

Thomas soon blew their cover. "Yeah, and we can't wait to find out what it is."

Jonathan slowly unwrapped the paper to reveal a box. It was actually quite heavy for the size of it. The box was about 15 inches tall, 12 inches wide and five inches deep. Jonathan really had no idea what was in the box. Neither did anyone else except Gloria. Jonathan opened the box and pulled out a large album. He noticed right away that it had about 50 pages and was professionally done. On the cover, it read prominently "Jonathan Blake."

Jonathan opened to the first page. There he saw, facing him, a picture of himself at the age of six months.

"What is it?" Patty asked.

"This, it looks like, is a comprehensive album of my life," Jonathan said, as he slowly paged through the album. He flipped to the last page. There was an 8.5x11 of last year's family portrait. In between were pictures of Jonathan and his parents, Jonathan and Gloria's wedding picture, pictures of all of the children, special events in their lives, and reproductions of awards and certificates Jonathan had earned. This was a very thorough examination of Jonathan Blake's life—and he loved it.

"This is really terrific, everyone," he said.

The others all left their seats and gathered as they could around Jonathan to see the pages as he went through them one by one. There was his birth certificate, pictures of him as a boy, his parents, Edgar and Charlotte, Albert and Jonathan at Delbarton and Princeton, Jonathan and Gloria when they were younger, and, of course, pictures of Jonathan and Gloria with the kids.

"Thank you all so much," Jonathan said. Then he turned to Gloria. "Thank you, Gloria. I will cherish this." As he said the words, he realized that he wouldn't cherish it for very long. Even now, Jonathan's body was continuing to deteriorate at an even more rapid pace. The cancer was ravaging his body. The pain relievers that Dr. Kidman prescribed him helped a little, but there was still incredible pain most of the time. Just then, he felt a sharp pain under his ribcage.

"Well, let's take a break from this for a few minutes. We've all opened the presents that we are going to tonight. Let's get some more coffee or whatever, and then we'll get back together for the 1995 Fireside Chat."

The group broke up, and Gloria began collecting dirty dishes to take into the kitchen to get a head start on the dishwashing, with Samantha and William helping her. Patty announced that she was going to go get into the new pajamas she had just opened as her gift.

"That's a great idea," Jennifer said. "I think I'll go put on my 'jamas and bathrobe too. It will be great in front of the fire."

Thomas was digging into his fourth piece of apple pie. Thomas was the kind of person who could eat and eat, four or five pieces of pie at a sitting, and never seem to gain any weight. Jonathan had been the same way. A combination of good genes and an active lifestyle kept the weight off so they could enjoy all of their favorite foods anytime they wanted without the guilt of knowing that they might gain extra pounds.

Scott, who had to watch his weight, kidded Thomas. "I wish I could eat 14 pieces of my favorite dessert. I'd weigh 400 pounds if I ate like you do, Thomas."

"Such is the luck of the draw in life, Scott," Thomas replied.

Jonathan was struggling to get up off of the couch.

"Here, Dad, let me help you," Michael offered.

"Thanks, Son," Jonathan said as he reached out to let Michael take a hold of his forearm. "Just help me up a bit, and then I can make it the rest of the way by myself." Michael followed his dad behind the couch and toward the door just to make sure he didn't fall. He really wished Jonathan wasn't so proud so he would use his walker. At least here in his own home with his family, he wouldn't have to worry about his reputation. He knew better, though. It wasn't as if Jonathan was proud in a bad sense; he just didn't want people taking pity on him. Struggles are a part of life for everyone, and he could get through them as well as the next guy, he reasoned.

When everyone had finished their break, they gathered again in the living room. Patty and Jennifer were all situated with their pajamas and bathrobes on, the two most comfortable of the family, for sure. Every year, the Fireside Chat was a highlight for the family. It is where they talked about the blessings and challenges of the previous year, family issues, and a look forward to the new year. Jonathan would usually lead off the discussion, and then it would pick up from there. Everyone was encouraged, no, expected, to take part in the conversation, at least in some part.

"Welcome to the 1995 Fireside Chat everyone," Jonathan began. "As the head honcho of this family, it is my privilege to start by giving an overview of the year as I saw it. 'A Year in Review,' if you will. It is my point of view that 1995 was a very good year for us in the Blake family." Many of the family who were listening would disagree. Though Jonathan would soon list the positive events of the year, they still saw the primary event of the year as the diagnosis of Jonathan's cancer. This overwhelmed every other aspect of the year. Jonathan would help them keep perspective as he continued, though.

"First of all, I think 1995 is the year in which I was able to spend the most time yet with my family. My wonderful bride and I were able to start the year with a fantastic two-week cruise. The sun was warm and bright while you all suffered here in the frozen tundra. Gloria and I celebrated 35 absolutely wonderful years of marital bliss with one another by having a terrific little party with a few hundred of our closest friends. Thank you, Michael, for organizing that," he said, nodding in the direction of his oldest son. "That will be a night for the memory books.

"The spring also brought with it the final Delbarton graduation of this next generation, as Thomas finally accomplished the task. Now, it will be another 20 years or so before that happens again, and it had better happen again. Perhaps this new baby will be a boy, then just 18 years to go.

"The month of July brought an exciting Fourth of July celebration and, of course, a few days later, the real fireworks of July, the wedding of Ms. Samantha Blake and her esteemed husband, the Reverend William Moore."

"Here, here," Michael said, thumbs up in the air.

Jonathan continued. "Your mother and I took a few days on Martha's Vineyard after the wedding to rest our tired bodies, and that was a special time for the two of us. Also, shortly after the wedding, I found out that Scott and Jennifer would give to me my first grandchild. This has to be one of the greatest joys a father can have, so it ranks high on the 1995 highlight list. There wasn't much action through the fall until we had a splendid Thanksgiving, with great food and warm fellowship with one another. I, again, won the football pool we had for the Thanksgiving games, if you remember, staking once more my claim as the best football prognosticator in the family, including Albert Manning, who always tries to lay claim to that title. By the way, mentioning Albert reminds me, I had a super hunting trip with Albert this year, as well as our annual fishing trip to Upstate New York.

"Where was I? Oh, yes. That brings me almost to the end of the year. The trip to Captiva was extraordinary, don't you all think?" The rest of the family smiled and shared their agreement. "The flight down, the weather, the time together, the food, the walks on the beach… It was all just perfect."

Jonathan had finished all that was good with 1995, and all were in agreement with him. He knew that he had to discuss the negative as well, so he had planned to talk about his illness, his impending death, and all of the ramifications of those circumstances. He had debated about doing it on Christmas Eve, not wanting at all to ruin the night, but this was the Fireside Chat where they dealt with the business of the family's year. He knew that he had to. It helped that the Blake family had always dealt with situations head-on, in an atmosphere of open communication, so he knew that the family would be able to handle what would come along. Also, throughout the year, since finding out about the cancer, Jonathan had taken the time to talk to each of the kids one on one about the issues of his death. They had talked about it, and he was sure that there would be no new surprises tonight.

"Of course, the real shock of this year was finding out about my illness. Now, I don't want this to be sad. I really don't. There are some things I want to say to you all, things that need to be said on Christmas. You know, life is a lot bigger than we make it out to be. Our existence is not limited to this finite earth. We just seem to spend most of our time here acting like it does. I remember when I was a little child. Old age seemed like a million years away to me. And certainly, at that young age, one doesn't ever think that he will actually ever become an old person. One can't even fathom the thought.

"As a teenager, there is so much life and vitality and energy that you are too busy to think about eternity and how you are living. Then you get married, have kids, and start building a life. It takes all of your attention, if you're not careful. It appears to be so important. It is, I know, but all the while you are worrying about life, the ironic thing is that life is slipping through your fingers. Every now and again, you notice it is happening, you think about it for an hour or an evening. Maybe you have a talk with your spouse or a close friend. Then, it's back to the fast lane of life.

"Here I am, 57 years old. I won't be here in six months. Yes, I could have remained healthy, but the result would have been the same eventually. Sooner or later, it catches up with us all."

Jonathan stopped to think about what he wanted to say next. The top log on the fire rolled off and hit the retainer. Everyone looked and then brought their attention back to Jonathan. "I guess what I'm trying to say to you kids is to not take life for granted. Don't ever stop reflecting on what life is really all about. Christmas reminds us what life is all about. It reminds us that God loves His people very much. So much so that He sent His only Son to save us. You know, in an odd way, I'm looking forward to death. Once you resign yourself to the fact that it is going to happen, you begin to wonder what it is going to be like in the afterlife, what God will look like… I have a lot of questions for Him." Jonathan now had a smile on his face. Everyone else was puzzled at how he could be talking about his own death and be smiling. He noticed their quizzical looks and answered them. "Hey folks, we need to accept this. Besides, you're all next. Everybody dies."

Jonathan got back on track. "So, here are some rules to live by after I'm gone. First of all, I've decided on who is in charge—and—after much thought, it will be your mom." Gloria thanked him for being so kind. "And I have placed all of your financial affairs under Michael's directorship. You will all find out the specifics after the funeral. That's how I want it, but a sneak preview is in order. I'm giving a lot to charity. Mom will get most of it. You will all have a trust that will provide an income that increases through the years until you can have full discretion over it at a later time.

"You all have some exciting times ahead of you. Make the most of them, knowing that you never know when God is going to call your number. You have a great head start in life, so don't throw it away. I think that's about all I can say. Life is shorter than you ever think it will be, so make the most of it and remember what it is all about."

Michael spoke for the rest of the family. "Dad, we don't know how the next few months are going to play out, but, and I know that I can say this for everyone here, we all love you very much, and we appreciate you more than you could ever imagine. You have been so good to us and have done so much for us. We want to say thank you."

"Well, I appreciate that very much, and I want you to know that I love you all more than life itself."

It was an awkward finish, but Jonathan had said what he wanted to say. It was time to get to bed because they had another long day tomorrow. They watched the fire some more and finished their desserts and coffee.

Jonathan was walking out the door to bed and turned to tell the group that he had only one more instruction. "Oh, and starting next year, William is in charge of the reading of the Christmas story. Think you can handle that, Preacher?"

"I'm sure I can," he said with a smile.

Jonathan and Gloria went up to bed, and the others followed shortly thereafter.

December 25

I T IS VERY rare that one knows when their last Christmas will be. It is also an eerie feeling to try to bask in the joy and revelry of one of the year's most joyous holidays, one that celebrates the coming of the Christ Child, and at the same time, being tempered by the knowledge of your own impending death. All one can do is make the most of the time. Not so much for your own sake but for the sake of those around you, those who will live on, the memories playing over and over in their heads until, at last, it is their turn.

Such was the mood of Jonathan Blake at Christmas 1995. Having enjoyed tremendously the family vacation in Captiva, he was now feeling the effects of his disease full force. Jonathan's mobility was very low now. The doctor had even brought a walker by the house one day. Jonathan had tried it once when no one else was around to see him struggle. He didn't want the others to see their father and husband, the one who had been for so long the strength of the family, reduced to a contraption to help him in the simplest of life's tasks—walking. He had pulled it out of the front closet, the one he had placed it in the minute Dr. Kidman had left the front door, and tried to make his way through the front foyer. It did make it a little easier to walk, he had thought to himself.

Something happened, though, that first time he tried it, that was too much for Jonathan's pride. As he made his way across the front foyer, he passed a full-length mirror that Gloria had put in, mainly to check herself one last time before receiving guests, checking for a flaw in her wardrobe, makeup, or hair. As he passed the mirror, he turned and looked. What he saw amazed and astonished him. Here he was, Jonathan Blake, the once strong and virile young man, athletic warrior, wealthy and respected businessman, who now saw something entirely different as he gazed upon his image in the mirror. He was very gray-headed, his weight had dropped considerably, he hunched over as he walked, and, to top it all off, this walker! His robe cinched tightly around his waist, he was glad he wasn't yet reduced to a nursing home, wandering aimlessly around the halls, his hospital gown draped loosely, waiting for death to envelop him.

And yet, he looked at himself. The thought of not being in a nursing home was merely consolation, and futile consolation at that. He knew by the meager form in the mirror that this was one fight in his life he would lose. He had known that his life was systematically being drained from him over time, but this moment was when it all crashed down on him at once. He had gripped the walker with all the strength he could muster and, with all he had in him, lashed out with fury and frustration. "Damn," he said as he threw the walker against the wall. He had determined right then that he would never use the walker again. He limped over to the walker and picked it up. He dragged it over to the closet and placed it where it would remain until after his death.

This moment, perhaps more than any other recent occasion in the life of Jonathan Blake, demonstrated the mentality of one who was seeing his life slip away and realizing there was nothing he could do about it, while at the same time being required to participate in holidays and events of joy, requiring him, at least in his own mind, to be strong and happy. It was difficult, to say the least, but Jonathan Blake would do his best to leave the memory of a father who cherished life and lived it to the fullest.

By 8 a.m. Christmas morning, the family had all woken up and arrived downstairs in the living room to gather around the tree to open presents, drink hot apple cider and hot chocolate, and eat the assorted muffins Gloria had baked for the morning. They finished opening the rest of their presents, and the rest of the day was spent enjoying one another, playing pool, watching football, and talking politics with Albert Manning once he arrived. Albert was a strict Republican partisan, much more so than any of the Blakes, but they loved and sometimes laughed at his passion for the whole thing. Albert always provided a lively atmosphere wherever he went, and the Blakes loved to him have him around. He was as much a part of the family as anyone.

Albert brought gifts for all of the family, but the highlight was the antique shotgun that he had found for Jonathan. Albert thought it would look good in Jonathan's study, and Jonathan loved it. "Albert! I have been looking for one of these. It is fantastic. Thank you very much."

"Well, old boy, I figure that with all of the sitting in duck blinds that you and I have done, this would make a good gift."

"It isn't a good gift, Albert; it is the perfect gift."

The Blakes and Albert ate a roasted chicken dinner, then retired to the living room for a Christmas carol sing. Jennifer was actually a very good pianist, and so she accompanied the family. They sang all of the great Christmas songs and drank hot apple cider. They concluded, as they did every year, with "Silent Night."

Another Christmas was drawing to a close. The family stayed for a while then all went to their respective homes. Albert was the last to leave. He and Jonathan sat in Jonathan's study, talking. Albert smoked what he called his "Christmas cigar." Although Jonathan was done with his cigars and had been for months, he could still enjoy the smell of being with Albert while he had one. They talked a little about business, but they mainly spent their time remembering all of their hunting and fishing trips, all of the animals they bagged and fish they caught as well as the ones that got away. They laughed; they almost cried. They wondered what had happened to many of the people they had come across over the years. Albert stayed until 11 o'clock before leaving. Both he and Jonathan were enjoying the time together so much. Finally, Albert left. It would be the last significant conversation that he would have with his best friend.

After Albert left, Jonathan went back into his study. Gloria was already in bed. He turned on the gas fireplace and sat down in his chair. He thought back and replayed almost every scene that he could remember from the past few days. He just so badly wanted to experience life over and over, knowing that he couldn't.

Soon he was weeping, his head in his hands. He cried for about 10 minutes, and then he was just too tired to cry anymore. He thought about his vast wealth and how it couldn't help him at all. So many people think that if they only had money, that they would be able to conquer anything. He thought about how wrong those people were. All wealth did was allow him to buy more possessions, none of which mattered anymore. When it came down to the real issues of life, the important issues such as happiness, meaning, and a man's relationship with God, money counted for nothing. He had, on more than one occasion, heard Reverend Wilton say that no one is rich or poor in front of the throne of God. Jonathan could buy anything he wanted on this earth except more time. He finally shut off the fire and headed upstairs. Jonathan Blake's last Christmas was over.

January 1, 2:30 p.m.

THE REST OF the family was still inside enjoying New Year's Day by eating snacks and watching football, but Jonathan wanted to take a walk. He could barely walk, which was actually a shuffle, but he felt it was in him today. The temperature had warmed up in the past few days. There was still snow on the ground, but Jonathan planned to walk on the drive, which was meticulously plowed. It was as black as black could be, with not one speck of snow on it. He told Gloria that he was going to take a short walk, so she helped him to bundle up warmly. As soon as he began down the drive, he turned and looked back at the house. There in the front window was Gloria, worrying about him. She was so afraid that he would fall. He was determined not to.

As he walked slowly along, he surveyed the land that his father had purchased and built their grand home on so many years ago. He knew almost every inch of the property in detail. He looked at the trees that he used to climb in as a boy. He saw one in particular that he and Albert had built a fort in at one time. He laughed thinking about it now. There was the lake where one year his Dad had stocked trout and used it to teach Jonathan and his sister to fish. Jonathan had done the same thing for his children. There was an open field where Jonathan and his friends used to gather on Saturday afternoons to play touch football and the spring and summer games of baseball. This had been his family's land for decades. It probably would remain so for many years and generations to come. His turn to live on it and enjoy it was coming to an end. He was thankful to God for allowing him to have lived such a blessed life.

Jonathan walked all the way to the gate. He remembered when they had to build the new one. All of this property had been groomed to what it had become by either Jonathan or his father. He loved Three Lakes. When he got back up to the house, Gloria was still standing in the window, watching. Jonathan laughed. She had always had a bit of worrier in her, but she would have nothing to fear today. He had made it back safely. Just a stroll to look at his land under a close, scrutinous, and reflecting eye one more time before he would pass away from this life and into the next. He had enjoyed every minute and every step.

January 23

JONATHAN WAS ALONE at Three Lakes today. The cold New Jersey winds were blowing, keeping Jonathan on the couch in his office safely under a blanket. He liked to get out of bed and at least go to his office, though his cancer was rapidly bringing the end about. Since his walk on New Year's Day, Jonathan had been virtually immobile. Gloria was in Morristown today, working with the mission and doing some shopping. She hasn't liked leaving much lately, wanting instead to spend as much time as possible with Jonathan.

Jonathan was lying there stone-faced and thinking diligently about the end. He would alternate between anger, gratefulness, and sadness. He really desperately needed to talk to someone, one who could understand, one who could empathize with him. He decided to call Reverend Wilton.

Jonathan slowly arose from the couch and went to his chair by the desk. Sitting down, he picked up the phone and dialed Reverend Wilton's home number.

"Hello?" It was the Reverend's cheerful voice. Jonathan loved that voice, and today it was more precious to him than ever. So often, that voice had been an encouragement, a source of strength to Jonathan and his family.

"Hello, Reverend Wilton," Jonathan said in a strained voice.

"Jonathan? Is that you?"

"Yes, it is. Do you have a few minutes?"

"Of course, Jonathan, what is it?"

"Well, frankly, I'm feeling a bit scared, a bit angry... a bit of many emotions actually. I just needed someone to talk to, I guess."

"How are you doing physically, Jonathan?"

"That's the problem, Reverend. It is getting very bad. I can barely move. As you can tell, I can barely speak." Jonathan's voice began to crack in emotion. "It is obvious that I'm going to die soon."

"I'm sorry, Jonathan. Would you like me to come over to Three Lakes and spend some time with you?"

"No, that's quite all right. There is no need for you to do that."

"It is no problem at all, Jonathan. I could be there in less than a half an hour."

"No, perhaps you could encourage me. Pray for me, perhaps."

"Surely, Jonathan. You know that I believe, and you do as well, that it gets darkest just before the storm. The tempest rages, and all one can see is the dark, the desperate, the tragic, and the pain. Yet, it is in those times that we hold fast to faith, for faith will see you through. Remember the Bible says that we rejoice in sufferings because suffering produces perseverance, and perseverance produces character, and character produces hope, and here is my favorite part—and hope does not disappoint us.

"Jonathan, you are deep in the swells of perseverance, the waves of suffering washing over you, but there is hope, my friend. I know you must feel like it is easy for me to say these things, and the truth is that it is much easier for me to say them than for you to experience them, but the words are truth."

"Yes, I know. And sometimes, in between doubt, I do have faith. I just don't know why it has to be so hard, why there has to be so much pain."

"I don't know either, Jonathan." The Reverend's wisdom had ended, and the reality of the pain had taken over. Yes, the words were true, but in a time like this, they were just that, words.

"Reverend Wilton? Will you pray for me?"

Here was a man, one in the last, painful stages of life, reaching out to another frail human to beckon the grace of the unseen God to have mercy and meet him in his time of need. The kind, compassionate old man did just that, praying passionately for his younger friend. The words were offered in faith that they would be heard and received just the same.

"Thank you," Jonathan said as Reverend Wilton finished.

"Jonathan," he said with a deep grievous sigh, "it is the very least I can do for you. Any time you want me to pray for you or just to talk, please, call me."

"I will. Thank you."

"Goodbye Jonathan."

"Goodbye Reverend Wilton."

Reverend Wilton was leaving on a short trip in a few days and made a mental note to call Jonathan again as soon as he came home. Jonathan went back to the couch and fell asleep. The goodbyes he just exchanged with his minister would be the last.

February 2

G LORIA WAS READING a book to Jonathan in the library around 7:30 in the evening when they heard the front door slam shut. "I wonder what that was?" she asked, knowing full well that it was the front door.

"Probably one of the kids," Jonathan surmised. It shouldn't be Thomas as he was to be with friends until tomorrow morning.

"I'll go see," Gloria said, rising then disappearing out the library door. Just as she turned the corner into the hallway, Samantha's familiar voice rang out.

"Mom? Dad?"

Gloria caught up with Samantha in the living room entrance.

"Well, hello, Samantha. What brings you home?"

"Hi, Mom. William is at a meeting tonight, and I wanted to talk to Dad a little bit. Is he awake?"

"Yes. He's in the library. I've been reading a book to him. His eyesight is failing him now."

"Let me guess," Samantha said. "Poetry."

"Of course," Gloria responded as she smiled.

"Arnold?"

"Some, a bit earlier. Go ahead into the library. He'll be so glad to see you. I have some things to take care of in my office. Tell him I'll be back in to read in a little while."

Samantha bounded into the hallway and down toward the library. Gloria went to her office. As she came into the library, Samantha noticed her dad just looking at the book he held in his hands. He wasn't reading it, just looking at the closed book.

"What are you doing, Dad?" she asked.

"Samantha. Hello. I'm just looking at this book." Jonathan's speech was slow and pained. Gasps came at regular intervals.

Samantha sat down next to the couch in the chair that matched it. "What is so interesting about that particular book?"

"Oh, it isn't this book." He paused. Samantha didn't know if it was to think or to collect the energy for the next sentence. "I'm just thinking about books in general."

"You sure love books, Dad."

"Mmmm," he hummed in agreement. "I couldn't have lived in a better house than this one, what with all of these books here at my disposal." He said this waving his hand as best as he could at the thousands of volumes that surrounded him. "I owe all of this to your grandmother. She was an even greater lover of literature than me. She had such a wide collection that I have had to add very little to it since she died."

"I bet you've spent thousands of hours in here, haven't you?"

"You know, when you kids were little, I would put you to bed, and then your mother would go to bed. Sometimes I just couldn't sleep, and I would spend hours every night in here. I would pore over poetry, classical fiction, so many wonderful volumes. It was such a release for me from the stresses of work. And when I was a child! Your grandmother would bring me in here, and we would pick out 10 or 15 books. Some of them I would read myself. Some she would read to me. We would spend so much time reading." Jonathan was longing for a distant time. Now he could barely see enough to read the title on the cover, much less the words inside.

He realized he was talking about himself, and that Samantha probably didn't come over to do that, so he asked her what it was that brought her to Three Lakes this evening.

"I just wanted to talk to you."

"What about?"

"A few things. I know you are getting sicker. I want to make sure that I tell you that I have appreciated this past year so very much. I feel like all the past hurts and desires to know you have all been reconciled. I wish we had more time, but…" She drifted off, falling silent.

"But I'm dying, yes."

She nodded. "So, I wanted to say thanks. Thanks for noticing, and thanks for being humble enough to take the initiative. I think so highly of you for being such a great man. You weren't just a great businessman, but a great father as well."

Jonathan was getting a bit of energy now. "Thank you, Samantha. That means so much to hear you say that."

"It's what I feel. I also want to tell you how much I appreciate your relationship with Mom. William and I have talked many times about how we would like our relationship to emulate much of your relationship. I always have respected the way that you treated Mom. It was a great example to me to see how a man should treat a woman. It gave me a standard by which to judge the one who would become my husband." Jonathan listened. "William and I are very happy together. And, as much as you say it would be hard being in the ministry, it is working out very well for us. We enjoy it."

"No tough times yet?" Jonathan asked.

"Sure. There are struggles: People problems and the like. But all in all, it is very rewarding."

"You know that soon you'll be able to do whatever you like."

"What do you mean?"

"I mean that you'll have the money to do whatever you like."

"Oh." Samantha thought to herself that she would prefer to have her father over any money he would leave her. "Well, we are doing what we like, Dad. I imagine we'll do this the rest of our lives. It might change a bit in the specifics, but we're right where we want to be right now."

"Good," he said. Jonathan reached out his hand. Samantha took it in hers. Jonathan's hand was cold. She put her other hand over it to warm it. Together they sat holding hands and talking for another 10 minutes or so. They talked about times when Samantha was growing up, vacations the family took together, people who had influenced their lives. Eventually, Gloria made her way back into the library.

"Hi, you two. I made some hot tea. Would you like some?"

"Not for me, Mom. I need to get going. I still have a couple of more stops before I go home. Thanks, though."

"I would love some tea," Jonathan said.

Samantha kissed her mother and father goodbye, then left to run errands while Gloria and Jonathan spent the rest of the evening reading and drinking tea.

February 3

J ONATHAN WAS EATING virtually nothing anymore, but Gloria liked to try to get him to drink warm liquids, especially on colder days. Perhaps it didn't provide real help, but it made Gloria feel better. Today happened to be particularly cold, so she decided to bring Jonathan some hot tea in his room. After making the tea, she squeezed a quarter of a lemon into the water and added a touch of honey. It was just the way Jonathan liked it.

As she got to the top of the stairwell and turned toward their room, she could hear the music coming from their stereo. She smiled at Jonathan's passion for classical music. He had always loved both poetry and classical music. He always said of them that they were like lovers who strolled hand in hand through the park.

As Gloria turned into the room, she saw that Jonathan was awake. It was about 6 o'clock. She had eaten alone as she had frequently as of late, while Jonathan merely lay in his bed. He turned slightly as she entered. "Hello," she said. "I brought you some tea."

"Thank you," Jonathan said, barely audible. He stared straight ahead. Gloria set the tea on the nightstand next to the bed. She felt and saw that Jonathan was hot, so she went into the bathroom and brought back a cool, wet washcloth.

"Here you are, Love," she said as she sat down on the bed next to him and gently placed the washcloth on his forehead.

"That feels good," he said. She then took the cloth and dabbed all over his face and neck. Jonathan closed his eyes and leaned his head back. When she was done, Gloria took the washcloth into the bathroom and placed it on the counter.

Back in the bedroom, she sat down on the chair next to the window. She would often sit there now and read while Jonathan slept. She waited to see how he would be this evening. Some days, they would talk. Others, they would just sit in the room together. Still others, Gloria would read poetry to Jonathan. Jonathan enjoyed it all. He wanted Gloria always by his side in these last days.

For a few moments, Gloria sat wondering what Jonathan would do. Finally, he opened his eyes and looked at her, then motioned ever so slightly with his finger for her to sit by him. She came over and sat fully on the side of the bed where she slept. He reached out and took her hand.

"You know I love you?" he asked.

"Yes. I do."

"You mean everything to me," he said a few moments later.

"I know."

"It has been a good life."

"Yes, Jonathan, it has been a very good life," Gloria responded, tightening her grip on his hand, tears running down her cheeks.

Jonathan saw the tears. "Don't cry, Gloria."

"I can't help it, Jonathan."

Jonathan turned and looked forward again. "Yes, it has been a very good life." For the next few minutes, they sat together listening to music. Finally, Jonathan turned one last time to Gloria.

"Gloria?"

"Yes?"

"I don't know how much longer I have. Not much, I suppose. I want to make sure I tell you something."

"What, Jonathan?"

"Goodbye."

Gloria half smiled, half cried. Jonathan had rarely left the house without first telling her goodbye. He was good about that.

She reached up and put her palm to his cheek, looking straight into his eyes.

"Goodbye, Jonathan." He smiled as best he could then turned again to look straight ahead and soon fell asleep.

They had said goodbye to each other now. Gloria was glad about that. She felt some finality. She got up and went downstairs to pick up a book to read upstairs, make a few phone calls, and shut the house down for the night.

February 4

S COTT AND JENNIFER made their way to Three Lakes after going out for lunch with some friends after church. Gloria had called them the night before and suggested that they come soon if they wanted to talk to Jonathan before he died. She knew that he wasn't going to last long, if even through the next week.

Scott and Jennifer had wanted to spend some time with Jonathan anyway. The last year had been a growing time for them as a couple, and it was in no small part because of Jonathan's willingness to challenge Jennifer with her propensity to not forgive Scott and to encourage Scott to put Jennifer back into a place of devotion in his life. Surely, getting pregnant had been a wake-up call to them, but Jonathan's concern and his willingness to assert himself into it without becoming intrusive had proven to be particularly helpful to them, and they wanted to thank him for it.

Scott parked the car in front of the main door, and they got out. Jennifer, now within a month of delivery, more waddled up to the house than walked. Scott walked beside her, close enough to hold her up if she were to slip. When they got to the door, they grabbed the handle to go in, but it was locked, so they rang the bell. In a few moments, Gloria answered the door.

"Hi, Mom," Jennifer said, announcing their arrival.

"Hello, you two. Come in out of the cold." Gloria moved out of the way so Scott and Jennifer could come in. They each took their coats off and placed them in the closet.

"That's sure a pretty maternity dress," Gloria said looking at Jennifer.

"Thanks. It's new. Scott picked it out for me."

"I always knew you had fine taste, Scott," Gloria flattered him.

"How's Dad?" Jennifer asked, quickly changing the subject.

Gloria grimaced. "He's not going to make it much longer, Jennifer. He can barely move. He can hardly see. He's just about gone. Go in and see him, though. He can hear and acknowledge and speak a little if he has the energy at the moment. Give it a try. He'll be glad to see you both. He's up in the bedroom."

Scott and Jennifer went upstairs to Jonathan's bedroom. The door was ajar. They pushed the door open to see if he was awake. His eyes were open. The room was light with the sun coming in through the window. The room smelled a bit, though they knew not what of. Jonathan's head moved slightly to the door. Not much, just slightly. His eyes caught Jennifer's as she moved around the end of the bed, Scott directly behind her. Jonathan managed a smile, be it ever so small.

"Hi, Dad," she said.

"Jonathan. How are you?" Scott regretted the words the moment he said them. *How are you?* he thought to himself. Absurd question to ask a man on his deathbed. Jonathan replied to neither of the greetings.

"Dad, I know that you are tired, so we'll go soon, but we wanted to tell you something." She could tell Jonathan was listening by his eyes. "We want you to know that we have been getting along so much better this past year." She looked quickly at Scott then back to Jonathan before continuing. "I feel like our lunch together that day really helped me to realize that I was holding grudges against Scott. And I realized how detrimental it was to our relationship. I've been working on being more forgiving, and things have really improved for us. Scott feels the same way, and he's so glad that you encouraged him along the way too."

Still nothing from her father. "Dad. I know we don't have much more time, so we came to tell you that we love you and that you have meant so much to us. Don't worry about us. We're going to make it. We promise. And we're going to be great parents to this grandchild of yours." Jennifer was almost pleading with Jonathan to hear. Now she couldn't tell if he was able to or not. She had said what they came to say, so now she didn't know what to do. She had expected more of a conversation.

Jonathan raised a finger. It was almost as though it were his sign that he had something to say. Scott and Jennifer both looked at him, anticipating.

"You'll make it." He pronounced in a gruff, barely audible voice.

Jennifer began to cry. "Yes, Daddy, we'll make it." She held his hand. Scott put his hand on her shoulder.

In a few moments, Jonathan was asleep. Scott and Jennifer went back down to the living room where Gloria was waiting.

"How was he?" Gloria asked.

"Oh, at first I thought he heard us, then I wasn't so sure. Then he finally responded." She sat down in a chair. Scott sat on the couch at the other end from Gloria. "He just isn't the same old Dad anymore."

"No, honey, I'm afraid he's not."

"I didn't know he had gotten this far along," Scott said.

They realized that they had probably said the last things that they would to Jonathan. Death would be merely the formality to follow. Scott and Jennifer spent another 20 minutes with Gloria before going home for the day.

February 5

JONATHAN WAS UPSTAIRS. He was almost gone now and barely conscious. His eyesight was failing him, and breathing was difficult, painful almost to the point of being unbearable. Gloria was downstairs paying bills. After she sealed the envelope to the phone company, she noticed that she was out of stamps. She opened the drawer in her desk, hoping to have a few extras lying loose there. As she lifted up the papers on the top, she noticed her stationery. The letter she had written Jonathan and had intended to give to him was still there. Her heart raced. She knew that he didn't have much time left, and she was so disappointed that she had forgotten to give it to him. She especially had hoped to do it so nicely, perhaps lay it on his food tray when she made him breakfast in bed some morning. She had hoped to talk about it. Now, Jonathan was barely able to hear, much less talk.

Gloria took the letter out of her drawer and walked quickly upstairs. The room was dark. Jonathan lay on the bed. Gloria turned on the lamp by her side of the bed and sat down. Jonathan rustled. "Jonathan?" she said quietly.

Jonathan woke up but said nothing. His eyes were like slits. He was conscious. "Jonathan? Are you awake?" He nodded slightly. "I wrote you a letter. I actually wrote it a few months ago and intended to give it to you sooner but…" she hated to admit it, "I forgot. I want to read it to you."

She took Jonathan's right hand in her left and held the paper in her right. Jonathan's eyes moved back and forth as she read. Midway through, a single tear formed and fell slowly down his face and off his jawbone. It left a trail that Gloria saw when she was done reading the letter. She looked in his eyes. "Did you hear me, Jonathan?" He squeezed her hand slightly. "Did you understand?" Again, he squeezed.

Gloria set the letter down and hugged her husband of close to 36 years. Jonathan didn't move at all. He couldn't. The end was soon to come. Gloria knew it and didn't want to let him go. "I love you so much, Jonathan," she said. Jonathan didn't hear it.

February 6

D R. WALTER KIDMAN had arrived at Three Lakes around 7 o'clock in the evening after receiving a call from Gloria. She knew that Jonathan was in the final stages of dying, and she wanted Dr. Kidman to be there. After checking all of Jonathan's vital signs and a few other routine tests, he was sure that Jonathan wouldn't last more than a few more hours. He put the end of his stethoscope in his pen pocket and turned to speak to Gloria.

"May I speak to you outside the room," he asked in a whisper to Gloria.

Once outside the room, he gave Gloria the news. "You'll want to call the other children," Dr. Kidman said to her. "He most likely won't make it through the night, if even a few more hours. He is so weak, and his body is just shutting itself down. There is nothing I can do except administer medication to ease the pain."

Gloria nodded and turned to go to the phone at the end of the hall. Dr. Kidman could hear the quiet cry of a woman about to lose her love. Gloria picked up the phone and in the next five minutes reached Jennifer, Michael, and Samantha. They and their spouses were now on their way.

Back in the room, young Thomas sat on the side of the bed next to his father. Knowing that Jonathan would probably die soon, Thomas had elected to live at home this quarter and commute down Route 206 to Princeton rather than live in the dormitory. He reached out and grasped his father's hand. After clasping it in between both hands, Jonathan's eyes opened, barely. He looked over at Thomas.

Barely able to form the words on his lips, Jonathan mustered the strength to say what would be his last words. "I won't be here long, Thomas. Please remember that I always loved you. I always will."

Thomas rolled over and lay next to his Dad. "I know, Dad." Thomas could hear his father's faint heartbeat through the thin pajama top. They lay there together, just the two of them, for over 10 minutes. Gloria had come and looked in but decided to let Thomas have his time with Jonathan. She and Jonathan had already said their goodbyes.

"Thanks for loving me so much, Dad. Thanks for taking me fishing so much. Thanks for giving me so many opportunities." He was speaking to himself now, as Jonathan lay there unconscious. "I guess I never appreciated all we had…"

Suddenly, Thomas noticed that he no longer heard his father's heart beating. He quickly rolled off of the bed. "Dr. Kidman!" he said loudly as he moved toward the door. Dr. Kidman had been sitting in a chair in the hallway, just outside of the room. He met Thomas face to face as they reached the door at the same time.

"Dr. Kidman, Dad isn't breathing."

Walt Kidman came into the room and checked for himself. Indeed, Jonathan was dead. Dr. Kidman took Thomas into his arms. "I know, Thomas, there is nothing we can do. He's gone." He held young Thomas for a time and then moved toward the bedroom to confirm Jonathan's death. "Thomas, will you get your mother? She went downstairs a few minutes ago." With that, he passed into the bedroom.

Moments later, after checking him and confirming that, indeed, Jonathan Blake had died, Gloria came and stood next to him. They both said nothing for a few minutes, instead just looking at Jonathan.

Finally, Dr. Kidman broke the silence. "Gloria. Jonathan was a fine man." He turned and put a hand on her shoulder. "I need to go and call the funeral director to come and pick up the body. You'll have some time with him. About an hour. The kids will be here soon. I'll wait in the sitting room next to the front door if you need me. You should probably leave the gate opened so the funeral home can get in."

Gloria responded, "Okay. Thank you."

"Call me if you need me," Dr. Kidman said as he went to make his phone call and wait for those who would take the body.

As he walked down the stairs toward the main foyer, Samantha and William came through the front door, followed minutes later by Michael and Patty. Shortly thereafter, Jennifer and Scott arrived. Jennifer moved slowly, her pregnancy making it hard to do otherwise. Nonetheless, they, too, went upstairs to join the rest of the family bedside the bed that cradled Jonathan's body. There they were, Gloria, Michael and Patty, Jennifer and Scott, and Samantha and William. Samantha noticed that Thomas wasn't there. "Where's Thomas?"

"He's in his room. I'll go get him," Gloria said as she began to circle around the bed.

"No," Samantha said. "I'll go get him."

Gloria stopped and Samantha disappeared down the hall toward Thomas's room. After Thomas and Samantha arrived back in the master bedroom, the family stayed with Jonathan's lifeless body, talking rarely, until the funeral director arrived to take the body. Dr. Kidman came in with Sam Winston, the funeral director, and waited. One by one, the kids and Gloria said their last words to their departed father and husband then left the room.

Once Jonathan's body had been taken away, sometime around 11:15, the family gathered in the living room. Everyone just sat there, not saying a word, every bit of emotional energy sapped from them. Gloria spoke first. "Listen, we had better all get some sleep; the next few days are going to be hectic and traumatic. Why don't you all sleep here tonight, and we can begin making arrangements for the funeral tomorrow."

"Yeah," Michael said as he stood up, "that's a good idea."

The family all slept at Three Lakes that night, and for the next few days, made the final arrangements for the funeral. It was a sad, busy time.

February 10, 1 p.m.

I T HAD BEEN four days since Jonathan's death. Three, if you count only full days. The funeral had already been planned. Jonathan and Gloria had arranged all of the details last summer. Jonathan's final tribute in death, his funeral, would be as were most of the events in his life, rigorously planned. He and Gloria had spent much of one evening and all of the following day deciding just what music would be played, who to invite, who would speak, where it would be held, where the reception would be, etc. Very few in this life have the luxury of planning their own funeral.

Even those stricken with terminal disease, those who could, like Jonathan, rarely do. They live in denial, hoping that it won't really happen or just plain don't want to, realizing someone else will be forced to do it for them in the days following their death. Not Jonathan. He wanted a hand in it all.

This day was as every funeral day should be but everyone hopes won't be. It was drizzling an icy rain, and bone-chillingly so. The snow had melted, and a warm front had come in late January, only to turn dramatically colder the beginning of February. Thirty-two degrees and raining. It spoke of death and dreariness in and of itself. New Vernon Presbyterian was too small to hold all of the people the funeral expected, so it was held at the Presbyterian church on the Green in Morristown. The 400 mourners had arrived and were seated by 12:55, as Jonathan had been sure to include an admonishment to be on time and prompt in the announcement. Those who knew him best recognized this well-known time manager's own hand in the prompting.

The sanctuary held the family and friends of Jonathan Blake. All came to pay their respects to a man who made their lives richer for having known him. They came from all classes of life. Many of Jonathan's distant relatives were not wealthy but commoners, some blue-collar workers. There were politicians and television personalities and, of course, many from the publishing world. They would all this day celebrate this individual life that had come into their own. They would reflect one last time on the meaning of Jonathan's life and one more time on the meaning of their own.

Jonathan knew that this would be the case, so the funeral was not designed to focus on him as much as it was to focus on the larger issues of life and death, meaning, and eternity—topics that people so often neglect in the midst of getting through each day. The music was lofty, centered on themes of victory over death and the triumph of God in bringing men and women into eternal life. Nothing was holding Jonathan Blake back now, and he wanted to remind his earth-bound friends that in the midst of their sorrow, they must know that they, too, would one day pass through this mystery, death—that journey that everyone loathes—and come into the reception of eternal life. He wanted them to focus on the frailty of this life but also on the certainty of the life to come. He wanted to tell them to trust in God and make the most of their lives they have now.

Reverend Wilton came to the pulpit of this old stone building to begin the service wherein they would lay to rest their old friend. He came slowly, carefully, his own years showing as he walked. He rested both hands on the sides of the wooden pulpit and, looking over the crowd gathered, began.

"Friends. Family. We come here this afternoon to give our friend Jonathan Blake over to his Maker. Yes, he is gone already, but this is the time for us to let him go. It is also a time for us to reflect. We shall this day say goodbye one last time to Jonathan but hello one more time to our own inability to live here forever. The scriptures tell us that it is appointed for man to die once and then face judgment. As surely as you are here today, Jonathan has gone to be before his Maker. I know, having known Jonathan for so many years, that today he is in heaven with God. We live so longingly after this temporal life. Why is that? Why do we pursue something so relentlessly that one day, be it soon or be it later, will be ripped from our hands no matter how hard we try to grasp for it? This is the question Jonathan wanted me to ask you. Jonathan wanted me to remind you that there is much more to your existence than the size of your house or pocketbook. There is much more to your happiness than the completion of your latest adventure or vacation. There is family. There are friends. There is the responsibility to leave this world a better place than it was when you arrived. There is a God whom we will one day answer to, and therefore, we must serve while on this earth of His. I believe that Jonathan Blake lived these virtues.

"Born into wealth, Jonathan didn't have to struggle financially as many do. But his struggle was self-inflicted. He decided early on that he wouldn't drift through life secluded in his material possessions but would think and act as a man with responsibility to his God and fellow man. He determined to never pass through this life without confronting the issues that present themselves to all people. Many would scoff that that is impossible for a man like Jonathan Blake, but I can tell you as his minister for so many years that Jonathan was a man who struggled for good in a world gone awry. There are so many things that he did in his life that only he, Gloria, his God, and I know about. It would be wrong for me to tell you, but let it be said that Jonathan was a man who bettered mankind through his work and his life."

Reverend Wilton continued on for some time, and the congregation reflected on their own lives, just as Jonathan had hoped.

Businessmen pondered whether or not their own lives really made a difference. The few politicians in attendance rethought silently about how they governed. Was it out of expediency or for the good of the people who elected them? Did they realize that there was a higher Governor still than they? Reverend Wilton's sermon was having just the effect Jonathan and Gloria had hoped it would.

When Reverend Wilton was finished, the congregation stood to sing a hymn. When they were through, they sat, and many turned in their program to see that Albert Manning would speak next. Jonathan's oldest and dearest friend moved to the front as the congregation took their seats. Albert stepped to the lectern, his own face looking older today, slight bags under his eyes from the few days of barely getting any sleep. His hair was graying, slightly thinning, but he maintained his regal look nonetheless. He paused before beginning, looking out over the assembly. He thought to himself how he never would have thought this time would come. But here he was. Wiping a small tear from his right eye, he began. "From John Greenleaf Whittier. This poem of friendship entitled 'A Legacy.'

> *Friend of my many years!*
> *When the great silence falls, at last, on me,*
> *Let me not leave, to pain and sadden thee,*
> *A memory of tears,*
> *But pleasant thoughts alone*
> *Of one who was thy friendship's honored guest*
> *And drank the wine of consolation pressed*
> *From sorrows of thy own.*
> *I leave with thee a sense*
> *Of hands upheld and trials rendered less—*
> *The unselfish joy which is to helpfulness*
> *Its own great recompense;*
> *The knowledge that from thine,*
> *As from the garments of the Master, stole*
> *Calmness and strength, the virtue which makes whole*

And heals without a sign;
Yea more, the assurance strong
That love, which fails of perfect utterance here,
Lives on to fill the heavenly atmosphere
With its immortal song.

"The calmness, strength, and love of unbridled friendship. Jonathan Blake and I have been the best of friends for close to 50 years, if that can be imagined. Through these years, we have tried much and achieved much, at least in the way of the world. We have walked side by side for all of those years. My position has been one of the 'out front,' if you will. I have much joy in shaping public opinion through my speaking, my writing, and my political involvement. Who is it that shapes the shapers, you may have often wondered. For me, I have always been shaped by my friend and mentor, Jonathan Blake. He was the much better man of these two Delbarton and Princeton graduates. He was a man of impeccable character, and I was always questioning and following his rock-grounded values. He was the strong, quiet type, and I was the one who would be shaped by his inner strength and given to verbalizing that in the public square.

"I owe much to my friend for his help in shaping my public life. He was always the listening ear and the forceful, steady, and thoughtful response. For that, I am ever grateful. But where I am most grateful is for the many, countless hundreds of small moments and weekends, holidays, and quick or lingering lunches where Jonathan Blake was simply my friend. He has been gone a mere three days, and how I miss him already. 'The calmness and the strength, the virtue that makes whole.' It was great in Jonathan Blake. How I loved to fish and hunt with him. It started with his father taking us two squirrely boys out for weekends away. It continued for the years to come. We just enjoyed being together. And now, he is gone.

"The brilliance of the light that was the life of Jonathan Blake will live on. It will live on in his family, of course, and it will live on, at least for some time, in the minds of those who knew him through his newspapers and civic involvements. But there is another place in which the brilliance of that life will always shine, and it is the most important place for me. Jonathan Blake lives on in my mind in memories and in my heart in love."

Looking upward, Albert Manning spoke his final words. "I miss you, Jonathan."

At the end of the funeral, Reverend Wilton directed everyone to the graveside where Jonathan's body would be laid to rest. They were free to join the family there, or they could proceed back to Three Lakes for a reception in one hour.

Before the casket was closed for the final time, Gloria placed two items in with Jonathan. The first was the letter she had written to him in the middle of the night. This she carefully placed in his inside left coat pocket, close to his heart. The second item was the photo album she had made for Christmas. Though she hadn't told Jonathan, she had two made, one for her to keep, the other to place for all eternity in Jonathan's casket.

Most of the people at the funeral joined the procession to the gravesite. In their car, Michael and Patty drove silently. The rain was coming down hard now, the skies almost black. It was barely 2:30 p.m., and it was as dark as 6:30 in the evening. Like the rain pounding the windshield, Michael's mind pounded him with memories of his father. He began to silently sob as he remembered so vividly the time Jonathan had bought for him a puppy for his seventh birthday. What a sacrifice giving a 7-year-old a puppy is. The thought is that the young one will learn responsibility by taking care of the new animal. The reality is that the older takes most of the responsibility himself. Michael had made it clear for months that he desperately wanted a puppy for his birthday. All through it, Jonathan and Gloria had made sure that Michael's hopes were not set too high for fear of being let down. This was all typical Mom and Dad stuff, but young Michael didn't know any better. When the big day came, they had a full-blown birthday party with all of Michael's friends. There were balloons and cake and ice cream. To throw Michael off even more, Jonathan had even gone ahead and gotten Michael's number two request. This had brought the boy some joy, but it was obvious that he was disappointed.

Later that evening, Michael was reading in his room, and Jonathan came in to sit beside him on the bed. "How are you doing, birthday boy?" Jonathan asked.

"All right, I guess. Thanks for the birthday party. It was fun."

Jonathan led him even further with, "Did you get everything that you wanted?"

Michael paused. "Well… no, I really didn't."

"Oh?" Jonathan asked.

"No. Remember, I really wanted a puppy, but that's okay, I guess." Michael was trying hard to be appreciative, yet not covering his disappointment very well.

"I see," responded Jonathan. "Say, I'm wondering if you could take a minute and help me with something."

"What, Dad?" came the reply.

"Oh, just a box I need some help with in the garage."

"Okay, let me put my book away." Jonathan waited while Michael put his book on the shelf and then bounced his way past him into the hall.

"Wait for me," Jonathan called to his young son. They soon arrived in the garage.

"Where's the box, Dad?"

"Oh, it is right over here," Jonathan said as he led Michael to a box on the side of the garage.

"Can you lift it up for me?"

"Sure." As Michael lifted the box, the bottom had been cut out, and it revealed a small cage with a beautiful cocker spaniel puppy inside. Michael's eyes grew as big as silver dollars. "Dad!" he exclaimed, "He's great!"

Michael's tears now streamed down his face as he drove. Patty sat sideways in the seat, quietly gazing at her husband. She saw the tears and felt the pain almost as much as Michael felt it. She reached out her hand and placed it on Michael's forearm. She dared not say a word. "He was such a great dad," he said. He would have made a wonderful grandfather… and now he's gone. It's not fair for him. It's not fair for us."

He paused. He looked out the side window. "It's not fair for the grandkids. They'll never know him. Never even a chance." He then drifted off again into thought. The rest of the 15-minute drive was spent with Michael recalling events of his youth and Patty sitting silently beside him.

The graveside service was short. After the group arrived and gathered around the grave, Reverend Wilton started by reading from Ecclesiastes:

> There is a time for everything, and a season for every activity under heaven: a time to be born and a time to die, a time to plant and a time to uproot, a time to kill and a time to heal, a time to tear down and a time to build, a time to weep and a time to laugh, a time to mourn and a time to dance, a time to scatter stones and a time to gather them, a time to embrace and a time to refrain, a time to search and a time to give up, a time to keep and a time to throw away, a time to tear and a time to mend, a time to be silent and a time to speak, a time to love and a time to hate, a time for war and a time for peace. What does the worker gain from his toil? I have seen the burden that God has laid on men. He has made everything beautiful in its time. He has also set eternity in the hearts of men; yet they cannot fathom what God has done from beginning to end. I know that there is nothing better for men than to be happy and do good while they live. That everyone may eat and drink, and find satisfaction in all his toil—this is the gift of God. I know that everything God does will endure forever; nothing can be

added to it and nothing taken from it. God does it so that men will revere Him.

Reverend Wilton continued, "It is time to lay Jonathan Blake to rest, to commit him to God and to say our goodbyes. Goodbye, Jonathan." Reverend Wilton then turned to Albert Manning. "Albert?"

Albert Manning had written and committed to memory a poem for his dear and beloved friend. The rain drizzled into his face as he closed his eyes and spoke for those gathered. His words rang true for each and every one of their feelings.

> *About two paths that cross in time,*
> *One often wonders why,*
> *The time therein becomes too short,*
> *And then a haste goodbye.*
> *But allotted is the course we live,*
> *Take it we must do.*
> *In the end, what can I say,*
> *Of cherished time with you.*
> *To make the most of every day,*
> *And live it to the full.*
> *Never must we let ourselves*
> *Wander into a lull.*
> *The day will come to bid adieu,*
> *Forward I look not.*
> *Say I must, the happiness*
> *You give, could never be bought.*
> *Then when you a vision only,*
> *In my mind do stay,*
> *The times we spent will always last*
> *As each goes their own way.*
> *Ah, but when the Lord comes back*
> *To bring about the end,*

Of course desire longs for Him,
But we'll also be with friends.

When Albert had finished, Reverend Wilton gave the customary closing. "Ashes to ashes, dust to dust. Lord, into Your hands, we commit the spirit of our beloved Jonathan. May You in Your grace receive him into your everlasting kingdom. Amen." Albert and Reverend Wilton exchanged hugs with the family members, and then the family took condolences from the rest of those who had come to the graveside. In a few moments, they began to return to their cars for the trip back to Three Lakes. It was getting very cold, and the rain was beginning to pick up even more, which made them want to get indoors.

After the reception, back at Three Lakes, the few members of the Blake family and a few close friends spent some time together drinking coffee, reminiscing, and grieving together. After a time, only Albert was left with the family. He asked Gloria if she would gather the family together.

"Of course, Albert. Where?"

"Wherever you please, Gloria, but it needs to be in a room with a television and VCR," he said.

"I'll gather them in the living room."

"Good. I have something for you all."

After Gloria had gathered the family into the living room, Albert standing there waiting for them, he directed them to the television and video cassette recorder. "One day a few months ago, your father asked if I might help him prepare a final message for you all. We spent the afternoon at my home, and we recorded this message. I have had copies made for each you, as you will want to keep this." He reached down and pressed the power button to the television and then pressed "play."

Quickly the image of the departed Jonathan came on the screen. He looked pale, wrinkled, old, a man beaten down by the weather of sickness. He looked into the screen and spoke to his family.

"Gloria, I already miss you." He smiled. She smiled, too, but cried. She stuck her tissue to her face. Gloria had no idea that Jonathan had done this.

"I miss you too," she whispered.

"To the rest of you, I miss you very much as well. I know the pain and sadness you must feel now. I would as well, if it were one of you and I remained. Yet I take some serious reflection to the words of the poet Joseph Addison. He said:

> *When I look upon the tombs of the great, every emotion of envy dies in me; when I read the epitaphs of the beautiful, every inordinate desire goes out; when I meet with the grief of parents upon a tombstone, my heart melts with compassion; when I see the tomb of the parents themselves, I consider the vanity of grieving for those whom we must quickly follow: When I see kings lying by those who deposed them, when I consider rival wits placed side by side, or the holy men that divided the world with their contests and disputes, I reflect with sorrow and astonishment on the little competitions, factions, and debates of mankind. When I read the several dates of the tombs, of some that died yesterday, and some six hundred years ago, I consider the great Day when we shall all of us be contemporaries, and make our appearance together.*

"The prose speaks for itself. Yes, I am gone, but you have lives to live yourselves, and they will in the end seem like extraordinarily short lives at that. Make the most of them. Lay aside those things that betray the truly important concerns of life. Remember character, honor, and integrity. Be examples to those around you of lives given to the Lord.

"Remember the words of Oliver Wendell Holmes: 'What lies behind us and what lies before us are tiny matters compared to what lies within us.'

"You will all have trials in this life. That is a given. It matters not that you do but how you handle those trials and who you are as you do. May I present to you all one last challenge to always be in the process of personal inner growth, on the road to the kind of transformation that changes the world around you.

"Kids, you are now the possessors of greater wealth than many would ever know. Until now, you have lived with the benefit of your mother and my toil. Now, much of that wealth is yours. This happened to me as well, and so I know that, used properly, much good can come from your inheritance. May I remind you of the words of, I believe, Ralph Waldo Emerson: 'The true measure of a man's wealth is in the things he can afford not to buy.'

"I don't believe that this will be much of a problem for you. Your mother and I have raised you right, and we are proud of the way you have all turned out. They are words to heed, nonetheless, in the face of the temptation to materialism.

"And now, my unofficial last will and testament:

"To Gloria, I leave the many wonderful memories of a life filled with love and laughter. I leave you forever with my heart of gratitude for your partnership in this joy we call life.

"To Scott, I leave patience and love and the willingness to be so.

"To Jennifer, I leave forgiveness and the capacity to extend it.

"To Michael, I leave a quiet but steadfast spirit to always do what is right. I know you will.

"To Patty, I leave a tender heart and a willingness to serve others, as you already do.

"To Samantha, I leave you the knowledge that I tried and succeeded in knowing you.

"To William, I leave tenacity to remain a minister of the gospel in light of the course of humanity, and I leave the desire to lead others to a better place.

"To Thomas, I leave a full life ahead of you with many choices to be made in the coming years. Choose well and wisely, my Son.

"Goodbye, my family. I love you, and I'm sorry that I have departed so soon. Hold on to one another and love one another deeply."

There was no one in the room without a tear in their eye. Jonathan paused and then looked back up to the camera.

"One last thing. No matter how broke he tells you he is, don't ever lend one red cent to Albert!" You could hear Albert on camera laughing with his old friend Jonathan. Typical of Jonathan, he broke the sad moment with a perfectly placed sense of humor. The family laughed a bit. The old saying that laughter and sorrow are cousins proved to be true this day. Albert rewound the tape and pushed the "eject" button.

The family sat quietly for a good five minutes or so. Gloria noticed the clock read 5:30 and suggested that they retire to the dining room for some dinner. Gloria had a caterer she used frequently to prepare some food and leave it in the ovens so they could eat about that time. The family realized they were indeed very hungry and acquiesced to her suggestion.

March 7, 4:30 p.m.

GLORIA AND JENNIFER pushed the door gently open, revealing the baby in his crib. "Shhh. He's sleeping," Jennifer whispered to her mother. They were inside the nursery Jennifer and Scott had prepared for their baby, the first of the Blake grandchildren. It was the room right next to the master bedroom in their home. Jennifer had decorated it with her mother, mostly in primary colors. There were teddy bears of all shapes and sizes all around the room.

They walked over to the crib, each standing on one side facing each other. Jonathan Blake Rogers, two days old, lay quietly sleeping under his blanket, thumb firmly in his mouth, unaware of his mother and grandmother.

"He's beautiful," Gloria said softly.

"He really is," Jennifer agreed. "Look at how small his hands and feet are. I can hardly believe it. He looks like a little doll."

"I think he looks like your father," Gloria offered.

Jennifer wasn't quite so sure. "I've tried to see it in him. I think he has Scott's eyes and nose. Maybe he has the Blake mouth, though. I just don't know. It is so hard to tell yet."

"Well," Gloria responded, "He has Jonathan's name; I'll hope that he has his features." They both smiled. After a few more moments, Gloria again spoke. "He would have loved him so much."

Jennifer looked up at her mother. Both of them were crying. "I know. He would have been the best grandpa. I wish he could have seen him. One month. He missed seeing him by one month. He should have been able to see him."

"Sometimes life doesn't work that way, honey," Gloria reminded her oldest daughter. "This baby won't know his Grandpa Blake, but he'll know lots about him. I'll make sure of that. You will too, I know. He'll also get lots of love from his aunts and uncles and especially his dear old Grandma." She paused. "Yes, this baby will get lots of love. We'll take very good care of him." Gloria reached over and took Jennifer's hand. "Come on, honey, let's go out and drink some coffee. Little Jonathan needs some peace and quiet so he can sleep."

With that, they turned out the light, exited, and shut the door behind them.

March 7, 8:30 p.m.

G LORIA STARTED UP her driveway after passing through
the gates at the entrance to Three Lakes. It was three days shy
of one year ago when Jonathan found out that he had cancer and
would die. The past year had been a whirlwind. It had obviously
been dominated by Jonathan's impending death and the sadness of
that. But there had also been so much good. There was Thomas's
graduation, the anniversary party, the wedding, and of course now,
the new baby. As she drove slowly up the drive, she reached up and
touched the necklace Jonathan had given her at their anniversary
party. She began to cry again.

As she rounded the last turn in the driveway, the house came
into full view. She had left a lot of lights on, as she didn't like coming home to a dark house. When she got to the garage, she opened
the door and pulled into her spot, then closed the door behind her.
She got out of her car and walked up the stairs to the mudroom
door. From behind the door, she heard a noise and smiled. Opening
the door, she was greeted by Sunny, her new golden retriever. Gloria
had decided a few weeks ago that she didn't like being home alone,
so she invested in a new friend. She went to a local breeder and
purchased Sunny, and they had hit it off from the very beginning.

Sunny couldn't possibly know what Gloria had been through
in the past year or how much pain there was in Gloria's heart,

but one thing was certain: Sunny was glad that Gloria was home. Gloria bent down to say hello, and Sunny licked her face. "Come on, Sunny girl, let's get you some food, and then we'll make a fire and listen to some sad music." Sunny liked that idea, and together they went into the house.

ABOUT THE AUTHOR

CHRIS WIDENER IS widely recognized as one of the top personal development influencers in the world. He's been named one of the top 50 speakers in the world, one of *Inc.* magazine's Top 100 Leadership Speakers, and is a member of the Motivational Speakers Hall of Fame. Chris has written 21 books that have been translated into 14 languages. Chris also has a small boutique coaching practice where he works one-on-one with successful entrepreneurs and executives to help them improve their lives and businesses. Chris and his wife, Denise, reside in beautiful Scottsdale, Arizona.